QUEEN ANNE'S LACE

SUSAN WITTIG ALBERT

QUEEN ANNE'S LACE

BERKLEY PRIME CRIME
NEW YORK

BERKLEY PRIME CRIME
Published by Berkley
An imprint of Penguin Random House LLC
375 Hudson Street, New York, New York 10014

Library of Congress Cataloging-in-Publication Data

Names: Albert, Susan Wittig, author.
Title: Queen Anne's lace / Susan Wittig Albert.
Description: First edition. | New York, NY : Berkley Prime Crime, 2018. |
Series: China Bayles mysteries
Identifiers: LCCN 2017028400 (print) | LCCN 2017031280 (ebook) |
ISBN 9780698190306 (eBook) | ISBN 9780425280058 (hardcover)
Subjects: LCSH: Bayles, China (Fictitious character)—Fiction. | Women
detectives—Texas—Fiction. | GSAFD: Mystery fiction.
Classification: LCC PS3551.L2637 (ebook) | LCC PS3551.L2637 Q44 2018 (print) |
DDC 813/.54—dc23
LC record available at https://lccn.loc.gov/2017028400

First Edition: April 2018

Printed in the United States of America
1   3   5   7   9   10   8   6   4   2

Cover art: *Illustration* copyright © by Joe Burleson;
Lace background copyright © by Sh.Olga/Shutterstock
Cover design by Judith Murello
Book design by Tiffany Estreicher

PUBLISHER'S NOTE: The recipes contained in this book are to be followed exactly as written.
The publisher is not responsible for your specific health or allergy needs that may require
medical supervision. The publisher is not responsible for any adverse reactions
to the recipes contained in this book.

For Natalee Rosenstein, gratefully

QUEEN ANNE'S LACE

Prologue

Pecan Springs, Texas
1885

It was a mistake to think of houses, old houses, as being empty.
They were filled with memories, with the faded echoes of voices.
Drops of tears, drops of blood, the ring of laughter, the edge of
tempers that had ebbed and flowed between the walls, into the
walls, over the years. Wasn't it, after all, a kind of life?

Key of Knowledge, Nora Roberts

 If Annie Laurie's house could speak, it would have said that
she was a contented woman.

She rose before the sun every morning to prepare her husband's
breakfast. Douglas always went out to his blacksmith shop the very
first thing, to see that the fire was started in the forge and his smithy
helpers were at their tasks. Then he would come in for the good food
Annie had ready for him—eggs and bacon, grits, and biscuits with
redeye gravy—before he began the day's work. And there was always
plenty of work to do, because Douglas Duncan was the best blacksmith in the village of Pecan Springs, Texas. Annie wasn't the only one
who had this opinion, and to prove it, there were the customers lined
up waiting in the dusty alley behind their house at 304 Crockett Street,
eager to have their horses shod or their implements mended or their
wagon wheels repaired.

Their house. Annie loved the house Douglas had built for her. It was a fine, two-story dwelling with walls made of square-cut limestone blocks and a white-painted wood-frame veranda across the front, draped with ivy and honeysuckle. Behind the veranda were two large rooms side-by-side, one of them a sitting room, the other a dining room, with high ceilings and tall, deep-set windows in the outer walls. Behind them were a bedroom and a large kitchen and pantry. Above, there was a full second-story loft that Annie and Douglas planned to partition into bedrooms for their children.

The house was in a lovely setting, too. It faced Crockett Street, which was lined on both sides by large live oak trees that made a graceful canopy over the brick pavement. On the east side of the house was a garden, and behind it on the alley were Douglas' smithy and the commodious stone stable where he kept his sleek, spirited horse and a shiny black buggy with red-painted wheels. On the other side of the garden hedge was a large, yellow-painted frame house where Adam and Delia Hunt lived with their little girl, Caroline. Adam Hunt had been Douglas' best friend since their boyhood days and the two men often went fishing and hunting together.

All day long, as she went about her own activities, Annie could hear the musical *clang clang clang* of Douglas' hammer, and her heart swelled with happiness. Her husband was an excellent provider. He gave her a generous household allowance and hired a woman to do the cooking and the laundry so that, when Annie's housework was done, she could spend the rest of day doing what she most loved: making fine laces. For Annie, lacemaking was a challenging craft that kept her fingers nimble and her mind sharp, while Douglas saw it as a dainty lady's hobby that gave his wife something to keep her hands busy before she became occupied with a growing family.

But in the Duncan household, all was not work. On mild Sundays, Douglas would drive them in the buggy west along the Pecan River. Or north, to the village of San Marcos, or east across the San Antonio Road to the blackland prairie. Or they might take a picnic basket to the spring, where they spread a blanket in the shade, ate Annie's fried chicken, and enjoyed the breeze while Douglas played his guitar and sang. His father and mother had come to America from Scotland, and he loved the old Scottish ballads—"Highland Mary," "My Love Is Like a Red, Red Rose," and his favorite, which always brought tears to Annie's eyes:

> Maxwelton's braes are bonnie
> Where early falls the dew
> And it was there that Annie Laurie
> Gave me her promise true
>
> Gave me her promise true
> Which never forgot will be
> And for bonnie Annie Laurie
> I would lay me down and die.

Annie hoped to give Douglas the son he wanted, but it had taken many months to conceive. While she was waiting, she continued to make lace—such beautiful lace that, while at first she gave it away, her friends and their friends soon clamored to buy it. Douglas wasn't a man to be offended if his wife brought in a little extra money doing something she enjoyed, and he allowed her to keep what she earned. It gave her great pleasure to use it to buy little things for the house and for Douglas and herself: a white silk parasol, for instance, that she trimmed with frills of her very own lace.

But Annie was impatient to get her family started, so one afternoon shortly after their third anniversary, she walked down Crockett Street to call on Mrs. Jane Crow, who ran a boardinghouse on the next block. A plump, kindly woman with brown hair pinned up in a shaggy knot, Mrs. Crow had hung a sign on her porch rail: *Herbs & Herbal Remedies For Sale.* She grew a great many herbs in the garden behind her house and sold them to Mr. Jackson, the village pharmacist, and to anyone else who came to her with a request.

Annie found Mrs. Crow sitting in a rocking chair on the porch with her knitting, a kitten playing with the ball of yarn at her feet. "What can I help you with, my dear?" Mrs. Crow asked.

"I'd like to buy some herbs," Annie said. Her mother was dead and her aunts lived far away, but she remembered hearing them talk about plants that were useful to women in their childbearing years— plants that could help you conceive. Or could help if your monthly was late, or too heavy or too scanty, or didn't come at all.

"What exactly are you looking for?"

"Red clover, perhaps," Annie said. "And nettle and yarrow, too, I think." She paused, frowning. "I'm sure there's something else, but I can't quite remember—"

"Ah." Mrs. Crow picked up her ball of yarn and pushed her needles into it. "You and your husband are wanting a baby?"

"Yes," Annie said, relieved that she wouldn't have to go into a long explanation.

Mrs. Crow stood up. "I think I have what you're looking for, my dear. Of course, there are no guarantees, but we can try to give nature a bit of a boost."

A little later, Annie was on her way home with a large paper packet of dried herbs. On it was written: *Red clover, nettle, evening primrose, chaste berry, yarrow. Pour boiling water over a spoonful in a cup and steep for fifteen minutes. Drink twice a day.*

Annie brewed Mrs. Crow's tea, drank it as prescribed for several weeks, and was delighted when her next monthly didn't appear at the usual time. She waited until she missed the second, then sat down and wrote a thank-you note to Mrs. Crow. When her husband came in from the smithy that evening, she told him. He caught her up in his arms and whirled her around in an excited dance.

"A baby!" he cried. "Our baby. Oh, Annie, my dearest, dearest Annie, I *love* you!"

And then it seemed to Annie that their house was filled with such a great happiness that it should surely burst. Douglas never stopped smiling and she went about her work with a joyful song on her lips.

Later, she would tell herself that it was a very good thing that she couldn't look into the future and see what lay ahead. After the worst had happened, she would look back on those days with a wistful long-ing, wishing with all her heart that she could have held on to the good times and kept them with her forever.

Of course she couldn't. None of us can. But we can try.

Annie tried.

Chapter One

Queen Anne's lace (*Daucus carota*, aka wild carrot) traveled to America from Europe and hopscotched across the continent with a recklessly joyful abandon. Some herbalists speculate that its use as a morning-after contraceptive made Queen Anne's lace a valuable must-have herb for pioneer women, so they made sure to carry the seeds with them wherever they went. With this in mind, I suppose it's no surprise that we find this plant growing everywhere—along roads and in ditches, in farmers' fields and urban backyards.

Queen Anne's lace earned its common name from the lacelike delicacy of its doily-shaped white blossoms, each of which is centered with a single, tiny bloodred flower.

"Anne's Flower"
China Bayles
Pecan Springs Enterprise

I love Mondays. I really do.

Thyme and Seasons is closed on Monday and I can slop around in my grubbiest jeans and T-shirt, doing all the housekeeping I can't do when customers are asking for my attention every few minutes. On Monday, there's time to appreciate the old stone walls, the well-worn wooden floors, and the beamed ceilings that create a lovely setting for my herbal wares. I can dust the antique hutch and wooden shelves stocked with herbal vinegars, oils, jellies, and teas. I can rearrange the books in the bookshelf and tidy up the old pine cupboard that displays bath herbs, herbal soaps and shampoos, fragrances, and massage oils. I can restock the wooden rack that holds the bottles of extracts and tinctures and the large glass jars of dried culinary and medicinal herbs. I can rearrange the wreaths and swags on the walls and reorganize the buckets of fragrant potpourri in the corners, as well as tall stalks of dried sunflowers, baskets of dried Queen Anne's lace, Silver King artemisia, yarrow, and tansy. And when the weather's good, I can work outdoors in the herb gardens around the shop and replenish the shelves of potted herbs for sale—basil, parsley, sage, rosemary, thyme, chives—outside my front door.

No offense to my friends and customers: I enjoy you, and if I want to stay in the herb business, I *need* you. But if I were Queen of the World, it would be Monday all week long.

This particular August Monday was hot and steamy, so I worked outdoors for less than an hour, pulling weeds, trimming plants, and cutting some parsley, thyme, and rosemary for the tearoom kitchen. Then I cooled off with a little dusting and tidying up and planned to spend the rest of the morning peeking at my monthly income and expense reports, reviewing the tearoom menus that Ruby and Cass had proposed for the next couple of weeks, checking out a couple of things on the website, and looking over the handouts for September's classes on wreath-making. Lovely things. Lovely *Monday* things.

With this in mind, I took my laptop to the counter and sat down on my stool. Khat—our shop Siamese and quite an autocratic creature—jumped up beside me, placing a proprietary paw on the computer keyboard and watching with interest while I pulled up the previous month's financial data. I didn't need a degree in economics to see that while July's bottom line wasn't quite red, it wasn't quite as black as it should be. Sales had been a little slow, and on top of that, I had paid a couple of sizeable bills for the loft renovation, which happened because I decided that the empty space over our heads really ought to be generating some income. There was also a big bill for the veranda construction, which was rather a whim but has made an attractive difference in the street appearance of our shops.

I knew my building was old—well over a hundred years—but I didn't know much about its history. It has been extensively remodeled, of course, but it was originally built, I've learned, as a house. When I started planning the loft project, I happened to look at a photograph from the early 1900s and discovered that there had once been a wood-frame veranda across the front. I loved that veranda at first sight. No matter how much it cost, I had to have it.

And when the job was done and the building looked very much the way it did when it was first built, the Pecan Springs Historical Society installed a handsome plaque beside the front door. It says *The Duncan House, 1882*—Duncan, the name of the family who originally built the house. Jessica Nelson, a reporter from *Pecan Springs Enterprise*, wrote an interesting article on its history, with photos. I've framed it, and it's hanging on the wall behind my counter.

The loft is finished, too, and rented to Lori Lowry, a textile artist who uses it as a studio and teaching space. Which is a good deal for Ruby and me, for on top of the rental income, Lori's students like to browse through our shops and stop for lunch in our tearoom. The local weavers' guild is planning a show there in October, which will mean even more traffic.

I finished running the July numbers, frowned at them for a moment, then decided that if I didn't count all those extra expenses (which are really an investment in the building), the bottom line didn't look all that bad. Cheered up a little, I found the file of tearoom menus that

Ruby and Cass had emailed me for posting on our website, and began to study them. Khat and I were considering the merits of grilled chicken with carrot and couscous salad when Ruby came through the door from her Crystal Cave, which is also closed on Mondays. At six-foot-something in yellow sandals, she was dressed for her day off in a sleeveless yellow top and lipstick-red shorts. Her hair is the color of fresh carrots, finely frizzed, and today, her eyes were green (a sure sign that she was wearing her green contacts—otherwise, they may be blue or brown).

She leaned against the counter. "A little voice woke me up this morning telling me that today would be a good day to clean out the storeroom upstairs. If you're not doing anything, why don't you give me a hand?"

Cleaning out that storeroom had been on our joint to-do list for some time, but it had never seemed very urgent. "I *am* doing something." I pointed at the computer screen. "I'm doing menus. And then the website."

"You can do menus and the website later." Ruby stroked Khat's tawny fur and he began to purr. "There's not all that much stuff in that storeroom. It won't take more than a couple of hours."

"And then what?" I asked. "We don't really *need* the space, do we?"

Khat arched his back under Ruby's hand, turning up the volume on his rumbling purr. "Of course we do," Ruby said. "We can use it to store all the stuff we're keeping under the stairs."

"Then what will we put under the stairs?" There's a bathroom there—well, a toilet and sink. And piles of junk. When you sit on the john, you're staring at boxes and bins of our out-of-season decorations. Christmas lights, Halloween ghosts and goblins, Easter bunnies, stuff like that. "Most of our customers don't use *that* bathroom," I pointed out. "They use the restroom off the tearoom."

"Yes, but sometimes people have to wait." Ruby twiddled a frizzy lock of her red-orange hair. "There are times we could use a second bathroom. If we move the holiday decorations to the storeroom upstairs, we can put in a new vinyl floor and paint the walls. Maybe add a cabinet under the sink and some decent lighting, so it doesn't look quite so much like a toidy in the Pecan Springs jail."

"How do you know what a toidy in the Pecan Springs jail looks like?" I asked, interested.

Ruby rolled her eyes. "You know what I mean, China. Our customers will appreciate another bathroom. We'll be killing two birds with one stone."

It sounded to me like a whole flock of birds and a big basket of stones. Not to mention a lot of work. "Well, maybe," I conceded. "But we don't have the money to fix up the bathroom right now. And while the loft is air-conditioned, that storeroom isn't. It'll be an oven up there today. We'll roast."

Ruby pulled her gingery brows together. "China," she said seriously, "that little voice is telling me that we ought to do this *today*. Lori doesn't have classes on Monday, so we can haul that stuff out and not worry about getting in her way." She bent over and planted a kiss between Khat's charcoal ears. "You know what Benjamin Franklin said. Never put off to tomorrow what you can do today."

"I'm more familiar with Mark Twain," I countered. "Never put off to tomorrow what you can do the day *after* tomorrow." I thought for a moment. "Or was it Oscar Wilde?"

The Victorian-style shopkeeper's bell mounted to my front door tinkled pleasantly, and both of us turned around to look. But the door was locked and I had hung up the Closed sign to deter prospective customers. Nobody was there.

Khat arched his back, hissed, and jumped off the counter. Ruby frowned. "What's wrong with him? And why is your bell ringing?"

"Dunno." I shrugged. "Vibrations or something, I guess." I waggled my eyebrows. "And maybe Khat is telling us that today isn't a good day to clean out the storeroom."

"Maybe he's telling us that it *is*," Ruby said decidedly. "Come on, China. Let's do it."

I pressed my lips together. When Ruby has an idea, I can either stand back and watch or be a good sport and join the party. After a moment's reflection, I joined the party.

"If you insist." I closed the menu file and shut down my laptop. I glanced down at Khat, who was sitting on the floor, gazing fixedly at the bell. "Come on, Khat," I said. "You may find a mouse or two up there."

The bell tinkled again, affirmatively.

"You see?" Ruby said in a meaningful tone. "It's telling us that we're *supposed* to do this."

Looking back now with the wisdom of hindsight (funny how that works, isn't it?), I wonder what would have happened if Ruby hadn't listened to that little voice telling her that today was a good day to clean out that storeroom.

Or if I had said, *Sorry, Ruby, but I absolutely positively have to get these menus uploaded today*? How long would it have been before we discovered the wooden chest and the carton of old photographs? Maybe we wouldn't have discovered them, ever. How would that have changed what happened?

Or if I had removed that bell.

We'll never know, of course, because Ruby *did* hear that voice, and when she asked me to help, I *did* say yes. We *did* discover that chest, and after that, the photos. And the bell continued to ring.

And thereby hangs a tale.

BUT before I tell you what happened when Ruby and I went upstairs, it might be helpful if we took a few moments for introductions. If you're a regular visitor to Thyme and Seasons, you know who we are and what we're all about, so you have my permission to skip the next dozen or so paragraphs. If you're new to Pecan Springs or just want to see if anything's changed since the last time you were here, you're invited to read on.

My name is China Bayles. In a previous incarnation, I was a criminal defense attorney with a large Houston law firm that catered to big bad guys with bottomless pockets who could hire our top-dollar dream-team defense. There were a lot of things I enjoyed about being a lawyer—and yes, money was certainly one of them. In those days, I was as ambitious and greedy as anyone else and willing to fight for my place on the ladder with whatever weapons it took. But after spending a decade of my life in that knock-down, drag-out environment, I began to wonder whether the justice I was engaged in seeking was the kind of justice we needed in this world—and whether Houston was the place I wanted to live for the rest of my days.

When the answers to both of these urgent questions finally came up *no*, I turned in my resignation, cashed in my retirement account, and bailed out. I landed in Pecan Springs, a small, friendly town just off I-35, halfway between Austin and San Antonio, at the eastern edge of the Texas Hill Country. I bought a building on Crockett Street and opened an herb shop I called Thyme and Seasons. When people ask me "Why herbs?" I give them the short answer: "Because plants don't talk back." When they ask "Why Pecan Springs?" I reply, "Because it seemed so crime-free and *peaceful*."

And then I laugh out of the other side of my mouth, because while Pecan Springs is a great place to live, it is not and never has been crime-free. Don't be fooled by the cozy images you see in the glossy *Why You'll Love to Visit Pecan Springs!* brochures handed out by the Chamber of Commerce. Our nice little town has its fair share of crime, just like every other nice little town, everywhere—maybe even a little more, since we're conveniently located in the I-35 Corridor, the narco-corridor, some call it: the main artery for the nation's south–north drug trade. If you come here expecting Mayberry, you'll be disappointed.

Pecan Springs and Thyme and Seasons were just the first of several major earthquakes in my life. After years of insisting that marriage required too many compromises, I married Mike McQuaid, whom I had met years before in a Houston courtroom. McQuaid is a former homicide detective, currently a private investigator with his own firm (McQuaid, Blackwell, and Associates) and an adjunct professor on the Criminal Justice faculty at Central Texas State University. We are the parents of two great kids. McQuaid's son, Brian, will be a sophomore at the University of Texas this fall, majoring in environmental science. He lives with his girlfriend in Austin. Caitlin, my fourteen-year-old niece and our adopted daughter, lives with McQuaid and me in a big Victorian house on Limekiln Road, about a dozen miles west of Pecan Springs. We share the place with a gloomy basset hound named Winchester, a grizzled orange tomcat named Mr. P, Caitlin's flock of chickens, and a legion of fugitive lizards escaped (or de-scended) from Brian's collection of reptiles.

And then there's Ruby. She is my business partner, sidekick, and owner of the Crystal Cave, the only New Age shop in Pecan Springs. Together Ruby and I jointly own and manage the tearoom behind our shops (Thyme for Tea) and a catering service we call Party Thyme. We also co-own (with Cass Wilde) the Thymely Gourmet, which delivers packages of healthy precooked food to upscale singles who want to eat right but don't have the time (or don't know how) to cook. Ruby has two grown daughters and a granddaughter, although you'd never know it to look at her. After an early divorce, she has managed to stay unmarried, although she is partial to intelligent men and cowboys. Just now, she is seriously dating a very nice guy named Pete who manages an olive ranch, a relationship that is complicated by the fact that the ranch is a couple of hours away and Pete's job doesn't allow him a lot of free time.

As you might guess from the fact that she owns a New Age shop, Ruby's lifelong passions include astrology, tarot, and the Ouija board. I sometimes imagine the interior of her mind as a large crystal ball, with images materializing out of the shadows, disappearing, and then reappearing as something else entirely. Sorry if that sounds snarky—it's not intentional. I admire Ruby's intuition and empathy. She can actually scan people's thoughts, although "off" is her default position on this ability. (She says she doesn't like to pry into her friends' secret lives.) I've known her to come up with some startling insights, based on ways of understanding the world that have nothing to do with the linear logic within which the rest of us poor mortals are trapped. While for me (and probably you), two plus two will only ever equal four, Ruby can just as easily make it eighteen-and-a-half—and more often than not, she's right. Wacky, but right.

This might also be a good time to introduce you to our building, for it is a character in this story, too. As I said, I didn't know much about 304 Crockett Street when I bought it, except that it was built of native Texas limestone sometime after the Civil War. In its first incarnation as a residence, it seems to have had two large rooms in the front, two behind, the loft above, and that lovely veranda across the front. There was a large garden on the east side of the house, and a stone stable for horses at the rear, on the alley.

Buildings change through time, just as people do, and the occupants have left their mark on this one, inside and out. At some point, a frame kitchen was added across the back of the house, the upstairs loft was partitioned into bedrooms, the veranda was removed, and the stable was converted to a garage. Later still, an architect bought the place and completely redesigned it. He turned the front two rooms into his office and studio, the back two rooms plus kitchen into an apartment for himself, and the stone stable-garage into a lovely guest cottage.

Ruby and I have changed this building, too. Her Crystal Cave takes up one of the front two rooms, and Thyme and Seasons the other. I lived in the architect's apartment until I married McQuaid. Now, our tearoom occupies that space, and we've expanded and modernized the kitchen. The guest cottage has become a bed-and-breakfast—or a classroom for our cooking classes, when it isn't occupied. The loft upstairs has had a full makeover. It is now Lori Lowry's textile arts studio.

The loft was one of my better ideas, if I do say so myself—although the renovation was more extensive than I'd originally planned. The old wooden staircase had to be brought up to code (building inspectors are fussy about things like fire exits). The extra air-conditioning required some serious rewiring, and the windows had to be replaced.

The flimsy interior partitions came out, revealing an expansive room with a pine floor and cypress rafters. There wasn't enough light, so I had the contractor install a row of skylights in the roof and enough track lighting to comfortably illuminate the whole space.

The loft seems almost custom-designed for Lori's studio and teaching space. The center part of the floor is filled with four floor looms, several tabletop looms, a couple of rigid heddle and inkle looms, a warping reel, and a half dozen spinning wheels. (Some of this equipment is on loan from members of the local weaving guild, who are Lori's friends and supportive of her work.) Lori installed shelves along one wall and filled them with an assortment of rainbow-colored yarns and threads and fleeces ready to be spun, a delicious temptation for Khat, who loves to play with the tag ends of yarn when he sees them dangling. She's turned the other walls into a well-lit gallery for her woven pieces and those created by her students and members of the local weaving guild. The whole place is totally gorgeous.

Which brings us to that storeroom.

WHEN the loft was renovated, I didn't get around to doing anything with the old storage room at the back. It's been a handy place to stash junk, some of it mine and Ruby's, some of it left over from earlier occupants. The loft is air-conditioned, but the storeroom isn't. When I propped the door open that morning so Ruby and I could work in it, the rush of heat felt as if it had accumulated from uncounted summers past. It was hotter than the dickens—and dark as the inside of a cow, until I remembered that there was a bare bulb hanging from the ceiling. I reached up, found its chain, and yanked it.

The naked bulb revealed a shadowed, low-ceilinged space running the full width of the building, about six feet wide, with shelves along the back wall. It smelled of musty old papers and summer's heat, with an oddly sharp top note of lavender and the elusive bouquet of hot dust and dead mouse. I expected Khat to rush in, eager to discover if there were any survivors (mice, that is) who might require his immediate attention. But oddly, he put one paw inside the door, took a sniff, and then decided he had urgent business elsewhere.

"Wonder what got into him?" Ruby asked as he zoomed past her at warp speed and vaulted down the stairs. Wrinkling her nose, she stepped into the storeroom. "Is that lavender I'm smelling?" Not waiting for an answer, she pulled out a cardboard box. "What's this?"

I opened the box and peeked in. "It's the extra craft supplies from that papermaking workshop we did a couple of years ago. I thought we gave it to the preschool over on Elm Street."

Ruby picked up the box. "That's where it's going now. I'll put it at the top of the stairs. Could you see what's in that crate? Maybe it's something we can throw away."

And that's how it went for the next couple of hours. We worked our way down the length of the storeroom, opening boxes and bags, identifying the contents, and making executive decisions. Some of the stuff went to the Dumpster in the alley, some of it went back on the shelves (neatly!), and some of it was going to Goodwill. The curtains from my former apartment, for instance, along with some pots and pans, a rolled-up section of carpet, Brian's old goalie mask, and a couple of boxes of games and puzzles—all bound for Goodwill.

I was beginning to feel like an archaeologist on a dig, for as we burrowed deeper into the storeroom, we seemed to be moving back in time. I discovered a *Life* magazine featuring the assassination of JFK, several copies of the *Pecan Springs Enterprise* dating back to the 1950s, a box of vinyl World War II–era records (Bing Crosby, Glenn Miller, the Andrews Sisters) that might be worth something at a yard sale, and a metal advertising sign for Coca-Cola that said *Refreshing Fountain Drink, just 5¢!* A collector might want that.

And then it got even more interesting. I turned up a 1930s Shirley Temple doll with only one hand but most of her curly blond hair; a campaign button for Franklin Roosevelt's first run for the presidency in 1932; and—folded into a cardboard dress box between several layers of tissue paper—a slinky silver flapper dress from the 1920s, with a silver headband and a red feather boa.

"Omigod," Ruby breathed, when I opened the box. "Let me see that dress, China! It's *gorgeous!*"

I held it up. It was made of some sort of sheer metallic fabric with skinny spaghetti straps and rows of layered silver tassels from the deep vee neckline to the hem. "It's totally *you*, Ruby," I said. "And it looks just your size. You have to try it on."

Ruby's eyes were shining. "Oh, wow," she breathed, and snatched it out of my hands. A few minutes later, she was back, a vision in silver tassels, her carroty frizz set off by the silver headband. "Twenty-three skidoo," she said, twirling the red feather boa. "Perfect for Halloween, don't you think?"

"You are the bee's knees," I said admiringly. "So now that we've found your Halloween costume, we can quit. Right?"

"Nah," she said. "We're almost to the end. I'll change and be right back. Bet we can finish in a half hour."

"Okay," I said, and went back to work.

There was more junk and more trips to the Dumpster, but more goodies, too. A copy of the *Austin Weekly Statesman* dated November 7, 1912, announcing Woodrow Wilson's election as president. A framed photograph of the 1906 San Francisco earthquake. A wooden stereopticon with a set of cards illustrating battles of the Spanish-American War. A cardboard carton printed with the words *Corticelli Silk Threads, Florence, Massachusetts*, and a picture of a kitten playing with a spool of thread. The carton was filled with old sepia-toned snapshots from around the turn of the century, judging from the costumes and the way the women wore their hair. On top was a photograph of a man, a woman, a baby, and a pretty young girl, sitting in an old-fashioned porch swing on what looked like the veranda right here at 304 Crockett Street. The man, smiling happily, had one arm around the woman's shoulders. She was holding a tiny, blanket-wrapped baby in her arms. The girl, dressed in a lacy pinafore, was holding a kitten. A shaggy dog lay on the porch beside the swing, and an old-fashioned bicycle leaned against the railing.

Ruby was rummaging in a box beside me. "This is nice," she said, holding up a long gray skirt, gored to fit smoothly over the hips and flared at the hem, and a white, lace-trimmed Victorian shirtwaist with leg o' mutton sleeves. "Looks like it might fit you."

I put the box of photographs back on the shelf, thinking that it would be fun to go through them on a rainy Sunday afternoon. "Sure," I said. "That'll be *my* Halloween costume. I'll go as Mary Poppins and you can be the Mad Flapper." I opened a round cardboard hatbox that held a woman's flat-brimmed straw hat with a red velvet band. It had once boasted a gray feather, but something had nibbled the feather to a stub and gnawed several small chunks out of the brim. "And here's my hat," I said, and put it on.

Then I found what looked like a small white umbrella. "Look, Ruby! A lace parasol." It was gray with dust and there were a few ragged holes in the lace trimming, but it was still very pretty.

20

"Oh, China, that's lovely!" Ruby said eagerly. "It must be *very* old. Parasols went out with bustles, didn't they? Let me see it." Ruby took it from me and strutted and twirled for a moment. "I think we should bring back parasols as a fashion statement. This makes me feel positively elegant."

"Looks like we're almost finished," I said. I dusted my hands and looked around. All that was left was a stack of old newspapers and the box Ruby was rummaging in, which appeared to be full of petticoats and camisoles, the same vintage as the Mary Poppins costume. "Let's take this box out to the table. We can go through it out there. If there's nothing we want, we can drop it off at the vintage clothing shop on the square."

Ruby took the box and left. As she went through the door, she accidentally kicked the prop and the door swung shut behind her, cutting out the light that had come from the loft. The naked lightbulb near the door had never done a very good job of illuminating the far end of the storeroom, and now the space around me seemed to close down like a dark cave. I turned, aiming to replace the prop that held the door open, but as I did, I heard something that stopped me dead in my tracks.

Somewhere, very close to me in the gloom, I heard a low voice, a woman's pleasant voice, humming a breathy snatch of melody—an old Scottish ballad, "Annie Laurie," that had been made popular by a folk group a few years ago. No words, just the low-pitched, melodic humming, a wispy, haunting sound deep in the shadows. And with it, the tantalizing scent of fresh lavender.

I sucked in my breath and the flesh on my arms broke out in goose bumps. Was I imagining this? Surely, I couldn't be—

No. I was actually *hearing* it. There was no one else in that storeroom with me, but someone, somewhere close by, was humming. As I listened, it grew louder, the melody carrying the words, unbidden, into my head. *And for bonnie Annie Laurie, I'd lay me down and die.*

I stood frozen, holding my breath, listening. The humming faded slightly, as if the woman had moved away from me. Then, at last, it faded away to nothing, and all I could hear was my ragged breathing and the pounding of my heart. I don't frighten easily, but I was honestly, genuinely, down-to-the-bone *scared*. Someone was here with me. Someone else was in this *empty* room.

I stood still, my mind a swirl of confused thoughts. "Hello?" I whispered. "Who's here?"

Nothing.

I tried again, louder. "Who's here? Who *are* you?" The words were a raspy whisper in a voice I barely recognized as my own.

But there was no answer. Only the dusty, lavender-scented silence and the banging of my heart against my ribs. And the echo of unspoken words. *And for bonnie Annie Laurie . . .*

The door opened and the light from the loft brightened the dimness around me. "Oops," Ruby said cheerfully. "Didn't mean to shut you in here all by yourself." She was a dark silhouette against the light. "Is that all? Are we finished?"

"Did you—" My mouth was dry as dust. I swallowed. "Did you hear anything just now?"

"Nope." She stood on her tiptoes to look on a shelf. "Why? What was I supposed to hear?"

"Maybe somebody . . . humming?" I rubbed my arms. Just a few moments before, the sweat had been trickling down my back, but now I was shivering. The storeroom felt as cold as a frozen food locker. "A woman. Humming."

And as I said the words, I heard it again. A woman's voice. That melody.

But Ruby didn't. "Nope, sorry," she said, pushing a stack of newspapers aside. "Maybe you were hearing the air-conditioning. It kicked on a minute ago, out in the loft. Feels cooler in here, too, don't you think?" She sniffed. "And I'm smelling lavender again. Wonder where it's coming from." She looked around. "Well, are we done?"

"I guess so," I said, and clenched my jaw to keep my teeth from chattering. I am willing to grant that an air conditioner can hum, but I seriously doubted that it could hum an old Scottish ballad. I was in no mood to argue the point, however. I was ready to get out of the storeroom, right *now*, before I froze to death.

"Wait." Ruby reached up to the top shelf and took something down. "This is really weird, China. I could swear we had cleared off all these shelves, but it looks like we missed something." She was holding a rectangular dark wooden chest with a carved lid, about the size of a briefcase. "Do you recognize this?"

"Never saw it before," I said. "But then, I've never gotten this far back in this storeroom." I shivered. Ruby's find was as good an excuse as any. "I've had enough closet-cleaning for a while. Let's take a break and see what's in it." Then, as if to underline my words, the lightbulb—which hadn't been very bright to begin with—gave a distinct *pop* and quit.

"Yes, let's," Ruby said with a laugh. "Obviously, we're done in here."

I followed her out into the loft and shut the storeroom door behind me, firmly. As far as I was concerned, whatever was in there could *stay* in there and hum to its heart's content. I didn't want to hear it.

Ruby put the chest on the nearest table. It was made of a reddish wood with a decorative grain—walnut, maybe. The hinged lid was fastened with a gold-colored hasp. The top was covered with a thick layer of dust, and I bent over to blow it off.

"Wait," Ruby commanded. She picked up a half-torn camisole from one of the piles of old clothes and wiped off the top, revealing a large carving. "A flower," she said. "Nice."

"Looks like Queen Anne's lace," I said. Of course, the carving might represent a dill blossom, which looks somewhat similar—but when I lifted the lid, I knew I was right. The box was crammed full of pieces of lace. No surprise, I suppose, since Queen Anne's lace (the plant) is supposed to be named for an English queen who made lace. The chest, which appeared to be very old, was probably made to store lace, which in times before ours had been quite valuable and was often stored in a locked box, to keep light-fingered ladies' maids from helping themselves.

"Look, Ruby!" I exclaimed, taking out a filmy embroidered net veil of gossamer-like lace, made of thread so finely spun that it weighed almost nothing in my hands. Then a lace baby's cap, several lengths of narrow cobwebby lace that might have edged a chemise, pieces of wider lace, lace doilies, lace fingerless mitts, several lace collars with matching cuffs. Some of the pieces were white, some cream-colored. The mitts were startlingly pink; one of the collar-and-cuff sets was black. All were intricately, beautifully worked. All clearly handcrafted, and undoubtedly antique.

"Wow, these are *gorgeous*," Ruby said breathlessly, laying a length of narrow lace on the table and tracing the filigree pattern with her finger. "They've got to be handmade, don't you think? You don't see anything like this nowadays." She picked up the black lace collar and held it for a moment, studying its intricate design. Then she dropped it quickly, pressing her lips together. "Sad," she murmured. "So . . . sad." Her voice sounded choked. "Terrible."

"What's terrible about it?" I picked up the collar, but couldn't see anything wrong with it. "Looks fine to me." I glanced back up at Ruby and was surprised to see her biting her lip as if against a sharp pain. "Ruby, what's *wrong*?"

Ruby didn't answer. Instead, she turned away so that I couldn't see her face. And I didn't get a chance to pursue the matter, because we were interrupted.

"Hey, you two," a woman's cheery voice said. "What's going on?"

Startled, I whirled. "Oh, hi, Lori," I said. "We thought today was your day off."

Lori Lowry is about my height and slender. She was dressed in a red sleeveless blouse, jeans, and sneakers. She wore no makeup, and her tortoiseshell glasses were pulled down on her nose. Her brown hair was sleeked back into a ponytail that emphasized the diamond shape of her face and made her look ten years younger than her actual thirtysomething. A popular artist and teacher in the Pecan Springs weaving community, Lori has had an unimaginably hard time of it in the past few years. Her adoptive parents, to whom she was very close, were killed in the tornado that tore through Joplin, Missouri. She was just learning to live with that loss when her husband, Damien, a well-known art professor at CTSU, died when a truck plowed into his vintage VW Beetle at a railroad crossing.

Lori was devastated by the tragedies. Suddenly, her parents and her husband were gone and she was all alone in the world. She spiraled into a depression that frightened all of us. Things got even worse a few months later, when she was diagnosed with stage-three breast cancer and had to undergo both a mastectomy and chemo. Hit by this triple whammy, she had to stop teaching and give up the lease on the building where she had her weaving studio and classroom space. She's officially cancer-free but still very fragile, and when we told her that the loft was available and that she was our first choice as a tenant, she was hesitant.

"I'm not sure I can make a commitment both to my weaving and my students," she said. "What if I try to go back to a full schedule and then have to quit?"

But when she decided it was time to put her life in order and return to her art, her circle of friends—which includes Ruby and me—got behind her a hundred percent. I gave her a break on the rent to get her started. A dozen of us pitched in to move the equipment up the stairs and set it up for her. And we've all helped advertise her classes. As a result, she has a full house for every class she teaches.

"It *is* my day off," Lori agreed. She dropped the bag she was carrying. "I spent the morning on the computer. My search for my birth mom, you know."

"Having any luck?" I asked hopefully. Lori is beyond intense in her search, which has become a consuming passion—an obsession, really. Her friends have been behind her all the way. We see her search as a way to help her heal from her devastating losses. Of course, it has its downside, too. What if her mom can't be found? What if she's dead? What if Lori really *is* all alone in the world? So my question wasn't casual.

"Well, maybe," Lori replied. "I could be getting closer. I think I've located my adoptive mother's sister."

"Oh, really?" Ruby said. "That's exciting, Lori!"

Lori nodded. "Aunt Josephine and my mom—my adoptive mom—

were estranged for years, so as a child, I never met her. I found her through a search on Ancestry dot-com and emailed her this morning. It could be another blind alley, but I'm hoping I can learn something from her. *If* she's the right person. And if she replies to my email."

Lori was fourteen when she learned that she was adopted. Her adoptive parents were living in Little Rock when they found her—a week-old baby—in a home for unwed mothers. The agency that handled the adoption is now defunct, and its records, if there were any, have long since disappeared. According to Arkansas law, her biological parents' names were removed from her birth certificate and replaced by the names of her adoptive parents, and all the court records and documents were sealed. Her adoptive parents hadn't known her mother, so they couldn't help. And now *they* were gone, too. There was nobody to answer Lori's questions—except maybe, just possibly, this aunt.

"Fingers crossed," Ruby said emphatically, holding up both hands. "Old Irish blessing," she added, and we all laughed.

Ruby has her own reasons for encouraging Lori in her search. Ruby got pregnant when she was a teenager, and her mother sent her to a home for unwed mothers, where she was forced to give up her baby for adoption. Her daughter Amy found her at last, and now there's little Grace, Amy's three-year-old daughter and the joy of Ruby's life. Ruby sees Lori's search from the point of view of a mother reunited with the daughter she thought was gone forever.

"Yeah, well, I'll get back to it tonight," Lori said. "I thought I'd take advantage of the free afternoon to warp one of the looms. It's not something I like to do when I've got a roomful of distracting students." She looked down at the lace spread out across the table. "Wow!" she exclaimed. "Where did you get all this *loot*?"

"We were cleaning out the storeroom," I said, and pointed to a couple of boxes by the stairs. "We'll get that stuff out of your way in a little while. It's headed for Goodwill. But you might be interested in this lace," I added, remembering that Lori had done her master's in textile history.

"It was all stuffed in that box," Ruby added, nodding toward the wooden chest. "We were just thinking that it looks like it's pretty old."

"Old is *right*." Lori pushed her glasses up on her nose and bent over the table. "And all handmade." She held up the filmy embroidered net veil. "This might be a bridal veil," she said.

Lori picked up another piece, then another. "Just gorgeous," she said. "You know, I really think they ought to be looked at by an expert. Some seem to be quite unique. And in amazingly good condition, too. A lot of very old lace is nothing but rags and tatters." She glanced at me. "Christine Vickery teaches textiles at CTSU—I had her for a couple of classes, and I know she's interested in lace. She might be able to tell us how these were made, and perhaps even when. Would you like me to ask her?"

"Oh, absolutely," I said. "Yes, please do."

Lori picked up her bag, found her cell phone, and snapped several quick photos. "I'll send her these. If she's interested enough to take a look, I'll give you a call and we can set something up." She straightened up with a sigh. "Well, if I'm going to get that loom warped today, I'd better get started."

"Have fun," Ruby said, as Lori went to the large loom on the other side of the loft.

I scooped up the laces and put them back into the chest. "Maybe I should take this home for safekeeping."

"Sure," Ruby said. "I guess we're done here for now."

I nodded. "Then let's tote those cardboard boxes out to my car. I'll finish the menus and email them back to you, then drop the boxes off on my way to pick up Caitie at rehearsal. We're giving her chickens a bath this afternoon. And Brian and his girlfriend are coming for supper this evening." The whole family would be there, gathered around the table—these days, a rare occasion. I was looking forward to it.

"Caitie's chickens are getting a *bath*?" Ruby gave me a disbelieving look. "I know your daughter treats those chickens like family, but isn't that . . . well, a little extreme?"

"Probably," I said with a grin. "But she's got her heart set on winning at least one ribbon at the county fair. So chicken baths are what we do."

Ruby rolled her eyes.

Chapter Two

Pecan Springs, Texas
1885–1888

Annie's pregnancy filled her with a surging joy that grew greater by the day. The baby would be a boy, she hoped— Douglas, after his father. If a girl, she would be Laurie, after Annie's mother. And now that they had finally begun their family, surely other children would follow in quick order. That's how it had been for her mother. The first child—a daughter—hadn't put in her appearance for several years, and then it was Katy bar the door. One baby every twenty-four months until there were nine and her father made his bed in the loft.

But Annie knew that Douglas Duncan would never be content to make his bed in the loft. He knew what he wanted and he wanted it *now.* He hated to wait for anything. For instance, he hated to climb out of his buggy and hold his nervous horse while the train rumbled past the railroad crossing just north of the International and Great Northern railroad depot on Sam Houston Street. So if he saw the locomotive coming, he would whip up his horse and race across ahead of it. Annie had tried to point out the danger, but he wouldn't listen. "My horse is the fastest in town and I'm tough as nails, Annie," he'd say, and bend to kiss her. "You've got nothing to fear, my girl."

But one July morning, Douglas and the locomotive arrived at the crossing at almost the same moment. Impatient to be on his way, he tried to cross, but this time, he wasn't fast enough. Douglas was dragged along the tracks until the engineer could bring the train to a stop. The horse was killed and the buggy was smashed to smithereens.

Adam Hunt, their neighbor and Douglas' closest friend, brought her the devastating news. A large, quiet man, ginger-haired and with a quick smile that lightened his deep-set eyes, Adam was weighted down by his own shock and sorrow. She saw it written across his face, plain as could be, before he ever spoke a word.

"Be brave, Annie," Adam said. He told her as gently as he could and caught her in his arms as she swayed and fell. He carried her to her bed and sent one of the smithy boys for Dr. Grogan, then stayed with her until he arrived. Later, he went to Carter's Pharmacy for the medicines the doctor prescribed, then waited to see if anything else was needed.

But Annie was in her seventh month, and her husband's death was more than she could bear. That night, the pains began. She went into early labor and the next morning gave birth to Douglas' child, a tiny boy who never drew a breath.

Her husband was gone and her baby, as well. Between one day and the next, within just twenty-four short hours, Annie's life was utterly changed.

TIME heals all wounds, people said. But people were wrong.

Three years later, Annie was still learning to live in Douglas' absence: to sleep in an empty bed and eat at the table by herself and try to imagine a future alone. She often remembered what Gramma Anne had told her when she was learning to make bobbin lace. Still a young girl, Annie would lean against her grandmother's chair, watching the gnarled hands pick up first this bobbin, then that, weaving them under and over, over and under, so quickly that Annie's eyes could scarcely follow.

"Magic," Annie whispered, as the pattern of tiny flowers and birds appeared, mysteriously, in the lace. "Gramma, it's magic!"

Her grandmother's smile lifted the corner of her mouth as her hands continued to move. "Well, yes, it's a little bit of magic. But more, it's paying attention. And understanding the pattern so well that your fingers know what to do before your mind can tell them." Her swiftly moving hands stopped, reversed the last two overs-and-unders, and did them again, the right way. She gave Annie a serious look. "And catching the little accidents before they get to be big ones. Sometimes you can work the mishaps into the pattern and make something new."

After Douglas' death, Annie often thought of her grandmother's words. *Sometimes you can work the mishaps into the pattern and make something new.* It could be a rule of life, too. But like any rule, it was easy to put into words and harder to put into practice. What could be the pattern of a life that seemed to promise so much—a caring husband, a baby son—and then be so suddenly, so tragically altered?

Sometimes, when her grief was the sharpest, Annie would take down the wooden casket with the flower carved on the lid. The flower was Queen Anne's lace and the casket was walnut, Gramma had said, made by *her* father—Annie's great-grandfather—in Massachusetts, just after the Revolutionary War. Annie kept the casket on the tall pine chest of drawers in her bedroom. It held Gramma Anne's collection of treasured pieces of laces, some of them brought from the Old Country. When she felt terribly sad, Annie would open the casket and take out the pieces one by one, appreciating the techniques and the expert workmanship, admiring the intricate patterns, loving each one because it had belonged to her grandmother.

But most of all, Annie loved the laces because each of them told a story—a *woman's* story. There was the fine, intricately embroidered net veil that Gramma's mother had made to wear as a bride. The crocheted lace for the nightgown she wore on her wedding night and gave to her daughter. Gramma's best lace cap. The delicate collar and cuffs that Annie's mother had crocheted. The tiny cap Annie had made for the baby she had lost, the ivory lace as fine as cobwebs. Gramma had often said that the experiences of a woman's life—hope and joy and love, pain and despair and grief—were stitched and woven and twisted and knotted into the lace she made and wore, and that those feelings lingered there like a faint perfume. The fragile ghosts could sometimes be felt much later, she said, by the right wearer, under the right conditions. Annie understood that, for she could no longer bear to wear the jet-black collar and cuffs she had made for her best dress during the year after Douglas died. Just a touch of the lacy whorls and black-beaded florets, and she was almost overwhelmed by the grief that had drowned her the whole of that year.

And life itself was like a lace, Annie thought as she turned the pieces over in her fingers, looking at the patterns, holding them up to the light. Lace was a delicate pattern of threads and spaces, sometimes familiar and expected, sometimes surprising. Life was a fragile weaving of words and actions and intentions around the absences that love—and hope and imagination—could fill with a magical promise for the future.

But in her life now, those spaces were merely empty, or filled with the sadness of loss and the ache of unfulfilled desire. Her husband and her infant son were lost to her forever.

Absence and emptiness. Unfilled spaces. Unfulfilled dreams.

* * *

WHEN most of a year had gone since Douglas' death, Annie had recovered enough to acknowledge that if she didn't take responsibility for putting her life in order, nobody else would. Empty and bleak as the future seemed, she had to face it, alone.

Annie was fortunate that the house Douglas built for her had no mortgage. But there was not a penny coming in and after some months her small savings were depleted. She let her maid go and began doing the housework and cooking—what little there was of it—herself. She got three leghorn hens and a rooster from a neighbor across the street and began her own flock of chickens, so she would have fresh eggs every day. She planted a vegetable garden outside the back door, where greens and peas and carrots and onions would be handy for the pot. And Tobias Sharp, one of Douglas' helpers, took over the blacksmith business, paying a small rent for the smithy and a commission on its earnings.

But it was her next-door neighbor, Adam, who did the most to help her get through the year after Douglas died. Adam owned the tack and feed store between Purley's General Store and the railroad tracks. He leased Douglas' stable for his horses and generously offered to do the little household repairs Annie would otherwise have had to pay for—over (she was sure) the objections of his wife, Delia.

Ah, Adam. After half a year or so, Annie understood that her feelings about him had changed. When Douglas was alive, he had been her husband's friend and a frequent visitor, and she had smiled at the sounds of men's voices and laughter in her kitchen. Now, despite her best intentions, she had fallen into the habit of listening eagerly for Adam's step outside the kitchen door. His presence seemed to fill the room, his voice made her shiver, and she was all too deeply aware of the male scent of sweat and tobacco. She tried to discipline herself against her heightened anticipation of his coming, but it wasn't easy.

"Please let me know if there's anything more I can do to help," he would say when he had finished the little chores she thought up for him. He didn't add, *Douglas would want me to do this*, but she knew that was why he came so often. She felt deeply grateful, but soon, she felt more, and she had to acknowledge the unsettling truth: she wished that Adam's visits were something more than ordinary kindness toward the widow of his best friend. This was not a truth she welcomed, for with it came an uneasy guilt.

Still, those moments were among the brightest in her week, and as she fell asleep at night, Annie often found herself thinking of the hint of laughter hiding in the corners of Adam's mouth, the gentle regard in his brown eyes, the attentive way he watched her, listening as she talked about her plans. Annie knew how dangerous it was to indulge in these imaginings, and often chided herself. Adam was a married man with a wife and a dear little girl and—while she might wish to read something different into his glances or his tone of voice—his attentions toward her were always entirely proper. Her feelings (she told herself) were simply the natural result of her loss and her desperate loneliness. As long as she kept them to herself, kept herself under control, and behaved as properly as he, there could be no harm.

When Annie recovered enough to make plans for her future, she turned to the lace that had once been a pleasing way to spend her idle hours. Now, it became something more important: a way to earn her livelihood. Her financial situation was still precarious, but with the income from the stable and the smithy and what she might earn from the lace, there could be just enough.

Before Douglas died, Annie had sold her best lacework only to friends. Now, as soon as she felt well enough, she put on her best dress and jacket, boarded the train to Austin, and—carrying samples of her work—visited Austin's two women's shops: Madame LaMode's Millinery on Pecan Street and Mrs. Turner's Ladies' Exclusive Dress Shoppe on Congress Avenue, just two blocks south of the new capitol building. She was surprised and delighted when both Mrs. Turner and Madame LaMode (whose real name was Gertrude Winkle) approved of her work and told her they would sell everything she could produce, at prices that surprised her. Lace, it seemed, was all the rage these days. Ladies were mad for lace parasols, lace-trimmed camisoles and chemises and negligees, lace gloves, veils, handkerchiefs, collars, lace on bodices and blouses, lace lavished on beautiful hats. Cheap lace was manufactured by machines so every woman could have a bit of lace at her throat and wrists, but the discriminating eye could easily see the difference between machine-made and handcrafted lace. The fashionable women of Austin were discriminating—and wealthy enough to pay the prices the shops thought fair.

When Annie realized that her lace business might actually turn into a paying enterprise, she gave it a name—*Annie's Laces*—and had some calling cards printed up. The cards had scalloped, lacelike edges, her name and address, and a pastel drawing of Gramma Anne's favorite flower, Queen Anne's lace. Within the month, she had more work than she could manage alone, so she hired a helper. When she needed more, an advertisement in the *Pecan Springs Weekly Enterprise* brought her girls who were already skilled with a needle and were glad to earn some extra money without going out to work as domestics.

Soon she was employing half a dozen, all working on a generous commission.

Annie's girls worked in the large sitting room at the front of the house, in comfortable chairs arranged where the sunlight gave them plenty of natural light for their lacemaking, with baskets beside their chairs to hold their thread, scissors, and other supplies. As they worked, they chatted and gossiped and often sang. In the winter and spring, they had read aloud from Louisa May Alcott's *Little Women*, the touching story of the four March sisters, Meg, Jo, Beth, and Amy. When Beth died so bravely—Annie herself had read that day, in a faltering voice—they all wept. This summer, they were reading Mark Twain's new novel, *Adventures of Huckleberry Finn*. Annie didn't think there would be any tears for that story.

The "girls" weren't all girls, of course. Opal and Ida Jean were the youngest, giggly twins at seventeen but skilled and quick with their crochet hooks and knitting needles. Mrs. Caldwell and Miss Windsor, both steady workers in Irish lace, were in their forties. Old Mrs. Hathaway came from across town and her niece, Mrs. Hannah Jenson, from Travis Street, the next block over. Both Mrs. Hathaway and Mrs. Jenson were bobbin lace makers, good ones, too, and every bit as adept and as fast as Gramma Anne. Annie herself made both *gros point* lace and embroidered net, which was in great demand.

Adam's wife, Delia, occasionally came from next door to join them in the workroom, but she wasn't as skilled, nor as interested, as the others. Golden-haired, with a delicate, heart-shaped face, Delia reminded Annie of the petted and spoiled Amy March. She hadn't the patience to pay attention to what her fingers were doing, so her crocheted laces were loose and clumsy. She was quick to criticize others' work and replied sharply when anyone offered her suggestions for improving her own—which she had no need to sell, so she couldn't be bothered to make it better. Annie couldn't imagine why Delia joined them.

Although Annie's conscience might prick her for her disturbing midnight imaginings about Delia's husband, she knew she had given her neighbor no reason to be jealous. But she was finding it increasingly difficult to manage the envy that flared up like an unbanked fire whenever she was in Delia's company. Her neighbor had everything any woman might want: a generous and attractive husband, a lovely child, a comfortable house, and a hired girl to cook the meals and do the housework. Delia's little daughter, sweet six-year-old Caroline, sometimes came to Annie's house to make lace. Annie, who believed that all children were by nature highly creative, was teaching her how to crochet, and her small fingers were already much more adept than her mother's. She had made a crocheted cover for Delia's pincushion and was working on a doily for her dressing table. Annie loved little Caroline and envied Delia the daily delights the child must bring.

But Delia seemed to care little for these blessings, and she often indulged in a litany of complaints. At the top of her list: the hired girl, Greta, who was insolent and had to be continually reprimanded (which Annie already knew, because she frequently heard Delia shrieking at the poor thing). Village life was boring and Delia wished Adam would buy a store in Austin, so they could move to the capital city. Or if not Austin, then to Galveston, where she had grown up and which she visited at every opportunity. She even complained about her husband, who (she said) rarely took her *anywhere* and was stingy when it came to new clothes and especially jewelry.

"Every girl likes a shiny bauble now and then," Delia would say, and sigh that she had none—although almost every time Annie saw her, she had something new. Pink mitts, to match a new dress, or a new hat or a pretty broach.

Annie thought her pretty neighbor was one of the most fortunate women on earth and simply could not understand her complaints. This was especially true when Delia confided that Adam thought they ought to have a second child.

"But I never intended to have more than one," she had added hastily. "Babies ruin your figure. And they take up so *much* of your time."

As Delia spoke, Annie thought of Adam, so generous and strong and yet gentle, and a sudden bitter longing swept through her. How could Delia refuse him? If Adam were *her* husband, she would welcome his child, his children—as many as the Good Lord cared to send them.

But that thought took her to another thought, and to a dark place that she could enter only in her dreams. Annie pushed it away.

Chapter Three

Queen Anne's lace or wild carrot (*Daucus carota*) is the foremother of those pretty deep-orange carrots (*Daucus carota sativus*) you're planning to cook for supper tonight. The plant first emerged in what is now Afghanistan and Iran and has traveled around the globe. Its long, spindle-shaped root is ivory or yellowish. And edible, but only when young, because the inner core becomes fibrous and woody as the plant grows.

After the potato, the modern carrot is the second most popular vegetable in the world. And it's not just orange! If you're looking for a way to entice your kids to eat more veggies, surprise them with a helping of purple (or red, yellow, or white) carrots. Whatever the color, this special vegetable is loaded with nutritious beta-carotene and a wide variety of antioxidants and other health-supporting nutrients.

> "Anne's Flower"
> China Bayles
> *Pecan Springs Enterprise*

"Hey, Mom!" Caitie threw her backpack into the backseat of my old white Toyota and slid in beside me. She was wearing green shorts and a bright orange tee that said *Kids Act Up!*

Caitie's casual greeting made my heart flip, as it always does. She has been a member of our family for three years now, but it was a long while before she could call me Mom. The word is still new and wonderful for me, too. As a young career woman with an all-consuming job, I'd put motherhood fairly far down on my agenda. And yet, here now is this miracle of a girl-child. I consider myself one of the luckiest women on earth.

"Hey, Cait." I patted her bare knee. "How was rehearsal?"

"It was great! I died today." She giggled. "I got to die *twice*."

"I hope you died well." I shifted into gear and pulled away from the curb. "Bravely, I mean. Without a lot of fuss."

"Oh, I did. Both times." Another giggle. "Everybody cried."

A half dozen years ago, a couple of drama professors from CTSU got a grant to restore the old International and Great Northern railroad depot on Sam Houston Street for use as a community theater. It was a brilliant idea, since otherwise, the I&GN depot would have been razed and a big chunk of Pecan Springs' history lost. Caitie is playing Beth in *Little Women*, the Depot's Summer Kids Theater production. The director says she's doing a fine job.

That's no surprise to me. Last summer, the kids put on *Peter Pan*. Caitie played Peter to thunderous applause, especially when she flew across the stage. She was a natural fit for the role. She's small for her age, slender and pixielike, with short dark hair, large dark eyes, and a marvelously expressive face. I often wish her parents could see her now and share my pride in their daughter's energy and courage. Miles, her father and my half brother, didn't come into my life until we were both adults, and he was killed before I had a chance to know him very well. I never knew her mother, either, who drowned in a boating accident when Caitie was very young. Their daughter is now ours, McQuaid's and mine. Our daughter, and very, very dear.

Caitie blew out her breath. "The only thing I don't like about the play is the costumes. They're so pretty, with all that frilly lace and ribbons. But the long skirt keeps tangling around my legs and tripping me up. I don't see how Beth could run in it, even if she wasn't sick a lot of the time."

"I don't think girls did much running in those days," I remarked, signaling for a left turn.

"Except for Jo," Caitie reminded me. "Jo was a tomboy. I wish they'd cast me to play her." She paused, looking down at her bare knees. "I'll bet girls had to wear those skirts to *keep* them from running," she said thoughtfully. "And to hide their legs. Back in those days, people weren't supposed to see anybody's legs."

I nodded, thinking about the long gray skirt that Ruby and I had found in the storeroom that morning. "If you were Beth and I were Mrs. March, we'd both be wearing long skirts—and I wouldn't like it, either." I wrinkled my nose. "Imagine trying to plant a garden in a long skirt. Or a bustle."

"A bustle!" Caitie hooted. "That would be like tying a birdcage to your bottom! How could you ever sit down?" She was silent for a moment. "Anyway, if I were Jo, I wouldn't have to die. I'd be in the play all the way to the end." She looked at me. "You haven't forgotten about the chickens, have you, Mom? Today's the day they're supposed to get their baths."

"I haven't forgotten," I said. Some girls love dogs, others give their hearts to horses. Caitie is crazy about her chickens—twelve, the last time I counted. As she did last year, she plans to enter her favorites in the poultry show at the Adams County Fair, which is a big event in our small town. The chickens have to be checked in at the fairground on Thursday morning, and Tuesday or Wednesday would have been a better bath day. But Caitie has orchestra and play rehearsal on those days, and I have to work. Bathing a chicken is definitely a two-person job (as you know, if you've ever done it), and today was the only day we were both free.

"That's why we're stopping at the store," I added, turning into the supermarket parking lot. "We need dish soap." According to the people who do this frequently, a mild dish detergent is preferred for bathing chickens.

"Super," Caitie said happily. "Dixie Chick just *loves* it when she gets a bath." She made a face. "Extra Crispy, not so much."

I pulled into a vacant spot beside a big black Dodge RAM crew-cab pickup with a baby seat in the cab and a bumper sticker with a photo of an assault rifle and the words *You Can Have My Gun When You Pry It From My Cold Dead Hands.* Texas is open carry now. Most supermarket chains have prohibited guns on their premises, but this store isn't one of them, so we might meet the driver of this truck cruising the diaper aisle with a baby in her grocery cart and an AR-15 slung over her shoulder. Personally, I don't think guns and groceries are a good combination so I don't usually shop here. But the store was on our way home and we were in a hurry. I was making an exception.

I turned off the ignition. "Dixie Chick and Extra Crispy are the only two you're showing this year?" Last summer, Caitie entered three chickens and walked away with a first, a second, and a big boost to her confidence. She also learned a lot about chickens from the other chicken fanciers who brought their best birds to the show.

"Uh-huh." Caitie made a face. "I promised Silkie-Poo she could go, too, but she's molting."

"Bad timing," I said. When Silkie-Poo is in possession of all her feathers, she looks like a white feather duster with feet—and five toes instead of the standard-issue four. When she's molting, she's covered with weird-looking patches of dusty black skin with prickly little pin-feathers popping out.

"That's okay," Caitie said confidently, getting out of the car. "I'm not sure about Dixie Chick, but Extra Crispy is going to bring home a *blue* ribbon."

WE live about a dozen miles west of Pecan Springs, down a gravel lane a half mile off Limekiln Road. Our nearest neighbors, Tom and Sylvia Banner, are well out of sight, and the sound of traffic on Limekiln Road is buffered by trees, so it's almost like living in the middle of the wilderness. The house itself is a large old-fashioned Victorian with a wraparound porch and a round tower, where Caitie has her round fairy-tale bedroom, painted her favorite shade of pink. Behind the house there's a garage, McQuaid's workshop, a barn, and Caitie's chicken coop. And my veggie and herb garden, where I grow quantities of some of the herbs I sell at the shop.

Caitie's chickens have hatched quite an enterprise. Last year, she and McQuaid installed a livestreaming "chicken cam" in the pen. The camera feeds images to Caitie's website—called Texas Chix—so viewers around the world can see what the "Chix" are up to at any given moment. The website features an "About the Chix" page, with photographs of each of the chickens; an "About Caitie" page (no photo, for security reasons); and her blog, *Chicken Scratches*, where she posts almost every week. Caitie loves answering emails from "friends and followers" who pester her with questions about raising chickens. The whole thing has become a valuable learning experience.

Extra Crispy is currently Caitie's only rooster. He is Mr. Personality Plus, a rather spectacular Cubalaya, which is a Cuban breed that dates back to the 1930s. A majestic fowl with a lipstick-red comb and a bright yellow beak, he sports a gleaming orange-red feathery drape over his back and wings and an elegant black tail so long that it sweeps the grass. Caitie hand-raised this gorgeous guy from a scrawny little chick and he's tame enough to ride around on her shoulder. A plus: Cubalaya roosters have no spurs, which means that Extra Crispy is less likely to rip the skin off our arms when we give him a bath, which he hates.

Chickens are dirty birds by nature. Caitie's flock's favorite spa is a bowl-like depression in the corner of their run, filled with dry dirt and wood ashes. On a hot afternoon, they can all be found there, blissfully tossing dust, fluffing feathers, rolling over, and playing dead. There's nothing more comical than a chicken indulging in a dust bath.

But chickens that are candidates for a blue ribbon need a real bath, which means water. Warm water. With soap. In good weather, Caitie and I do this outdoors, because some chickens resent the process. Winchester (our basset) usually offers to referee but I tell him this is not a game. He has to stay indoors.

Caitie filled a couple of large plastic totes with warm water (one for washing, the other for rinsing) and started with Dixie Chick, a plump, matronly Buff Orpington hen the color of an antique gold watch. Bathing is obviously on Dixie's bucket list. She loves her bath so much that she falls asleep the minute Caitie starts applying the soap to her feathers and doesn't wake up until she is fully washed and rinsed. Then, while I hold her, Caitie does her pedicure (chickens have really *dirty* feet), trims her bill, and rubs her comb and wattles with olive oil to make them glisten. To hasten the drying process, I lay a couple of towels on the grass and Caitie bundles her up like a chicken burrito, head sticking out of one end of the terry towel rollup, feet out of the other.

When Dixie Chick is drowsing in her burrito-wrap, it's Extra Crispy's turn. This guy doesn't take to bathing with Dixie's equanimity, and he expressed his feelings with indignant squawks and an irate flapping of wings. By the time we were finished, Caitie and I were nearly as wet as the rooster. But it wasn't long before both chickens were clean and popped into the clean cages that we set up on the picnic table so their feathers could dry quickly. To speed this along, Caitie went upstairs and got my hair dryer.

Today's baths are not quite the end of the process, however. On Thursday morning, Caitie will wash their chicken feet again and rub them with olive oil, check for poopee on their rear ends, and smooth Extra Crispy's tail with a silk cloth to make it shiny. (Don't ask me: all I know is that it works.) Then McQuaid will take her and her chickens to the fairgrounds for the big event. That's the plan, anyway. Like most plans around our house, it's subject to change.

While Caitie emptied the plastic totes and put things away, I went upstairs and changed into dry shorts and a T-shirt. When I came back down to the kitchen and looked at the clock, I saw that McQuaid would be home in fifteen minutes. Brian and Casey, his girlfriend, would be along shortly after. It was time to feed Winchester and Mr. P and start putting supper on the table.

Winchester is our new basset boy, a replacement for the late, lamented Howard Cosell—although no dog could replace Howard in our hearts. Winnie (whom we found at Basset Rescue in Austin) is only three years old. But he's already seen enough of life to be profoundly pessimistic about the future of our planet and all its resident species, and he frequently offers his opinion on the subject in melancholy bass-and-tenor basset bays. Winchester's personal issues are mostly territorial. He has staked a nighttime claim to the entire foot of our bed, insists on anytime access to McQuaid's leather recliner, and will lunge through the locked screen door whenever a squirrel or crow trespasses in his personal backyard. Another issue still under negotiation: the house rule that bassets are not permitted to have bagels or pizza. When Winchester stands on his hind legs, he is as tall as he is long—which is just tall enough to reach a slice of pizza left carelessly at the edge of the kitchen counter. His own personal rule: if you don't catch me eating it (or if I reach it before you do), it's mine.

In anticipation of dinner, Winchester was stationed beside his bowl, and when I came into the kitchen, he greeted me with an enthusiastic wag of his tail. He knows it's his bowl, because it has his name on it. W-I-N-C-H-E-S-T-E-R, in big orange letters. When I pour his dog food into it, he assumes his flat-basset position with his belly on the floor and a possessive paw on either side of the bowl, counting the kibbles as they cascade past his nose. Then, still prone, he gets down to business immediately and with serious purpose. He growls as he eats (to discourage interlopers), dispatches his dinner quickly, then licks the bowl inside and out. Bassets live for mealtimes.

We feed Mr. P (aka Pumpkin, because he's that color) on a shelf in the pantry, out of Winchester's reach. This cat is a crafty, battle-scarred old tom who showed up on our doorstep starved and sore-pawed and captured Caitie's heart. I tried to talk her into a kitten instead, but she shook her head.

"He's just like me when I first came to live here," she said, clutching him defiantly. "He doesn't have any family. He needs somebody to adopt him. He needs *me.*" When he heard this, Mr. P turned up his purr another notch. He'd been on the lam long enough to know that he had lucked into the deal of nine lifetimes.

While the dog and the cat were making short work of their dinners, I got out the makings for a green salad and put rice into the rice cooker. The rice would accompany the Moroccan chicken and carrot main dish that had been simmering in the slow cooker all day. I lifted the lid and sniffed the blended aromas appreciatively. Lemon, cinnamon, coriander, cumin. Perfect. All I had to do was ladle it into a large bowl and let people help themselves.

I had set the table and was just finishing the salad—romaine, mushrooms, red onion rings, chopped tomatoes, sliced cucumbers, diced celery, and hard-cooked eggs—when the kitchen door opened and McQuaid came in. My husband is a big man, six-feet-two and broad-shouldered, with dark hair, pale blue eyes, and a knife scar (a relic of a run-in with a druggie when McQuaid was with Houston Homicide) across his forehead. A craggy-looking guy with a quick grin that never fails to light my fire.

"Hey, China." He came up behind me and nuzzled the nape of my neck. He spoke with his lips against my skin. "Caitie is out there with a hair dryer, blow-drying two damp chickens on the picnic table. You know about this?"

"I know." I turned into his arms. "You should have been here when the rooster got his bath. Cursing in chicken language. Wild wing-flapping. A tsunami of epochal proportions."

McQuaid kissed me. "Sounds like a helluva party." He chuckled and let me go. "Sorry I missed it. But them's the breaks." He opened the fridge, took out a bottle of Lone Star, and nimbly blocked Winchester with one foot. (Winchester makes a beeline for the fridge whenever it's opened, hoping to snatch an unwary slice of leftover pizza.) He popped the top of his beer and gave the table settings a curious glance. "One, two, three. Four and five?"

"Brian." I began slicing the last hard-cooked egg. "And Casey."

There was a silence. "Ah," McQuaid said thoughtfully. "I think I knew that. But I forgot." After a moment, he cleared his throat and started again. "Casey is a lovely girl, really. And smart as the dickens. I don't blame Brian for being smitten. Just takes some getting used to, that's all. Makes me feel old, I guess. My little kid with a live-in, when he's hardly old enough to vote." He swigged his beer. "I hope they're being . . . well, careful. Taking precautions, I mean."

"I'm sure they are," I said cautiously. "Both of them are serious about school. And Casey is premed." Which meant, I was sure, that she knew more about the birds and bees than I did at her age. (Not much of a comparison, actually, since I knew next to nothing.)

"Right. But accidents happen." He said this with a sheepish twist, and I remembered that he had once told me that Brian had been an accident. McQuaid's first wife, Sally, had not wanted children, and after Brian was born, she had announced that her little boy would be an only child. To make her point irrevocably clear, she'd had her tubes tied—without discussing it with McQuaid.

"I imagine they know what they're doing," I said in a reassuring tone, putting the salad bowl on the table. Our son Brian had brought his girlfriend to see us several times since they'd moved in together. McQuaid was absolutely right. Casey was as gorgeous as a fashion model, with an athletic figure, satiny dark skin, and very short black hair that accentuated the angular contours of her face.

"I had it cut really short so I don't have to fool with it," she'd told me the last time they visited. "Between tennis and my classes," she added ruefully, "I have more than enough to keep me busy." That was an understatement. Casey is at the University of Texas on a tennis scholarship, which adds hours of practice and competition to the heavy load of her academic program.

McQuaid turned the frosty beer bottle in his fingers. "Do you suppose they'll be together this time next year?"

The question was unanswerable, but I knew what had prompted it. McQuaid was wondering if Brian and Casey were considering marriage. And what he would say if the subject came up.

"I can't even guess," I said honestly. "They're young and living away from home for the first time. They're exploring their freedom. But they've both got years of college ahead of them."

"I just hope the boy remembers that," McQuaid said, and swigged his beer again.

I didn't say "He's not a boy," because I knew that McQuaid knows that, too. As you might expect, Brian's choice of a live-in girlfriend has given both of us something to think about. But the question itself raises a question. Would we have to "think about" how we feel if Brian had moved in with a white girl?

In the end, though, we've agreed that our son's choice of someone to love is *his* choice. All he needs to hear from us is that his family loves and trusts him and is firmly in his corner. He can work out the rest—whatever that might be—on his own.

McQuaid changed the subject. "We wrapped up the last interview on the fraud case this afternoon. Got the background work done last week, so all we have to do is write the report and we're done."

He and Blackie Blackwell, his partner in their private investigations firm, had been hired by a large Austin law firm to do background checks on two dozen witnesses, conduct interviews, and prepare questions for depositions in a criminal fraud case the firm is preparing for trial. It's the kind of job McQuaid enjoys, for it requires him to use all his investigative and interrogative skills. It's the kind of job I approve of, too, because investigating and interrogating aren't usually hazardous to my husband's health. The other kind involves guns and dangerous people.

"Got another client lined up?" I asked, reaching into the cupboard for dessert dishes. I'd baked a peach-and-carrot cobbler the day before. There was plenty left, so we'd have that for dessert, with peach ice cream.

"Nope." McQuaid put his empty beer bottle in the recycle bin. "But Blackie's been tagged by Foremost to investigate an insurance scam in Lubbock. He left for there this morning and plans to be gone a week or so. He said to tell you that Sheila's feeling a little bit better. She's supposed to go back to work tomorrow, but he'd be grateful if you'd keep an eye on her."

"I'll be glad to." I chuckled. "But she won't like it."

Sheila is Blackie's wife, Pecan Springs' first female police chief, and now the first *pregnant* female chief. She and Blackie are expecting a baby in November. Just last week, Smart Cookie (as her friends call her) put on a maternity uniform and broke the news to the city council and the police department. Her announcement, as you can imagine, caused a stir. This is, after all, good-old-boy country, and when it comes to running their cop shop, good old boys quite naturally prefer that other good old boys do it. Sheila's job has held its challenges from Day One, and her pregnancy is making it several orders of magnitude more difficult. There are those in the department and on the council who would like to treat her as if she has a disability that disqualifies her as chief—or maybe it's a communicable disease and *she* should be quarantined (in case pregnancy is contagious).

Smart Cookie's comeback: "Hey. I'm not disabled. I'm not sick. I'm pregnant. If you don't know the difference, ask your wife. Or your mother." Of course, all of this opposition makes her stubbornly want to appear as "normal" as possible. So even though she's had a problem with persistent morning sickness—hyperemesis, the doctor calls it— she hates to miss work. And she won't like the idea that her absent husband has asked a friend to keep an eye on her.

But at least she knows that she's working under a departmental policy that is friendly toward pregnant officers. She and other members of the department developed the policy last year, and the council approved it a few months ago. Sheila says she's a test case—a "trial balloon." I tell her she's not that big yet. Just wait another couple of months.

SUPPER was on the table when Brian and Casey arrived. Brian is almost as tall as his dad, with the same dark hair and pale blue eyes, the same firm jaw and broad shoulders. Together, they make the kitchen seem crowded. Casey filled the glasses with ice and poured the iced tea, McQuaid summoned Caitie from her chicken grooming session, and we all sat down to supper. The Moroccan lemon chicken with rice was a hit, everybody enjoyed the salad, and the peach-and-carrot cobbler provided a colorful conclusion.

As always at our house, supper was a time for everyone to share what was going on in their lives. McQuaid related a sanitized version of a recent missing-person investigation, and I told about finding the chest of lace in the storeroom (but omitted the spooky bit about hearing a woman humming, which would no doubt evoke hoots of laughter). Casey reported on her recent tennis match, and Brian recounted a funny story about a guy who came into the garden supply where he works part time, wanting to buy "real cow poop," not that "dried-up crap in a plastic bag." And Caitie described our tussle with Extra Crispy and invited everyone to her play. "It's a week from Friday," she said importantly. "Please come and watch me die."

As our guests left, Brian gave me an extra hug. "Thanks, Mom," he whispered in my ear. "You guys are great. I really appreciate you."

"You and Casey are the ones who are great," I said, meaning it. "Come back as often as you can."

Lori Lowry phoned just as McQuaid and I started the kitchen cleanup, so I left him to it and went into the dining room to talk to her. "Just calling to let you know that Professor Vickery got the photos of that lace," she said. "She says she'd love to have a look at them. She's free tomorrow afternoon—okay if she drops by the shops, around four? I'll be between classes and we can meet upstairs."

"Super," I said. "It'll be good to talk to somebody who knows about this stuff."

"Christine Vickery is the right person," Lori said. "She did her thesis on lacemaking as a women's craft in Ireland and America." She paused, and a different energy came into her voice. "I've had some good news on my birth mother search, China."

"That's great, Lori! Who have you found?"

"Aunt Josephine! She was my adoptive mother's sister, although they were on bad terms. She lives in Waco—and she's willing to tell me what she knows about my adoption."

"Woo-hoo," I said. "Atta girl!"

"I'm not getting my hopes up, of course. But this search has taught me that you never can tell what'll happen when you pull on a thread. It might unravel a whole new series of possibilities."

"Sounds a little like a detective story," I said. "You are the detective and—"

"And my mother is the missing person," Lori said with a laugh. "Yes, that's exactly what it is—a detective story. Anyway, after we talk to Professor Vickery tomorrow, I'm driving to Waco to see if Aunt Josephine can give me any clues. She's even invited me for supper."

"Fingers crossed," I said, repeating Ruby's old Irish blessing. "I hope she can tell you something useful."

"I do, too," Lori said. "But whether she does or not, it'll be interesting to meet her, after all these years. Her email seemed friendly." She sighed. "I'd love to have even a little bit of family."

Sometimes even a little bit of family can be just what we need to set things right, I thought as we said good-bye. Lori's mention of Professor Vickery had reminded me of the laces, so I took the wooden chest to the dining room table and opened it to have another look.

Caitie came to prop her elbows on the table and watch me take out the lace, piece by piece—some two dozen in all. The largest was the embroidered net veil, the smallest a six-inch strip of narrow cobwebby lace. There was a lady's lace cap with long ribbons, a baby's lace cap, the black lace collar that had made Ruby so inexplicably sad, and the pink fingerless mitts, made of silk yarn. And something I hadn't noticed that afternoon: a single gold-filigree earring with a shiny pink stone, stuck in one corner of the chest.

"Just one earring?" Caitie asked, picking it up. She held it up, turning it to catch the light in the gold lacework around the pink stone. "It's pretty. I guess the other one got lost, huh?"

"Probably." I turned the lady's cap in my fingers. "Gosh. I wonder how old this is."

"It looks like what Mrs. March wears in *Little Women*," Caitie said, dropping the earring back in the chest and taking the cap from me. "That would make it *really* old." She ran a finger around the frilly lace edging. "Somebody went to a lot of trouble to make this, didn't they?"

"I'm sure," I said. "Hours and hours of work, all by hand."

"A woman?"

"Most likely." I began putting the pieces of lace back in the chest. "A professor from the university is coming to have a look tomorrow. Maybe she'll be able to tell us something about the person who made these."

Caitie nodded and straightened. "I'd better practice my violin. There's orchestra rehearsal tomorrow. And I want to put some more chicken pictures on my website." She began ticking things off on her fingers. "Play rehearsal on Wednesday. The chickens go to the fair on Thursday morning. And on Friday evening, we go back to the fair to see what I've won." She grinned confidently. "And celebrate a blue ribbon. Maybe two."

I laughed. "Haven't you heard the old saying? Don't count your chickens before they're hatched. You never know what might happen."

I was joking. But I was right.

Really. You just never know.

Chapter Four

Now that Annie was alone and had only herself to rely on for her living, her little lacemaking business became not just the center of her life but her sustenance, as well. As long as there was a ready market for her lace, she felt she should be able to manage.

So on an early July morning, she prepared to take the train to Austin to sell the laces that she and the girls had finished in the past two weeks. She pinned up her auburn hair and put on her gray poplin traveling suit with a lace-trimmed white shirtwaist, gored skirt, and jacket. The bustle was back, but Annie's sympathies lay with the Rational Dress Movement and she refused to wear the ridiculous wire contraption, which made sitting terribly uncomfortable. She also preferred a simple wide-brimmed straw hat with a red velvet band and a modest gray feather to the more lavishly decorated hats that were in fashion. Her only pieces of jewelry were the simple gold earrings and gold lapel watch that Douglas had given her for their first anniversary. She had buried her wedding ring with her husband.

The summer day promised to be bright and hot, but the air was still reasonably cool when Annie folded the laces into tissue paper and packed them in a wicker basket. With her white parasol over her shoulder, she walked the six blocks to the railroad depot on Sam Houston Street, to catch the nine a.m. northbound train. The International and Great Northern railway had reached Pecan Springs just six years before, linking the village to Austin (thirty-five miles to the north) and San Antonio (thirty-five miles to the south). Its arrival had transformed the sleepy hamlet of five hundred souls to a bustling, prosperous village of nearly twelve hundred. A hotel had been built beside the small spring-fed lake for which Pecan Springs was named, and tourists were flocking to the cool, crystal waters. A teachers' college was under construction north of town on Cedar Ridge. The presence of tourists, students, and faculty members promised to change the village and make it grow even faster.

Annie always took a seat by the train window so she could enjoy the sight of the rolling, cedar-clad hills and limestone bluffs to the west. She wiped the coal dust from the seat before she sat down, then settled back, enjoying the pleasant view and the rhythmic *clackety-clack* of the wheels as the train took her northward to Austin, with stops at stations in San Marcos and Kyle and Buda to pick up passengers and freight. In the old days, before the train, the trip to Austin by horse and buggy took all day—if you were lucky. Now, the train trip took just ninety minutes. It wasn't yet eleven o'clock when she stepped from the coach car at the new buff brick railroad depot at Congress Avenue and Pine Street, north of the Colorado River.

If Pecan Springs was prospering in this second decade after the War Between the States, Austin—the capital of Texas—was booming. The station platform was crowded with bales of cotton and bushel baskets of chili peppers, peanuts, and yams, all destined for Dallas and Houston and points farther north and east. Some people still thought of Austin as a cow town, but the population had already reached nearly fifteen thousand people, some four times what it had been when the war ended. The city streets were crowded with horse-drawn wagons, trolleys, horse and buggies, and bicycles. The dust rose in clouds, and the sky shimmered with the usual Texas summer heat. But there was an energy in the air that gave Annie the sense that today, in this bustling city, anything was possible.

Holding up her gray skirt to keep it out of the dirt and avoiding piles of steaming horse manure as she crossed the streets, Annie walked up the wide gravel path along Congress Avenue. There was a spring in her step and a smile on her lips, for she was anticipating the pleasure of accepting the money from the sales of her laces, along with several special orders. Mrs. Turner might report: "Mrs. Hillary would like you to make the laces for her daughter's trousseau negligee." Or Madame LaMode might say, in her fake French accent, "Mademoiselle Campbell weeshes me to tell you zat she adores ze lace-covered parasol you made for her and wonders if you would consent to make another for her deerest friend." Annie would smile and nod and make notes in the little book in which she kept her orders—neatly and with care, because she was a businesswoman now, earning her own living, and it was important to keep track of everything.

But instead of a cheerful smile and a special order, Mrs. Turner—a gray-haired woman in her sixties—wore a somber look as she handed Annie the envelope with her payment and some disquieting news.

"The doctor says I must have a rest, so I've decided to close the shop." She sighed apologetically. "I've loved your laces, but I won't be taking any more, I'm afraid."

Annie was startled, then concerned. Mrs. Turner had been her very first Austin customer and she depended on the dress shop as a regular market. "Of course I wish you the very best," she said, and then asked the question that worried her most. "Do you think another shop will open here?"

"Oh, most assuredly," Mrs. Turner said. "Mr. Josephus Ward, from Dallas, has purchased the lease to this building and intends to open a haberdashery." Another apologetic smile. "But Austin is growing fast and someone is sure to open another dress shop soon, I should think. I hope this won't be a hardship for you, my dear."

A haberdashery! But that was only *men's* clothing! Still, Annie tried to cover up her apprehension. She lifted her chin, summoning a brave smile. "Oh, no. No hardship at all. I know how much work you've put into your shop, Mrs. Turner. I hope you enjoy your rest."

Annie wasn't feeling so brave when she stepped back out to the bright, bustling street. But she reminded herself that Mrs. Turner was right. Austin was flourishing—witness the "university of the first class" that was being built on forty empty acres north of the new state capitol. Oh, and the plan to build one of the largest dams and electrical generating plants in the world—yes, in the *world*!—just upstream of the city on the Colorado River. Soon, very soon, someone was sure to open another dress shop.

In the meantime, Annie was certain that Madame LaMode would take what Mrs. Turner couldn't use. Picking up her pace, she turned the corner at Hickory and started down the block. But when she reached the millinery shop, she was stunned to see that the display window was dark and empty and there was a Closed sign on the door. A note tucked into the door frame directed her to the barbershop across the street, where the barber handed her a cigar box and an envelope with her name on it. There was money in the envelope and a few unsold laces in the box, smelling of cigars. There was also a note.

It read simply, *My daughter has fallen ill in New Orleans and I must go to her. I do not plan to return.* Au revoir. *Gertrude Winkle.*

Annie gasped. *Oh, no—not this one, too!* She stared incredulously at the note, feeling as though someone had just punched her in the stomach. Somehow, she managed to thank the barber and went out onto Hickory, where she stood for a moment, trying to decide what to do. Usually, she treated herself to a nice lunch on her visits to Austin. But the two envelopes she had picked up contained a total of just seven dollars, more than half of which had to be shared with the ladies who had made the lace. Her chief source of income had just vanished, and there was no quick or easy way to replace it. The sensible thing to do would be to pick up a twenty-cent sandwich at the Pork Barrel on the corner of Congress and Hickory, go back to the station, and wait for the afternoon train.

But that would feel like a defeat, wouldn't it? And this—well, it wasn't a defeat. It wasn't! She had just met a temporary obstacle, that's all. She had lost everything in the world when she lost Douglas and their baby boy. Compared to that, this little setback was only a bump in the road.

Defiantly, she straightened her shoulders, crossed the street, and marched up the block to the imposing Driskill Hotel, recently built at the corner of Brazos and Pecan. The cost of lunch in the ladies' dining room—a whole dollar—was outrageous. But the table was spread with a snowy damask cloth, the crystal goblet held cold water and little cubes of real ice, and Annie's meal of veal cutlet, mashed potatoes, fried okra, and baked apple was served on the hotel's elegant gold-rimmed china. Placing the damask napkin on her lap, she glanced around, noticing the other women. They were all beautifully dressed—

out-of-town visitors, wealthy enough to afford one of the lavish rooms upstairs at the Driskill, which were rumored to cost as much as four dollars a night. As she ate, she tried to pretend that she wasn't a working woman who had just lost her job—*both* of them!—but was one of those ladies of leisure, come to Austin to enjoy some sightseeing.

After lunch, still trying to keep up her private pretense, Annie put up her parasol and strolled north on Congress Avenue to observe the newly built state capitol building. Dedicated just three months before, the building was constructed of native red granite dug out of the hills to the west of the city. It was immense—the *seventh* largest building in the world, it was said—with an astonishing 392 rooms and a dome that rose a breathtaking three hundred feet in the air. It was topped by a huge statue of a woman. Her upraised hand held a star, representing the Lone Star State.

Annie stood for a few moments, gazing wide-eyed at the awe-inspiring dome. But if she had hoped that some of the Lone Star's proud bravado might rub off on her, she was disappointed. The impressive size of the capitol building only made her feel small and insignificant, and the heat—the sun had slid behind clouds but the air was heavy and sultry—was making her light-headed. The hem of her gray poplin skirt was dirty, her hair straggled in damp curls around her face, and the underarms of her jacket were wet. Wearily, she turned and trudged back down Congress to catch the train to Pecan Springs, wishing she hadn't spent that small fortune on lunch at the Driskill when a Pork Barrel sandwich would have done just as well.

To make matters worse, as she sat in the station waiting for the train, Delia Hunt came tripping along and plumped herself down on the waiting-room bench. She looked cool and summery in a pink ruffled dress with (of course) a stylish bustle that required her to perch on the very edge of the bench. Her golden hair was caught in a pink net snood and she wore pink lace mitts—the very latest fashion—and smelled of a flowery perfume. She was carrying a basket filled with several parcels and chattering like a jaybird about what she'd bought and how much everything had cost and how annoyed Adam would be when he saw the bills—especially for the new earrings she had just purchased and that now dangled from her pretty ears. Pink amethysts, set in delicate gold-filigree lace.

Delia pouted. "Adam always tells me I shouldn't spend so much. I try to be good and mind him, of course—until I'm tempted past all resistance." She touched one earring. "I can simply never say no to a pretty pair of earrings, and these were only ten dollars. Real amethysts, too."

Ten dollars. Annie pulled in her breath. She and her girls had to work for a week to earn ten dollars!

"And anyway," Delia went on, "I needed something to go with this dress. Caroline and I are taking the train to Galveston tomorrow. With luck, we'll be there for a couple of months."

Delia had grown up in Galveston, and she returned every so often to visit her sister. Annie often thought that Pecan Springs must feel like a frontier village compared to Galveston, which at the last census had been the largest city in the state. Brightened by tropical flowers, it was also the most beautiful, everyone said, and certainly the most cosmopolitan, since it was a seaport and entertained people from the farthest-flung corners of the world.

Delia was smiling. "Of course, while I'm there, Clarissa and I will be going to all the best parties. The summer season isn't as grand as the winter, but it's still a great lot of fun." She turned to glance down her nose at Annie and, for the first time in a while, seemed to *see* her. She frowned at Annie's sweat-stained jacket and straggling hair.

"I wonder at you, Annie," she said. "I really do. Your husband's been dead for—what? Two years? Three? Isn't it time you fixed yourself up and went looking for another one? It's rather brave of you to try to manage on your own, of course. But that's no kind of life for a woman. Like it or not, we all have to marry, if we can. And if we can't—" She gave a short, brittle laugh. "Well, as I said, that's no kind of life, is it? But then, I imagine you've already found that out."

Annie sucked in her breath. She had always tried to return Delia's habitually disparaging remarks with something polite and neutral. But it didn't matter what she said. Delia was a silly chatterbox, impervious to even the most barbed rebuke. She was either completely unaware that her remarks might be hurtful or she didn't care. Annie had always suspected that it was the latter.

And this afternoon, the secret resentment she often felt toward Adam's wife suddenly bloomed into a hot red coal burning deep inside her. In Delia's pretty, perfumed shadow, Annie could no longer pretend to be anything other than she was: a poor-as-a-church-mouse widow whose chief source of income had just vanished. A woman who needed a husband.

Annie was too angry to risk an answer. Without a word, she rose and walked away. And when the train arrived, she chose a seat next to a portly gentleman who smelled of garlic and cigars, so Delia could not sit beside her.

Chapter Five

The ancient Chinese sailors who used ginger to prevent seasickness were right. Ginger's antinausea action relieves motion sickness and dizziness (vertigo) better than the standard drug treatment, Dramamine, according to one study published in the British medical journal *Lancet* . . . In addition to motion sickness, the researchers recommended ginger capsules, ginger tea, or ginger ale for the morning sickness of pregnancy. Some doctors now recommend it for nausea associated with chemotherapy.

The Healing Herbs,
Michael Castleman

I didn't sleep very well that night. In my dreams, I was back in that dark storeroom, the scent of lavender heavy around me. I was searching for something—what it was, I had no idea—pawing futilely through mountains of boxes and bins and piles of newspaper. I tossed and turned until Winchester abandoned the foot of the bed and McQuaid shook me awake to tell me that I was having a bad dream. When I finally woke a little after six, a haunting fragment of the Scottish melody I'd heard in the storeroom was running through my head. *And for bonnie Annie Laurie, I'd lay me down and die.* As I dressed (my usual shop outfit: jeans, sneakers, and a green Thyme and Seasons T-shirt), I found myself humming it.

Downstairs, I fixed a quick breakfast for McQuaid, Caitie, and the animals. I was on my way out the door, heading for the shop, when I got an anxious telephone call from Connie Page, Sheila's longtime assistant at the Pecan Springs Police Department.

"China, I just got off the phone with Sheila. She planned to come in early today, but she called to say she'll be late. She's been throwing up all night, and she didn't sound good at all. I'm worried about her. Blackie's out of town on a case, and I can't leave the office—we've had a couple of crises already, and there's another one brewing. We can certainly use her here, but if she's sick, I hope she won't push herself. Can you stop at her house and see what the situation is?"

Of course I could. And if Sheila had been throwing up, I knew what she needed. I went back in the house and took the last two bottles of my homebrewed ginger ale out of the fridge. Ginger is the best thing for nausea, but the ginger ale you find in grocery stores is either artificially flavored or doesn't contain enough ginger to get the job done. On the other hand, pregnant women need to be careful when they use ginger, since researchers say that in high doses (2000 or more milligrams a day), it can cause uterine cramping and even miscarriage. I also filled a baggie with dried peppermint from the canister I keep in the kitchen for making tea. There's more than one way to treat a case of nausea.

Twenty minutes later, I was parking behind Sheila's black-and-white cop car in the drive at her house on Hickory Street. I went around the back, opened the gate, and saw Rambo, Sheila's fearsome-looking Rottweiler, sitting on the porch step. Rambo works the day shift in the PSPD's K-9 Unit (nights, too, when there's an emergency), so Sheila's being late to work meant that the Rottie wouldn't be punching in on time, either.

Rambo scrambled to his feet as I came up the steps, gave an eager welcoming *woof,* and escorted me to the kitchen door, even pushing a little. Rambo looks like a vicious junkyard dog, and when the occasion demands, he can act like one, too. With bad guys, he is all teeth and threatening snarls, but with friends, he's a sweetie with exquisite manners. And like all Rotties, he has a very strong sense of responsibility, especially for Sheila's welfare. Now, he stood beside me, pressing against my knee and whining, his stub of a tail wagging so hard that it wagged his whole rear end. Rambo has been clocked at twenty-five miles an hour and he can clamber up and over a six-foot-high chain-link fence. But while he has many talents, he can't open a latched door. Obviously, he was asking me to do that for him. I felt a prickle of apprehension.

I knocked several times but didn't get any answer, and the prickle became an urgent concern. Sheila's squad car was in the drive, so she was still here. Rambo was outside, so she had gotten up to let him out. She had talked to Connie, as well. So where was she?

I knocked again and gave a loud *yoo-hoo*, then turned the knob and pushed at the door. It wasn't locked. "Let's go in, Big Guy," I said.

But Rambo didn't need my permission. He had already shoved past me through the open door, dashed across the kitchen, and was pounding up the stairs.

I found Sheila on the bathroom floor, Rambo frantically licking her face. Half-dressed and barefoot, she was just beginning to come around, and was dazed and only semi-coherent. Normally, she is downright beautiful, tall and willowy, with blond hair that she wears twisted up in a bun, blue eyes, a fetching nose, and full lips. This morning, her hair was down and disheveled, her face was ashen, her eyes barely focusing, her pulse fast and slight. There was a deep cut over her ear and she was bleeding badly. From what I could manage to get out of her, I guessed that she hadn't been able to keep any meals down the day before and hadn't kept herself hydrated. She had fainted, fallen, and whacked her head on the edge of the bathtub.

"I have to get dressed . . . go to work," she said in a blurry voice, as Rambo whined worriedly. She struggled to push herself up but fell back dizzily. "Help me up, China," she whispered. "Please . . ."

I didn't try. We were way past the point where ginger ale or peppermint tea would get Smart Cookie on her feet and into her uniform.

"Lie still, sweetie," I commanded, reaching into my jeans pocket for my phone. I knew that Sheila wouldn't want to alert the dispatcher, who would spread the news all over the department quicker than you can say 911. So I called Connie.

"Oh, dear God," Connie said breathlessly, when she heard my report. "I'm so glad you're there, China! Is she all right? Sounds like a concussion. Is the baby—"

"No idea," I said, breaking in. "We need to get her to the hospital. Can you handle the dispatch yourself? She'll want us to keep this under wraps until we know something definite."

"Will do." Connie stopped babbling and became all business. "Somebody will be there in less than five minutes, China. Hang tight."

I ran into the bedroom, pulled a blanket off the bed, and covered Sheila, who was shivering. I encouraged Rambo to curl up as close as he could get, to keep her warm. Then I made a compress out of a damp washcloth and pressed it against the gash in her scalp. All the time, I kept telling her that she was going to be just fine once EMS got an IV into her and pumped her full of fluids.

I hoped to God it was true.

When Sheila was in the ambulance and on her way to the hospital, I put Rambo in my Toyota and dropped him off at the K-9 facility, telling the supervisor that the chief wanted to board him overnight for a day or two. Back in the car, I took a few moments to phone McQuaid. I told him about Sheila's accident and asked him to get in touch with Blackie, who was working that new case up in Lubbock. Then I phoned Ruby to ask her to open the shop for me, and explained why.

When I got to the hospital, Helen Berger, a friend and fellow herb guild member, was on duty in the ER. She told me that they had already taken Sheila upstairs for a CT scan. I hung around for a while, pacing the floor and biting my nails, before deciding that since I wasn't helping matters, I might as well go to the shop. I gave Helen my number and Connie Page's and asked her to get in touch with both of us when there was news.

"I hope we can keep this quiet for now," I said in a lower voice. "Jessica Nelson from the *Enterprise* monitors the EMS runs in town. I wouldn't be surprised if she popped in to see what's going on."

"I understand," Helen said gravely. "Patient privacy is a watchword around here."

It's good to have friends in the right places.

At the shop that morning, it was business as usual, except that the Library Reading Circle was meeting for lunch in the tearoom. It's a largish group, so Cass and Jenna, her helper, were already setting up for it. On the menu: an easy chicken and pesto wrap, tomato basil soup, and fruit. Several of Lori's students came in and went upstairs to the loft to work on their weaving projects, and Ruby was teaching her Tuesday morning meditation class in the Crystal Cave's back room. Khat, as usual, was stretched out on the windowsill beside a pot of bright green parsley, napping in the sunshine. It would have been a lovely morning, if I hadn't been so uneasy about Sheila.

And then something happened to ratchet up my uneasiness a few dozen points. Merilee Kaufman, one of my frequent customers, dropped in on her way to work at the antique shop on the square. While I was ringing up her purchases—a box of mini lavender soap bars and a bottle of eucalyptus oil—she asked me about our fall classes. "I heard that Kelly Sutherland is teaching wreath-making," she said. "Do you know when?"

"First and third Saturdays in October," I said. "The classes are all listed there." I pointed to the magnetic bulletin board that hangs on the wall at the end of the counter, where customers can easily see it. I had posted the list the day before and made a colorful caption for it—FALL CLASSES—using some handy magnetic alphabet letters I bought at the five-and-dime.

But what I saw jerked me back for a second look. Between the class list and this week's tearoom menus (fastened to the board with cute yellow smiley-face magnets) somebody had posted a photograph. I recognized it right away: the sepia-toned photograph I had seen in the box in the storeroom, the picture of the smiling couple with the baby and the little girl, sitting in the porch swing on the veranda—on *my* veranda. The photo was stuck on with a heart-shaped magnet, and behind it was a single sprig of lavender. Fresh-picked lavender, just out of the garden. And as I turned back to Merilee, the bell over my front door rang twice, emphatically, as if it were making a point. I looked to see who had come in, but the door stayed shut.

"Your bell is ringing but nobody's there," Merilee said unnecessarily.

"I know." I sighed. "I have no clue."

I had no clue to the photo, either. I had put the Corticelli carton of photographs back on the shelf in the storeroom, intending to take it home and go through it some Sunday afternoon. I remembered doing that, quite clearly. So how had that photograph gotten to the bulletin board? The simplest explanation was the likeliest one, I told myself, exchanging Merilee's purchases for her credit card. It had fallen out of the carton and Ruby or Lori had picked it up and stuck it on my board.

So a little later, when Ruby came into the shop to remind me that the Library Reading Circle was coming to lunch and we needed to take turns hosting the tearoom, I asked her about the photo.

"Wasn't me," she said. "And I don't know when Lori could have done it. It was on your bulletin board when I opened up this morning. I noticed it because of the lavender. It smelled very fresh, like it had just been picked."

Before I could answer, the bell over my front door gave a silvery, half-amused tinkle. Khat, who had been sound asleep on the window-sill, suddenly woke, gave a gruff *mrrrow!* and jumped to the floor. In an instant, he had darted out of the room.

Ruby looked at me and raised her eyebrows.

I shrugged helplessly. "I'll ask McQuaid to take a look at the bell. Maybe it's loose, and a vibration . . ." I let my voice trail off. She wasn't believing me anyway.

Ruby cast a pointed look at the bulletin board. "There's another explanation. But you're not going to like it."

That's when she told me about a few "little things" she had been noticing in the past couple weeks. A book left open, found closed. A chair moved, an arrangement of crystals scrambled, incense set burning on a high shelf. A shimmer, like the skirt of a long white dress, barely glimpsed. Little things, but inexplicable.

"You're saying we have a *ghost*?" I asked. I tried to make my question neutral, but I must not have succeeded.

Ruby pulled down the corners of her mouth. "Please don't make fun, China. The spirits don't like it when we laugh at them."

I wasn't laughing. I was thinking of the woman I'd heard humming in the darkness of the empty storeroom. "Why don't you consult your Ouija board?" I asked crossly. "And you didn't mention any of this to me."

"I haven't asked Ouija because we're not living in a *Ghostbusters* movie," Ruby said patiently. "In my experience, it's not a good idea to pry, or ask a lot of questions. Be patient, and if a spirit wants to get in touch, he—or she—will find a way to do it. And I didn't mention it to you because . . . well, you know. You're skeptical. I thought I'd keep it to myself until something happened—to you. And now it has. That photograph. And the bell."

Yes, of course I'm skeptical. I'm suspicious by nature, and as a lawyer, I have been trained to examine every statement, question every claim, find a rational explanation, construct a logical theory, and stick to it.

But there was that bell chiming. And Khat, normally the most self-possessed of creatures, suddenly spitting and darting out of the room. The ghostly humming I had heard yesterday, and the sudden drop in temperature in the storeroom. And now the photograph, and the fresh sprig of lavender.

In the cold light of day, of course, the idea of a ghost defied logic. And even granting that implausible possibility, there was the timing. Ruby and I had occupied this building for years with no evidence of anything out of the ordinary. Why this, why *now*?

I was about to ask Ruby that question, but at that moment the bell rang again, authoritatively. This time it announced an actual customer— Geraldine Castleman. She's a chatty lady who loves to discuss the properties of relatively unknown herbs, and our conversations can easily stretch to a half hour or more. This visit wasn't quite that long, but by the time Geraldine finished her shopping and left, Ruby had gone back to her shop to wait on someone. And when she popped her head in a half hour later, she had something else on her mind.

"Have you had any news about Sheila?" she asked.

I had, via a flurry of phone calls. Blackie had phoned to get my first-hand report of what had happened and tell me that he was on his way back from Lubbock and would get to Pecan Springs early in the evening. McQuaid called to let me know that Blackie's insurance scam investigation was something they couldn't put on hold, so he was driving up to Lubbock to pick up where Blackie had left off. He likely wouldn't be back until early the next week.

"Caitie will be disappointed," I said. "You'll miss the poultry show."

"I've already told her I'm sorry." McQuaid paused. "Listen, I've just dropped her off for orchestra rehearsal. Afterward, she's going to Karen's house. She wanted to stay all night, and after I talked to Karen's mom, I said okay. That way, you won't have to pick her up tonight and take her to rehearsal again in the morning. But I'm afraid you'll have to handle the chicken check-in at the fairground on Thursday morning. Sorry."

He didn't sound terribly sorry about the chickens, but it was no big deal. "We do what have to do," I said. "Drive carefully, sweetie. And call me when you get to Lubbock."

I had just hung up when Helen Berger called to say that Sheila didn't have a skull fracture—which was a huge relief—and her baby seemed okay. But her concussion had been diagnosed as moderate to severe and she had to stay quiet for a few days. She added that Jessica

Nelson had showed up at the hospital to find out what was going on. Helen had sent her away empty-handed, but she didn't think that was the end of it.

"Ms. Nelson is a persistent young woman, isn't she?" she remarked dryly.

"Persistence is her middle name." I paused. "How's Kevin, Helen? Is he feeling better?"

Kevin is Helen's grandson. Just as importantly, he is Caitie's first boyfriend. Caitie and Kevin, who are both exceptional young violinists, compete for the position of concertmaster in the local kids' orchestra. The concertmaster is the player who occupies the first chair in the violin section, helps everybody tune up, and plays the solo parts. Caitie had that place until Kevin moved to Pecan Springs a few months earlier. He had held the position until he got sick—headaches, blurred vision—and had to sit out several of the summer performances. Caitie was back in first chair again, but I was concerned about Kevin.

There was a silence. When Helen spoke, her voice was unsteady and I could hear the pain in it. "China, please don't tell Caitie about this yet. We're not ready to make a general announcement, but I think you'd better be prepared, since Kevin and Caitie are close. She'll have to know." She cleared her throat. "Kevin has a brain tumor. We're taking him to MD Anderson next week for surgery."

I gasped, struggling for words, although there's nothing you can say in a situation like this. I managed, "Oh, Helen, that's . . . that's *terrible*! I am so very sorry!"

MD Anderson is the University of Texas' cancer center in Houston, and one of the very best in the country. But a *brain tumor*! Kevin is a bright and talented kid, not just in music but in math, and a wicked sense of humor lurks behind that nerdish look of his. If I had invented a first boyfriend for Caitie, he would be a lot like Kevin.

"Please keep me posted," I added. "And let me know when you decide to get the word out."

"It'll be after the surgery," Helen said more briskly. "We'll know more then. Right now, the challenge is to keep from being over- whelmed. We're doing this one step at a time, as we see what's next. And hoping for the very best outcome, of course. We have a great team of doctors, and they're optimistic. We've caught the tumor early and we're all hopeful."

"Of course," I said emphatically. "Thank you for telling me. Please let me know when it's time to talk to Caitie about this."

After I hung up, I sat there for a moment, struggling with my feelings. Kevin's family was close-knit and loving and his grand- mother was a nurse. It wouldn't be easy, but whatever came, they would be holding hands all the way through, and the rest of us would be holding them in our hearts. When something like this happens, we're all part of the family.

And then, worriedly, I thought of Caitlin. She had already lost far too many of the most important people in her young life: her mother, her father, and her beloved aunt Marcia, who had taken her in and cared for her after her parents died. And then died, too, of cancer.

This wasn't going to be easy for Caitlin. Or for any of us.

HELEN had remarked on Jessica's persistence, which was why I wasn't surprised when the next telephone call came from Jessica herself. She covers local crime for the *Enterprise*, and we have connected several times on stories she was writing. She has a serious nose for news and she knows that Sheila and I are good friends.

"Do you know what's going on with Chief Dawson?" she demanded, without any introductory pleasantries. She likes to catch people off guard.

"Hello to you, too, Jessica," I said pleasantly. "Why? Is something wrong with the chief?"

"EMS took her to the hospital this morning."

"Gosh," I said innocently. "That's terrible! Did you ask at the hospital? I hope she's okay!"

"Nobody would talk to me over there." Jessica sounded disgruntled. "I was hoping you could tell me, China. What is it? What's going on?"

"Sorry," I said. "Wish I could help but I can't. If you find out anything, will you let me know?" I said good-bye, feeling pleased with myself for answering Jessica's questions without telling an actual lie. As I ended the call, my eye was caught by the photograph on the bulletin board. Even though Ruby had been positive that Lori had nothing to do with it, it wouldn't hurt to check.

But the lunch hour was more hectic than usual and I didn't see Lori until mid-afternoon, when she came downstairs to get a quick sandwich between classes. When I pointed to the photo and asked if she had put it there, she shook her head.

"No, sorry," she said. "Wasn't me. Maybe Ruby? She opened the shops this morning."

"She says it wasn't her." My voice sounded a little uneven, and I cleared my throat. And then, because I knew I shouldn't put her on the spot, I added, "Just one of life's little mysteries, I guess."

And the bell dinged, of course, cheerfully agreeing.

* * *

AT four, Ruby and I left Jenna in charge of the shops so we could go upstairs for the meeting with Professor Vickery. I didn't know the professor, so I had taken a moment that morning to peek at her bio on the university's website. She had earned her PhD in the textile arts program at Ohio State, and had been teaching courses in historical textiles for twenty years. She had written several papers on lacemaking, so if anybody could tell us anything about the lace, she was certainly the one.

Professor Vickery, a small, slender woman with attractively graying hair and dark-rimmed glasses, arrived a few minutes after four, and we introduced ourselves. Christine—she asked us to call her that immediately—took one look at the collection of lace items we had laid out on the table and exclaimed, "Oh, what a *treasure!*" She looked from one of us to the other. "Who does it belong to? Where did it come from?"

"It belongs to China," Ruby and Lori said together.

"We found it on a top shelf when we were cleaning out the storeroom yesterday." I nodded toward the door at the back of the room. "There's no telling where it came from or how long it's been there." I added, "The flower on the lid looks like it's hand carved."

"Queen Anne's lace, isn't it?" Christine asked. "Fascinating. You know the story behind the name of that flower?"

"I've heard that it was named for one of the two Queen Annes of England," Ruby offered.

Christine nodded. "Some say that, yes. Others say that it's named for St. Anne, the mother of the Virgin Mary. Who just happens to be the patron saint of lacemakers—so I think there's something to that connection."

"Lacemakers have a patron saint?" Lori asked. "I didn't know that."

I chimed in. "After the Protestant revolution in England, Catholic saints were politically incorrect. Some plants that were associated with them got renamed. Which could be why the flower got transferred from a Catholic saint named Anne to a queen with the same name." This was something I had only recently discovered. Even when you think you know everything there is to know about a plant, there's always something new to learn.

"Well, then, let's see what we have here." Christine got down to work immediately, identifying each of the laces by the way it was made—bobbin lace, needle lace, tatted lace, crocheted and knitted lace—and then by how old it was, generally.

"To get really specific about the age," she said, "I'd have to do a detailed study. But there are some things we can say about these right away." She held the lady's lace cap in one hand and what she called a fichu—a triangular lace scarf worn around the neck—in the other. "Judging just from the style, I think these are the two oldest pieces. They may have been made in the early 1800s. The fichu is tambour embroidery with silk threads on a fine net, and it's almost perfect. Which is amazing, given its obvious age. It's two hundred years old, give or take a decade."

"Somebody's family heirloom, I'm sure," Lori said in a tone that was almost wistful.

"Just imagine," Ruby murmured, fingering the lace. "A woman wore this, two hundred years ago."

"Tambour embroidery?" I asked curiously.

"That's right," Christine said. "To make it, a piece of net was stretched tight across an embroidery hoop—tight as a drum, hence the name, tambour. The embroidery was done through the spaces in the net, using a tiny hook and very fine silk thread, colored. Beads were often used, as well, and colored threads, especially gilt. The work was popular from the mid-eighteenth century until the 1830s." She made a face. "Then a Frenchman invented a machine that turned out a piece about a hundred and fifty times faster than a tambour worker."

Lori sat down at the end of the table. "That's the story of technology, isn't it? Machines replacing craftspeople." She waved her hand at the spinning wheel that sat off to one side. "Like the spinning machines that replaced the wheel." She paused, pursing her lips. "Although of course, spinning with a wheel replaced hand spindling."

"A natural progression, isn't it?" Ruby asked. "From spindle to spinning wheel to machine."

"Exactly." Christine nodded. "Several of my textile students are interested in tambour work as an art form. They're doing some interesting things with it." She pushed the older pieces to one side and pulled another group of laces toward her. "Now, these are from the middle of the nineteenth century, I'd say. They're mostly crocheted lace, some knitted, with silk, cotton, and linen thread." She picked up a cream-colored piece of airy filigreed lace and turned it in her fingers. "And there are several pieces of bobbin lace, like this one. Do you know how that's made?"

Lori nodded yes, but Ruby and I chorused "No," and Ruby added, "Tell us, please."

"The lacemaker worked on a pillow she held on her lap. The pattern—it was called a 'pricking card'—was pinned to the pillow. The threads were pinned over the pattern with large dressmaker pins. The thread was wound around little bobbins—bone, in the old days, later wood or even plastic. The lacemaker passed pairs of bobbins over and under each other, creating the stitches as she followed the pattern. The more pairs of bobbins, the greater the intricacy of the pattern." She put the lace on the table and smoothed it with her hand. "If you want to see a famous painting of the process, take a close look at Vermeer's *The Lacemaker*. It's quite beautiful. And accurate."

"I've always wanted to learn to make bobbin lace," Lori said thoughtfully. "Maybe now is the time."

"I'll be glad to show you what I know about it," Christine said. "One of my students is working with bobbin lace, and we've found several very good tutorials online." She gestured to the largest group of pieces. "Now, these look to be the most recent. They were made between 1860 and 1900, I'd say. This embroidered bridal veil—see the dual initials?—is quite lovely, and very well done. The quality of the other pieces is good, but perhaps a bit uneven. I wonder if these might be pattern samples." She leaned back with a smile. "But that doesn't make the collection any less valuable, of course. Altogether, China, I'd say that you have an important group here—not in terms of money, perhaps, but as an illustration of more than two centuries of women's needlework. You might consider framing some and hanging them in your shop. They'd make a lovely decoration. They could help to enhance the historical importance of your building, as well." She added, "I noticed that you now have a historical plaque beside the door."

"I'd love to do that," I said, struck by the idea. "You're right—they'd be gorgeous, framed."

"We could hang some in the tearoom," Ruby suggested. "There's more wall space there."

I nodded, agreeing. "I don't suppose there's any way to tell where the pieces were made."

"I'm afraid that's true," Christine replied. "Unless there's some external documentation—a list of the contents, say, or a diary. Many lacemakers kept records of what they made. It was a business, of course. Lace could be an important source of income."

"We haven't found a diary," I said. "All we have are the laces—and one earring." I reached into the chest and took it out.

Ruby peered at it. "Pretty! That's an amethyst, isn't it?"

"Looks like it," Lori said, as Ruby passed it to her. "What lovely filigree work."

"Do keep an eye out for some sort of written record, China," Christine said. "It would be wonderful to have some documentation, and family collections often come with a list." She picked up one of the early pieces, holding it up to the light for a better look. "Lace was such a precious luxury item, you know, and cherished. Pieces like these were handed down in the family and often mentioned in the owner's will, or in an inventory of the family's most important possessions. Lace could be the costliest part of a dress, and was frequently designed to be detachable—lace collars and cuffs, for instance—so it could be worn with several different garments." She picked up another piece. "Until machine-made lace came along, lace signified a certain level of wealth and social sophistication, so it was prized. Just that little bit of adornment on your dress suggested that you had a refined taste and could appreciate the finer things. Larger pieces like this one"—she picked up the embroidered veil—"were often used ritually and passed down from one generation to the next. Because they weren't in everyday use, they were a sign that you had enough money to buy something that you would use only once or twice in a lifetime. Or that you were an accomplished needlewoman and had the skill—and the free time—to make it yourself." She smiled. "Of course, if you could spend your time making lace, somebody else had to be doing your family's laundry and cooking your meals. There are layers of privilege here."

A chuckle ran around the table. "You said something about pattern samples," Lori said. "Are you thinking that some of these later pieces might have been work that was made for sale?"

Christine nodded. "It's possible. In both Europe and America, women were seriously interested in lacework as a means of making money. It was something they could do at home—and in the right market, it might produce enough income to make a woman independent. Just last week, I ran across an article that was published in the *New York Times* in 1900, encouraging women to take up lacemaking as a business opportunity. Around that same time, lacemaking classes were being taught in Boston and Philadelphia."

"But wasn't there plenty of machine-made lace available by then?" Lori asked.

"Oh, yes," Christine said. "Machine-made laces had simply eclipsed handmade lace by the turn of the twentieth century. But that didn't mean that women stopped making lace—luckily, because when machines came along, the craft was in danger of dying out."

"I suppose the machine-manufactured lace made handcrafted lace that much more valuable," I said. "Which might have encouraged people to do it."

"Exactly," Christine agreed. "In some communities, women got together and produced laces for sale—sort of like a co-op. Their success, of course, depended on whether they were able to find a reliable market for their work. That might have happened around here, I suppose. A group of craftswomen could have produced lace for sale in Austin or San Antonio—especially in San Antonio, where there was a community of wealthy Spanish women and a great many Catholics. Lace has always been important for religious vestments and altar cloths. The women might also have sent their work to Dallas or

Galveston. Until the 1900 hurricane wiped it out, Galveston was a more important social and business center than Houston."

"I wonder if that's what we have here," I said thoughtfully. "Maybe the Pecan Springs Historical Society knows something about it."

"That's why it would be so good to have documentation," Christine said. "I recently learned about a lacemaking group of a half dozen women in Dallas in the early 1900s. We were lucky with that group, for one of the women wrote letters to her sister describing her work, and the letters were saved. In the late 1800s, in several Catholic orphanages around the state, the nuns who had come from lacemaking centers in Ireland or Western Europe taught the girls to make lace. They were hoping to give them a skill that might help them earn money later in their lives." She paused, looking down at the pieces spread on the table. "I'd like to take these back to my office and photograph them for more study, if you don't mind. Some of the patterns are a bit unusual."

Ruby had been listening intently. Now, with the tip of her finger, she pushed the black lace collar toward Christine. "Tell us about this piece," she said. She sounded hesitant, and I remembered what had happened when she had picked it up the day before.

"Well, it's a crocheted collar, as you can see," Christine said. "It was made to be worn with an important dress, probably sometime before 1900. It's black, so it's probably a mourning collar. Women typically wore deep mourning—black—for at least a year." She smiled a little. "It was a practice that was begun, formally, with Queen Victoria. She wore mourning for forty years after Prince Albert died. She made widowhood socially respectable, you know. Until then, widows were often social exiles."

"There's something else," Ruby said softly. "You may think this is silly, but I've heard that sometimes traumatic events can create a psychic imprint on an item or object, sort of like . . . well, like energy fingerprints. When we invest a great deal of attention and emotion in something, we leave a deep impression on it. And that impression stays, even after we're dead." Gingerly, she touched the collar again. "Yesterday, when I picked this up, I suddenly felt as if I had lost . . . well, everything. I felt I was drowning in sadness. If this was worn for a long time by someone who was in deep mourning, that makes perfect sense—at least to me."

Christine raised an eyebrow and smiled slightly, and I expected her to pooh-pooh Ruby's remark. But she didn't.

"Other historians might not agree with me," she said. "But I've worked with women's clothing long enough to understand its importance. We care deeply about the clothes we wear, especially when we spend a great deal of time making something and when we wear it repeatedly, or for very special occasions. I've seen the kind of deep personal significance, and social significance, too, that's attached to certain costumes, especially ritual clothing. In our culture, that might be bridal gowns and veils, christening dresses, mourning wear, and the like. It's easy for me to believe that, when we are wearing these things, we may actually invest them with our emotional energy—happiness, grief, anticipation, excitement." She laughed a little. "Of course, my male colleagues and people who approach textiles as a science will laugh at this idea. But maybe you understand."

Ruby smiled gratefully. "Yes, I do understand. It's like smelling a faint perfume, maybe—very evocative. Or hearing an echo."

Hearing an echo? I thought of the quiet humming I'd heard in the storeroom, and the vagrant scent of lavender, and the photo on the bulletin board downstairs. I shivered. I don't like it when I'm confronted by things that are beyond my ability to explain. But I couldn't deny that they had happened.

"Something like that, yes," Christine said, replying to Ruby but answering my unspoken question. "I've felt it before, myself, in certain instances, when I was deeply involved with a piece—as if I were hearing an echo of someone's excitement or her eagerness, or her grief." She turned, regarding me with a small smile. "You're skeptical about this, China?"

"Of course she's skeptical," Ruby said firmly, and Lori added, "Skeptic is China's middle name."

"I'm afraid it's true," I allowed, although I considered mentioning what I'd heard in that storeroom. But I wasn't ready—at least, not yet. There was still a part of me that doubted what I'd heard. What I *thought* I'd heard.

Ruby reached out and patted my arm. "That's all right, dear," she murmured. "We love you anyway."

Chapter Six

Adam Hunt was not happy.

Oh, he was fully aware that his friends considered him a fortunate man, and he knew they had every good reason for their opinion. Hunt's Feed and Tack was going great guns and promised to grow even faster in the years ahead. He had a pretty, sweet-tempered daughter, Caroline, who was his dearest treasure in the world. And a wife who was beautiful to look at and for whom he provided a nice house and a hired girl to help with the work. He was, as his friend Doug Duncan used to say, holding a royal flush.

But as he walked out to his rented stable to check on his horses that August evening, Adam felt as gloomy as the sky overhead, which was the greenish-purple of an old bruise. The air was hot and heavy, with the bitter tang of smoke from a neighbor's cookstove mixed with the scent of wet leaves. A short, pelting rain had fallen that afternoon and another storm was brewing now, a bad one. It was likely to bring wind with it, and lightning. His big bay horses—Jack and Ace—were skittish about thunder and storms spooked them, even when they were safe in the stone stable, which was about as solid a structure as you could find anywhere. He'd give them some oats, settle them down. He opened the door and went into the stable, pulling in a deep breath of dusty hay and warm horseflesh. He was greeted by Jack's anxious nicker.

"Hey, boys," he said. "Just a little lightning and thunder. Nothing for you to worry about." He slapped Ace on the rump and hung a bucket of oats on the feed hook, then went on to Jack. "You, too, fella. Good roof over your head. Stout walls. Best damn stable in the whole damn town, boys. Guaranteed."

It was true, he thought, as he went out to the well and pumped up a bucket of water for each horse. Douglas Duncan had built the stable and the house and his small frame smithy in the year he and Annie got married. Doug had wanted a big house because he, like Adam, had planned to fill it with children. Then, when he lost his foolish bet against the railroad locomotive and his widow needed money to keep her going, Adam had been glad to lease the stable from her, even though Delia objected. But then Delia objected to pretty much everything he did these days. Nothing about him suited her.

Doug's widow. Annie. At the thought of her, Adam pressed his lips together. He made it a rule *not* to think of her, although that was getting harder all the time—and especially when he'd had one whiskey too many, as he'd had tonight. It wasn't Annie's fault, of course. She always acted properly toward him, exactly as a widow ought to act toward her dead husband's best friend. While Adam might wish to read something different into the way she sometimes glanced at him, he understood that it was his imagination and not her intent.

But so what if it was? Maybe it was okay to wish and want and imagine, as long as he kept himself on the straight and narrow. He had known Annie since she was a girl, but she had always been *Doug's* girl, and out of reach. He had even managed to keep his thoughts in check—until Doug cashed in his chips, at which point it suddenly became a damn sight harder. Annie was not just lovely but deeply desirable, with that auburn hair and those large dark eyes, remarkable eyes that seemed to fasten on him. A glance from those eyes made his breath come short. And when he'd caught her in his arms the day he brought her the news of Douglas' death, he couldn't keep himself from touching her face and throat after he'd put her on the bed, and dropping a kiss on her pale lips before she'd come around. He'd suffered with her, too, when she lost that little boy. A tragedy, pure and simple, for he knew how much she and Doug had wanted a child.

And now—well, now he had to admire her even more for the brave way she kept her little lacemaking business going, which was just about all she had to support herself in her widowhood, besides his lease for the stable and what Tobias paid her for the right to use Doug's smithy. Delia liked to poke fun at Annie's Laces, and say that it wasn't worth more than a hill of beans. But that was Delia, always scornful of other women's efforts when she herself didn't do much besides spend money and run back and forth to Galveston as often as her sister could arrange for a party. As she had done a few days ago, and taken Caroline with her.

Adam had once thought Delia was so beautiful and had been proud when she agreed to be his wife. But he had learned—a hard, hard lesson—that her beauty wasn't more than skin deep. His mother used to say that pretty was fine as far as it went, but it didn't go very far when it came to keeping a marriage together. His mother had been wiser than he'd given her credit for.

And that bitter truth had been imposed on him once again when he went through the bills this afternoon and understood how much Delia had spent on those amethyst earrings and that new pink dress.

And then there was the envelope he had found, and what was in it—especially that. Which was why he had downed a couple of whiskeys with the sandwiches the hired girl had left him for his supper.

Adam picked up the water buckets. The first heavy drops of rain were beginning to fall as he carried them into the stable.

AFTER her disastrous trip to Austin, Annie's week had gone downhill, and it got worse as the full realization of her situation began to catch up with her. She knew she had to come up with a plan that would carry her through until she was able to find more markets for the lace. In the meantime, she would have to dip into her tiny cash reserve to pay her girls the commission she owed them and explain that their two Austin shops had closed. Perhaps she would even have to let one or two of them go.

But she hated to do that. Her lacemakers were becoming quite skilled, and they worked together so beautifully, almost like a family of sisters—with the exception of Delia, who wasn't really one of them. What's more, they had come to depend on the work she gave them. She couldn't let them down. She would simply have to keep them on, all of them, if she could, for as long as she could. So she put off saying anything until she had a better idea of what new opportunities she might be able to conjure up.

On a stormy August evening a few days after her trip to Austin, Annie took a pencil and piece of paper and sat down at the oilcloth-covered kitchen table to make a list of as many possibilities as she could think of. It had been hot all day, and after supper, she had stripped down to her chemise and cooled off with a sponge bath. Now, she was wearing a loose cambric wrapper, pale blue and sashed at the waist, and she had pulled her hair back from her face with a blue ribbon.

She frowned down at the paper. The first thing she should do, of course, was to find a new market for the lace in Austin. Surely another shop would open soon. *Austin*, she wrote, and underlined the word.

But another and perhaps more immediate possibility was San Antonio, just thirty miles to the south, so she wrote *San Antonio*, and underlined that, too. She had never been to the city, but she knew it was almost twice as large as Austin and had been settled by the Spanish. Surely there would be a dress shop or a millinery shop that catered to fine Spanish ladies. The Spanish ranchers were rumored to have lots of money, so their wives might be able to buy fine handmade laces. And perhaps the churches, although she didn't have any idea how to approach them.

But even if she found one or two of the right shops and her laces were taken on commission, it would be at least a month, maybe even two, before they were sold and she was paid. Until then, perhaps she could place a mail-order advertisement in the *Austin Weekly Statesman*, or even a magazine. There was *Godey's Lady's Book*, for instance, the most widely read women's magazine in the country. *Mail order*, she wrote on her list. She frowned. But wouldn't that be expensive? And she would have to pay for a catalogue, which would mean costs for drawings and printing, as well as the advertising space itself. And that could take months and wouldn't produce any income in the meantime, when there were the girls to pay and her own living expenses to meet.

Annie leaned on her elbows, her head in her hands, feeling daunted and a little dazed. Since Douglas' death, everything had been in such a muddle. She had done all she could, but she seemed to be falling further behind. Perhaps Delia was right: a woman simply couldn't make it on her own in this day and age. A widow who had social position and money could afford to pursue her own interests, to do what she liked. But she had neither. It stood to reason that to have any kind of life at all, she ought to find a husband. A husband—the *right* husband, one with plenty of money—would allow her all the time she needed to do the work she wanted to do.

But her independent spirit balked at the thought of marrying a man just to gain his financial support. No! Whatever Delia said, she didn't need a *man*, she needed a change. Perhaps it was time to admit that Pecan Springs wasn't the right place for her business. The house, which was free and clear, was her largest asset. She could sell it and move to a city in the east or up north, where it would be easier to find shops that would market her work. St. Louis, maybe? As a girl, she had occasionally visited her cousins there and had liked the city. The money from the sale of the house would support her until she could get a new start. On her list, she wrote *ST. LOUIS* in capital letters and underlined it twice.

But even as she stared at the words, she knew she couldn't do it. She couldn't sell this house. It was her spirit, her life. It was filled with memories, with the echoes of Douglas' song. With sweat and blood, with the sweet ring of laughter and bitter tears of grief, with all the music of work and love and life that had been lived within these walls. She couldn't leave that, could she?

She crossed out *ST. LOUIS* and dropped her pencil. She would have to face her challenges *here* in Pecan Springs, not somewhere else.

It had rained that afternoon and the smell of wet leaves hung heavy on the air. Now, the evening sky had grown very dark, and the wind was picking up. Another storm was blowing in from the south, and Annie could hear one of the wooden stable shutters banging. She found a match and lit the kerosene lamp that hung over the table. Then, pulling her wrapper closer around her, she went to the open kitchen casement, thinking to latch it. But just as she put out a hand to pull the window shut, there was a blinding flash and an ear-splitting crack of thunder. Not thirty feet away, the large cottonwood tree beside her garden exploded in a violent shower of sparks, hurling chunks of splintered wood like flying rockets. Limbs crashed to the ground and the tree swayed and began to topple toward her house.

Annie gave an involuntary cry and stumbled back. For one heart-stopping moment, she thought the cottonwood was going to fall across the roof. But when it crashed to the ground, she saw that it had just missed. There was no immediate danger, but that didn't dispel the effects of her fright. Her heart was pounding and she was still trembling when, a moment, later, she heard someone banging at the kitchen door. She opened it to Adam, bareheaded and wet, his shoulders hunched against the rain. Behind him, she saw whipping trees, illuminated by flashes of blue-white lightning.

"Are you all right?" he asked urgently. "That cottonwood nearly took out your chimney."

"I'm fine," she said, opening the door wider. "Just a little scared." With a shaky smile, she put her hand on his arm. "Do come in, Adam. You'll be soaked to the skin."

His startled gaze took in her figure, and she dropped her hand, clutching the wrapper a little tighter against her, remembering that she wasn't dressed. A flush rose in her cheeks, and she half turned away.

"I'm not exactly presentable," she said in a low voice, "but you're welcome. The kettle's still hot. We can have tea."

He hesitated as if he might not accept the invitation, then seemed to change his mind. "Thanks," he said, and stood by the door, dripping. "When that lightning bolt hit, I was at the stable, fastening the shutters. I thought it had struck your house."

"Everything's all right out there?" Annie asked, disturbingly aware of the male scent of tobacco and something else. Whiskey? Yes, whiskey. She was surprised. Delia often said that she didn't allow drinking in her home. And then she remembered. Delia had taken little Caroline and gone to Galveston to visit her sister.

"There'll be some cleanup," Adam said. "That tree literally exploded. But once all the pieces are dried and cut to size, it'll be good stove wood."

Annie felt herself trembling. "You're wet," she said. He was wearing a light blue shirt, the sleeves rolled to the elbows, and dark canvas trousers. The shirt was plastered to his shoulders, and raindrops glittered in his dark hair. Still clutching her wrapper, she opened a drawer and pulled out a towel.

"Here," she said, holding it out to him. "Dry off. I'll find you one of Douglas' shirts."

She had given most of her husband's clothing away, but she had kept two of his favorite flannel shirts that she herself wore to sleep in on cold nights. She found one and took it to the kitchen and busied herself wordlessly with the teapot while Adam turned away from her and stripped naked to the waist. He rubbed himself down with the towel and shrugged into Douglas' plaid shirt. A few moments later they were sitting across the table from each other, cups in front of them. The rain was pounding against the windows. The thunder was a continuous mutter and the lightning flashed wildly. The air in the kitchen felt close and charged, somehow. It felt, Annie thought, as if something was going to happen.

"Tea's good," Adam said, not looking at her. Caught in a draft, the flame of the kerosene lamp flickered, and Annie was struck by the realization that he was very like Douglas. Not physically, of course. Her husband had been dark-haired and sun-browned and large. Adam's hair was fair and he was slender and wiry. But both were strong men of generous heart and optimistic vision who gave themselves fully to work and play. She remembered the many times the two of them had sat at this table, laughing, while she bustled around making sandwiches for them, or pouring coffee or slicing pie.

But tonight Adam's mouth had a grim set, and his forehead was furrowed. He reached into his pocket for a cigarette, and she got up to fetch him one of Douglas' ashtrays. Again, she caught the scent of whiskey. She sat down and watched him light his cigarette.

After a moment, she broke the silence. "I . . . I don't mean to pry, Adam, but is something troubling you?"

Adam seemed to consider her question, as if he were debating what to say. After a moment, he said, quite abruptly, "You sure you want to hear this, Annie?"

She didn't hesitate. "Yes, of course."

"You've known Delia for a long time." His glance lingered on her hair, her throat. "Did you know . . ." He pulled on his cigarette and blew out a stream of blue smoke. "Did you know she's been taking something all this time—something to keep herself from . . . from having a baby?"

His voice was taut and his words, slightly slurred, hit Annie like a fist. Her breath felt as if it were trapped in her throat. His gaze was holding her now with such intensity that she couldn't move, couldn't turn away, couldn't even drop her eyes. She was sure he wouldn't have asked her that question if he hadn't had too much to drink. He would probably regret it in the morning—if he remembered it. Likely he wouldn't.

She might have parried him, but she didn't. Perhaps it was that he was sitting in Douglas' chair, wearing Douglas' shirt, holding Douglas' cup. Perhaps it was the electrical storm outside, the flicker of the lamp over the table, casting a circle of warm, sheltering light over the two of them. Whatever it was, she felt a new and startling intimacy, and it emboldened her to answer in a way she would not, *could* not have otherwise.

Meeting his eyes, she said, "I know that she doesn't want a baby." As soon as the words were out of her mouth, she wished them back. This was dangerous, risky. And yet, there was a kind of wild pleasure in it that made her heart race, her breath come short.

He gave her a long, questioning look. "She told you that?"

She nodded. She could hear the pain in his voice, and the anger. And understood.

He tapped his cigarette into the ashtray. "Did she say why?"

She pressed her lips together. Delia's reason—that babies ruin a woman's figure—was too trivial to repeat. "I thought . . . perhaps she had a hard time with Caroline."

"A hard time with Caroline? I remember it differently." Adam's shoulders slumped. "I guess I wouldn't mind so much if she hadn't been lying to me all these years. I wanted another child and I thought she agreed." Annie thought he sounded disgusted. "But now I find out that she's been getting something from Mrs. Crow. To keep herself from getting pregnant."

Annie shifted uncomfortably. She wasn't surprised to hear that Delia was using something. Many women did. But she was surprised to hear that Adam was just learning about it. And even more surprised that he was telling her. He must be deeply troubled.

"Do you know what she's getting from Mrs. Crow?" she asked, trying to lighten the conversation. She chuckled wryly. "Not that I have any use for it, of course. As a widow."

For the first time, he smiled, and his voice lost some of its tension. "Well, you've been married, so maybe you had a use, then. Wild carrot seeds. 'Chew and swallow with water' was written on the envelope. 'To prevent conception.'" He drew on his cigarette. "Is this something women . . . do?"

Annie nodded. This hadn't been her problem, but she had listened when her mother and aunts and cousins talked. It was often hard to get a man to be careful—that is, to pull out—so if you didn't want a baby, you had to take whatever precautions you could. Wild carrot seeds were only one alternative. There were parsley, gingerroot, tansy, pennyroyal leaves. And if you didn't have those to hand, there were plenty of patent medicines that promised to help if you had missed your monthly. Some of them—like Lydia E. Pinkham's Vegetable Compound or Madam LeRoy's Regulative Pills—were usually available at Mr. Carter's pharmacy. You had to be careful, of course, which went without saying, didn't it? Some of the patent medicines might not be strong enough to be effective. Some of the plants were so strong that they could be dangerous. Women shared the information they needed to keep themselves safe.

He was watching her. She felt her heart flutter. "Yes," she said, after a moment. "Women do use them. After—" She took a breath. "Afterward."

97

"Ah," he said. "As a contraceptive."

She nodded, thinking that she had never heard that word spoken aloud. And then, impulsively and quite honestly, she said, "I can't believe that you and I are talking about this, Adam." She was surprised that her voice sounded so light.

"Why?" He frowned. "Do I frighten you?"

"No, not you. It's just . . . woman-talk, I suppose." She had been about to say that it was husband-wife talk. She had shared her efforts to conceive with Douglas, who had listened and understood. But perhaps Delia simply didn't feel easy about talking to Adam about such things. Or—Annie thought this more likely—she was deliberately concealing what she was doing. She didn't want him to know.

Adam gave her a thoughtful look, and the lines around his mouth softened. "Does it bother you? I'm sorry, Annie. Maybe we should talk about something else."

"No, it doesn't bother me." She looked away, hesitating. "I was the one who asked. I mean, I . . ." She twisted her fingers together, then unclasped them.

He chuckled low in his throat. "You know, I used to envy Doug." He put out a hand as if he were reaching for hers, then pulled it back and looked away. But he didn't stop the words.

"I envied his good fortune in having a wife who supported him all the way, in whatever he wanted to do. And I don't think I ever heard you criticize him. You were always so . . . so loving." His tone became regretful. "Not like Delia. My wife has never loved me the way you loved Doug. He was one lucky sonovagun."

Annie cleared her throat. Adam wasn't *acting* drunk, but she was sure he wouldn't be talking this way if the whiskey hadn't loosened his tongue. This conversation was taking them into places they shouldn't go. She thought of the moonlit nights, alone in her bed with her imaginings, and weighed the power of her desire against the weakness of her will. She knew she wanted him. She knew she should send him home right now, before this went any further.

But she didn't. She flexed her fingers, then picked up her cup and took a sip. She put it down again, carefully, and said, "I loved Douglas very much. He was my life, and I wanted his children. But he's dead now, and I—"

She raised her eyes to his and saw that he had read her naked glance and knew what she was about to say. He stopped her.

"Don't," he said sharply, and she flinched. He ground out his cigarette in the ashtray and pushed his chair back. "I'm sorry, Annie." He stood, not looking at her. "Thanks for the tea, but I shouldn't have come. Not tonight, not the way I'm feeling. I'll leave now. Tomorrow, I'll get Tobias to help me, and we'll cut up that tree and stack the wood to dry."

She felt a stab of disappointment, as sharp as a knife. She stood, too, tears welling in her eyes. It hurt to breathe and she felt lightheaded.

"No, please," she heard herself say, and the words came as a surprise. She put out a hand toward him, and her wrapper fell open. The lamp flickered again, and the darkness seemed to gather around them like an embrace. "Please, Adam, don't go. I—"

But he didn't let her finish her sentence. He was around the table in three steps, pulling her against him, holding her tight, fitting his mouth against hers in a kiss that surrounded her, encompassed her, filled her with a passion she had not felt since Douglas left her. She lifted her arms around his neck and arched against him, giving herself to his kiss, to him, without reservation. She would regret it later, she knew, but tonight she was helpless against her desires, and his. His hands were hard on her, all over her, rough, demanding. And then he was lifting her, carrying her to the bedroom. And in a moment he was naked beside her, over her. And then, with a low, deep moan, inside her.

Afterward, Annie lay in his arms, her head in the hollow of his shoulder. The last years had been a desert. But it was raining again and she was home.

Chapter Seven

For many centuries and in many different cultures, family planning was the most important medicinal use of the seeds of *Daucus carota* (also called Queen Anne's lace and wild carrot). The earliest written reference to this plant as a contraceptive can be found in the writings of Hippocrates in the fourth century BCE. In his authoritative book, *Eve's Herbs, A History of Contraception and Abortion in the West*, John Riddle (a specialist in the history of pharmacology) writes that the seeds of *Daucus carota* were among the most effective herbal contraceptives readily available to women. According to Riddle, "The seeds, harvested in the fall, are a strong contraceptive if taken orally immediately after coitus." The seeds have also been widely used to "provoke menstruation"—in other words, as an early-stage abortifacient.

In an apparent paradox, the leaves and stems of the plant (which contain smaller concentrations of the active plant chemicals) have traditionally been used to enhance fertility. I could find no research on the subject, but some herbalists speculate that a lower dose, such as that in a tea, might make the lining of the uterus more receptive to implantation. This may explain why some suggest that the plant was originally named for St. Anne, who was said to have conceived the Virgin Mary when she was well past childbearing age. She is invoked as the patron saint of infertile women.

"Anne's Flower"
China Bayles
Pecan Springs Enterprise

McQuaid had gone to Lubbock and Caitie had stayed over at Karen's, so I was alone in the house on Tuesday night, which made it a good time to start my column for the next week's *Enterprise* garden page and catch up on some necessary housework. Bassets are wonderful dogs, but they shed constantly. Every corner in our house is home to a thriving colony of Winchester's basset–fur bunnies. I've warned him that if he doesn't hang on to his fur, he won't have enough to keep him warm this winter, but he just keeps shedding.

For the *Enterprise*, I had decided to write a column about Queen Anne's lace, which was blooming along our lane. It's an interesting plant with a long history of medicinal uses, and even some culinary uses. Jelly, for instance. In an old book, I found a recipe that looked good and copied it out. Maybe over the weekend, I'd find time to make a batch.

But I only got about half finished with the column. Blackie called to say that he had returned from Lubbock and that the doctor had released Sheila. The baby seemed fine, and she and Rambo were both home. My mother called to ask if Caitie could spend a few days with her and Sam before school started, and Brian called to let me know that he and Casey were driving to Dallas to see Casey's sister and take in a Rangers' game. It was late by the time I got back to my work, and while I tried to stay with it, I kept nodding off. I finally gave it up and went to bed.

I was tired enough to fall asleep right away, even with Winchester taking over McQuaid's half of the bed. But I didn't sleep well. It was another night of dark dreams that sent me searching through endless shadowy places for that carton of photographs. Finally, I understood (with the kind of crazy conviction that sometimes comes in dreams) that the carton was under my bed. In my dream, I lifted the dust ruffle, bent over, and reached into the dark space to pull it out.

But as I did, I saw that a woman in a long, white dress was lying on her back under my bed, one arm wrapped around the carton, humming. *And for bonnie Annie Laurie, I'd lay me down and die.* She turned her head toward me, and terrified as I was, I couldn't look away. Her alabaster face was framed by long, loose auburn hair. Her eyes, deep-set and very dark, like holes burned into her face, were fixed on me. They seemed to hold me, draw me.

She stopped humming. There was a moment's silence as I stared at her, transfixed by fear. Then *Please*, she whispered, *Please.* Her voice was thin and high and her breath congealed in a puff of cold fog. I jerked back, but not fast enough. She put out an icy hand, its fingers as dry and cold as frozen bones, and seized my arm. Powerless to resist, I was being pulled under the bed and into her arms, while the bell on my shop door jingle-jangled wildly.

I was saved by that bell—but it turned out to be the alarm clock. It was six thirty, the sheets were all sticky and twisted around me, and that damned Scottish melody was lodged in my head again, like an old vinyl record with a stuck needle. I had to turn on the radio to blot it out.

When I went to put my sneakers on, I couldn't find one of them. I settled for sandals. I suspected it had gotten kicked under the bed, and I couldn't bring myself to lift up the dust ruffle and look.

I fed the dog, the cat, and Caitie's chickens, then nuked a breakfast burrito in the microwave and took it and my coffee with me. I don't think I've ever been more glad to step out of the house and into the brightness of the early morning. The sunshine filtering through the trees seemed to make a cheerful mockery of the dark dreams of the night and that frightening figure under the bed.

On my way to the shop, I stopped off at Sheila's to see how she was—and was relieved that she seemed her normal self. That is, she was still in bed but she was already working on her laptop, going through some files that Connie had emailed her. There was a pot of coffee and a plate of scrambled eggs on the bedside table and Rambo was stretched out on the floor.

But her doctor was insisting that she stay home for the rest of the week, and Blackie had appointed himself as the Enforcer. "I'm sorry that McQuaid had to pick up my investigation in Lubbock," he told me quietly, as he went with me to the door. "But I was afraid if I didn't come back and make sure Sheila stayed home, she would be in uniform and at the police station before sunup this morning."

"You can't keep a good woman down," I said. "Oh, and speaking of keeping it down," I added, "I left some bottles of ginger ale and a bag of peppermint tea on your kitchen counter yesterday. If nausea is still a problem for her, give them a try."

"Got it," Blackie said. He frowned. "I worry about the baby, you know. And her, too, of course. Sheila's not a twentysomething."

"That's true," I agreed. "But she's in much better shape than your average twentysomething. I doubt if many of them could run her usual four miles before breakfast. I'm sure she'll be fine—once she stops throwing up." I paused. "Let me know if you need anything, Blackie. I'm on chicken duty tomorrow morning, but I'll be glad to shop for you."

He raised an eyebrow. "Chicken duty?"

"Caitie's chickens. Adams County Fair. The big poultry show starts tomorrow. Caitie is aiming for at least one blue ribbon."

"Oh, right." He grinned. "Well, have fun."

"We will," I replied. "Extra Crispy and Dixie Chick have had their baths and their pedicures, and they're ready to strut their stuff."

"Atta girl." Blackie rolled his eyes. "You are gonna knock 'em dead."

"I hope so," I said.

Little did we know.

I love Thyme and Seasons first thing in the morning, when the shelves are tidy, the floor is nicely swept, the counter is neat, and the sweet morning light filters in through the east windows, casting a golden glow over the shop. Today, I was first to arrive and everything was blessedly quiet. Ruby and Lori hadn't shown up yet, Cass' kitchen was still dark, and Khat and I were the only creatures stirring.

The night's frightening dream lingered in my mind, but it had given me an idea. I would get the carton of photos out of the storeroom and bring it downstairs, where there was counter space and a better light. Between customers, I could sort and study the photos. If I got lucky, I might find something that would help us document the laces. There might be papers in the box. Maybe even a diary.

A reasonable plan, but I hesitated. Perhaps it was the dream, but I stood at the foot of the stairs, reluctant to go up. I wasn't terribly eager to open the storeroom door and step into the dark with only a naked bulb for light, which might burn out again and leave me groping in blackness. I might hear that ghostly humming and sense that some-one, *something* else was with me, that I wasn't alone.

Funny thing. Only two days ago, that room had been just another large walk-in closet, full of piles of stuff that had to be sorted and dis-posed of so we could make room for more stuff. Now, it was like one of those eerie rooms in a Stephen King novel, a dark place full of speaking shadows, where inexplicable things happen, a place that ex-ists well outside of everybody's ordinary comfort zone.

I thought of what Ruby and Christine had said about clothing being somehow invested with the emotional energy of the women who made it and wore it. Perhaps buildings, too, absorb the emotional energy of the people who live there. Maybe they hold energy in the same way a battery stores power, and release it under the right conditions, when somebody receptive comes along.

I frowned. One trouble with that theory was that the "receptive" somebody ought to be Ruby Wilcox, not China Bayles. Ruby is the one who's in touch with the Universe. I'm the skeptic, remember? I'm the realist, the pragmatist, the doubter who only believes in what she can touch, taste, smell, see, weigh, and measure. Why was *I* the one who had heard that humming? And why now? I've lived and worked in this building for years, and I've never seen a sign of anything out of the ordinary—until this week.

By this time, I had talked myself out of the notion of going upstairs to get that carton. It could wait until somebody else arrived and we could go into the storeroom together. Having made this executive decision, I headed for the kitchen, where I fed Khat, brewed myself a cup of coffee, and snagged one of the carrot mini-muffins Cass had baked for today's lunch. I popped it in the microwave for a few seconds, then, coffee and muffin in hand, I headed for the shop to set things up for the day.

The first phone call of the morning came before I'd even finished my muffin. Kelly Sutherland, who is teaching wreath-making classes at the shop this fall, was phoning to check on the dates. "I want to put the classes in my email newsletter," she said.

"Hang on a sec, Kelly," I said. Holding the phone in one hand and my coffee cup in the other, I turned to the bulletin board to check the list I had posted two days before under the attractive caption I'd made with red, yellow, and green magnetic letters: FALL CLASSES.

But FALL CLASSES wasn't what it said now. Now, the bright red letter F and two orange ss were turned upside down and pushed off to one side. The other letters were arranged in two new words: ALL LACES.

The family photograph that had been pinned to the board yesterday—the man and woman in the porch swing with a baby and a little girl—was still there, but it had been turned upside down and there were *two* sprigs of fresh lavender tucked behind it. And as I stood there, staring at the board, the bell over my door dinged gleefully. I was being laughed at.

I stood stock-still, feeling as though playful fingers had just reached through the curtain between the world we know and the world we don't and messed up my hair. Was this a message of some kind? For *me*? After a moment, I muttered something unintelligible and turned the photo right side up. The bell gave one final *ding*, sort of like a hiccup, and stopped giggling.

"I'm sorry," Kelly said hesitantly, on the other end of the line. "I didn't quite hear that. What did you say, China?"

I cleared my throat and tried again. "Um, looks like we're on for the first and third Saturdays in October, one to three in the afternoon. Are those dates still okay?"

"Yes, thank you," Kelly said. "I'll put that in the newsletter. I'm hoping for a good enrollment." She laughed lightly. "You want to know what I thought I heard, China?"

I didn't, but she told me anyway.

"I thought you said, 'The ghost did it.' Isn't that crazy?"

I made my voice firm. "Yes. It is *positively* crazy. Why would I say a thing like that?"

But that, of course, was what I had said. "The ghost did it."

Yes, the ghost. The ghost who hummed the Scottish folk tune in an empty room. The ghost who fetched a photo from the carton on the shelf and pinned it, not just once but twice—and with not just one but *two* sprigs of lavender—to the bulletin board. The ghost who re-arranged the letters to announce ALL LACES and then laughed at me. My dream ghost. The ghost I didn't believe in.

The ghost did it.

And at that thought, my lawyerly self jumped to her feet and shouted, *Objection! I object, Your Honor! The statement assumes facts not in evidence, authentication is lacking and improper.* Then added, for good measure, *Vague, and a waste of the court's time, too.*

My mouth tightened. My prosecutorial self had the more cogent argument, I was sure. *Assumes facts not in evidence*, very definitely. In fact, *facts not in evidence* is the very essence of ghosthood, is it not? If I were Her Honor, I would certainly sustain my objection.

But in this case, I was also the witness who had to testify to what I had heard. And as counsel for the defense, I was looking at the phys-ical evidence—the bulletin board, *my* bulletin board—right in front of me. I was in uncharted territory here, and I couldn't for the life of me see my way forward.

I said good-bye to Kelly, then aimed my cell phone at the bulletin board and shot a picture. Then I put the letters back the way they were supposed to be (FALL CLASSES) and took the photo down. I glanced at it again, then picked up my magnifying glass to study it. If the ghost— or something—was using it to communicate with me, I ought to take a better look. Who were these people? When was the photo taken? And why this particular photo, instead of another one?

A couple, sitting on a wooden swing on what was undeniably *my* veranda, with *my* front door visible to the left in the photo and *my* front windows behind the swing. Husband and wife, I assumed. A baby and a little girl. The man, his rather plain face transformed by a proud smile, was leaning toward the woman. I couldn't see her face because she was looking down at the baby in her arms, dressed in a lacy white cap and a lace-flounced dress and waving one tiny fist. The woman herself, apparently the baby's mother, was wearing a white shirtwaist and a dark skirt. Her hair was pinned up on top of her head, Gibson-girl style. The child, who might have been nine or ten, had pretty banana curls and was holding her kitten against her cheek. She was smiling, too.

A happy family, I thought, wishing I could see the woman's face. Hoping for some identification, I turned the photograph over. No names, just a penciled date in a spidery hand: June 10, 1890. I felt like an idiot even asking the question, but it followed on my theory of the case. *Was this a photo of my ghost?*

I thought for a moment, then took down the framed newspaper article that Jessica Nelson had written about my building, which was once a family's home—the Duncan family, according to the Historical Society's plaque beside the front door. I had read the article when it first appeared in the *Enterprise*, but I didn't remember the details. I skimmed it quickly.

And I found something. According to Jessica, the house had been built for his bride by a man named Douglas Duncan. He had also built a wood frame blacksmith shop on the alley behind the house, and a stone stable for his horses. Jessica had included several photographs with the article, but they were all of the building, then and now. No people.

The photo I was holding: Was it Mr. and Mrs. Douglas Duncan and their children? Was Mrs. Duncan my ghost?

Objection, Your Honor. Assumes facts not in evidence.

Sustained. But there she is, the woman in the swing. Or was. Perhaps. How could I know?

I couldn't, but maybe Jessica could. She picked up after just two rings.

"Hey, China," she said, "I just talked to the chief, at home. She says she's feeling fine and will be back in the office in a day or two. Does that square with what you know?"

"Sounds right," I said. "I saw her this morning, working from home. She seemed fine to me." I changed the subject quickly. "Say, when you were doing the research on my building, did you happen to see any photographs of the family that built it? People photos, I mean?"

Jessica took a moment to think. "Maybe one or two. I can have a look in my notes."

"Please do," I said. "Specifically, I'm looking for information about Mrs. Duncan. I'd like to know her name, her age, anything you can find out about her."

"I'll see what I can do." Jessica paused. "By the way, your daughter entered the poultry show at the fair last year, didn't she? Is she doing that again?"

"Oh, you bet," I said emphatically. "Dixie Chick and Extra Crispy are already bathed, combed, pedicured, and polished. We're taking them to the fairgrounds early tomorrow morning." I paused. "Why are you asking?

"Because I'm covering the fair, and I wanted to include photos of a kid or two. Caitie is super photogenic, so I was thinking of using her, if it's okay with you." She chuckled. "And Extra Crispy and Dixie Chick, of course."

"Covering the fair?" I couldn't resist a tease. "I thought you were the *Enterprise* crime reporter. Is something going on at the fair that the rest of us don't know about? Somebody pilfering fair funds, maybe? Criminal connivance at the carnival?"

"Oh, you are so funny," Jessica said sarcastically. "The truth is that there hasn't been a lot of bad stuff happening in Pecan Springs lately, and my boss doesn't like me to sit on my hands. So I'm covering the fair. I'll be looking for anything newsworthy. What kind of chicken is Dixie Chick?"

"She's a Buff Orpington. Extra Crispy is a Cubalaya rooster. His family immigrated to the U.S. from Cuba around the time of the Second World War. He's super elegant, with a tail you won't believe. He's definitely newsworthy."

"'A tale you won't believe,'" Jessica muttered. I could hear her computer keyboard clicking. She was making notes. "Why won't I believe his tale? Is there some sort of mystery about this particular rooster?"

"That's t-a-i-l," I said. "And there's no mystery. Extra Crispy loves to mug for the camera."

"Sounds great," Jessica said. "How about if I meet you tomorrow and get some quotes and a pic or two of Caitie and her chickens? If one of them wins a ribbon, I'll follow up with an interview and—"

There was a voice in the background and Jessica said something I didn't quite hear. Then she was back on the line. "Hark wants to know if your garden page is going to be late again."

"Tell him he can stop being snarky," I said. Hark Hibler is the editor of the *Enterprise*, Jessica's boss. My boss, too, since I write the garden column for the Thursday paper. I trade the articles for advertising for the shop, which is a pretty good deal, and definitely worth the time it takes. "I'm writing about a wildflower that's blooming along my lane right now," I added. "Queen Anne's lace—lots of history as a medicinal herb. The article is all but done, and I'll have photos. Maybe some recipes, too."

I was stretching the truth a little. The article wasn't anywhere near done, but I was planning on working on it tonight. I went on: "Caitie and I are checking her chickens in about eight in the morning. Want to meet us at the poultry tent?"

"Perfect," Jessica said. "See you in the morning."

I looked once more at the photograph, then took my purse out from under the counter and slipped the photo into it. I would ask Jessica to take a look. Maybe she would recognize the couple sitting on my porch. And the porch swing in the photo had given me an idea. I'd buy a porch swing and have McQuaid hang it on my new veranda, with a few pots of green herbs along the wall. It would be a nice place for customers to relax.

For the middle of the week, the shop was busy. Thyme for Tea is a nice alternative to the usual Tex-Mex or fast-food lunches for the women who work on the courthouse square or in the small office park at the other end of Crockett, so we had a steady stream of guests, as Ruby likes to call our customers. On today's menu, a spinach and carrot quiche, plus a salad and a carrot muffin. There's nothing quite like Cass' signature quiches anywhere in Pecan Springs. You can bet our guests were enthusiastic.

But I had that carton of old photos on my mind. Lori came in just after the lunch crowd finished, so I left Jenna to mind the shop and followed Lori upstairs. Feeling a little silly, I asked her to stand at the storeroom door and hold it open while I went in to get the carton. I was glad when she agreed without asking me why. I'd hate to have to tell her that I was afraid of the dark—or of ghosts.

I tugged on the chain and the overhead bulb came on. A few steps in, I reached for the carton of photographs that I'd put on the top shelf. But it wasn't on the shelf, it was on the floor—the same carton, with *Corticelli Silk Threads* printed on one side, and a picture of a kitten playing with a spool of thread. As I bent over to pick it up, I felt a chill draft on the back of my neck and arms and at that moment the bulb popped and the light went out.

I stifled a gasp. If Lori hadn't been holding the door, I would have been left in the dark. I wasn't going to wait around and see what happened next. I grabbed the carton and scurried out as fast as I could.

"Funny about that bulb," Lori said, frowning up at it. "We might want to check the socket. Ruby told me another one burned out when the two of you were cleaning in there a couple of days ago." She closed the door behind us. "Did you get what you were looking for?"

"I hope so," I said breathlessly. I did *not* want to go back in that storeroom again. I put the carton on the table and took a deep breath to steady myself. "Mostly photographs, I think. But I'm hoping maybe I'll find some information about the laces." Trying to act natural, I added, "You drove to Waco last night to talk to your aunt, didn't you? Did she have any clues to help you in your search?"

"Oh, yes." Lori pulled out a chair and sat down, her eyes shining. "China, I may actually have learned my birth mother's name!"

"Oh, my gosh." I sat down, too, and pushed the carton out of the way. "Really? That's wonderful!"

"Yes, really." Lori's voice was full of excitement. "And would you believe? Aunt Jo—that's what she asked me to call her—actually *knew* my birth mother!"

"Gosh, what a lucky break," I said. "And a surprise."

"Oh, it is! My real mother's name is Gatley. Laura Anne Gatley. She was young, Aunt Jo said, in her early twenties, and very pretty. She and her mother, Lorene, lived across the street from Aunt Jo in Sherwood, which is a small town outside of Little Rock. Laura Anne, my mother, had to give me up because she was unmarried and couldn't make a home for me."

"That must have been so hard for her," I said sympathetically.

"Well, it turned out to be hard for Aunt Jo, too." Lori picked up a piece of yarn and made a cat's cradle around her fingers. "When she found out that my birth mother was giving me up, she knew she wanted to adopt me, and she started working through an agency to make that happen. But my parents—my adoptive parents, I mean—heard what she was doing and put in their application, too. And because they were married and Aunt Jo was single, the agency gave me to *them*." She looked up at me, shaking her head. "Aunt Jo said, 'I was never so mad in my life. My sister—my very own sister!—snatched you right out from under my nose.' I wanted to laugh, but she was deadly serious. In fact, Aunt Jo was so angry that she refused to visit or even speak to my parents all during the years I was growing up. Can you imagine?"

"A family feud," I said with a wry chuckle. "Over *you*. And you never had a clue."

"Exactly. So that's why Aunt Jo knew my birth mother and my parents didn't. But when she heard about my search, she was more than glad to tell me what she knew. She actually cried." She bit her lip. "Well, we both did. It was a pretty emotional moment for me, as you can guess. Learning my mother's name." She paused and said it again, almost whispering. "Laura Anne. It's a pretty name, isn't it? And a lot like my own. I'm Lori Ann, you know."

"So now that you have a name, what's next?" I asked. "Do you have a strategy?"

"Several," Lori said. "I started with the Internet, of course. Her last name—Gatley—seems fairly unusual, so I thought I might get lucky right away. But Google didn't turn up any leads, so I tried the White Pages. No luck there, either, yet. But there are lots more ways to search, and I'll keep at it. I'm just so *happy* to have something to go on."

"Maybe she got married and took her husband's name," I suggested. "That can be a problem." In my former incarnation as a lawyer, I frequently had to search for witnesses. Searches for women are often complicated by marriage name changes.

"I thought of that," Lori said. "Sherwood has a local newspaper, so I'll start there. Also, now that I know my mother's name and the town where I was born, I might even be able to locate my original birth certificate. I'm planning to drive up there. When I do, I'll go to the courthouse and search the records for marriage licenses."

"You might check the local death records, too," I said gently. "She may have died."

Lori's mouth turned down. "You're right, of course. Or she might have moved away and *then* got married. And maybe divorced and married again. It could be a long search—but it feels like I'm on the right track at last."

I reached for her hand and gave it a hard squeeze. "I wish you all the luck in the world, Lori. I think you're going to succeed."

"Thank you." She brightened. "Oh, and Aunt Jo gave me a few things she's been keeping for me. She said she always meant to throw them out, but when she'd start to do that, a little voice would tell her to hang on to them." Lori bent over and took something out of her tote bag. "She gave me this." She laid a baby dress on the table in front of her, smoothing out the wrinkles with her hand.

"It's beautiful," I said, fingering the soft ivory material. It looked as if it was very old. The long skirt had an elaborate lacy panel in the front, and lace inserts on the puffy sleeves.

"A christening gown, Aunt Jo calls it, entirely handmade and handed down in my birthmother's family. My grandmother Lorene— Laura Anne's mother, that is—gave it and some other stuff to Aunt Jo, when they thought Aunt Jo was going to adopt me. But then the family feud started, and Aunt Jo was so angry with my adoptive mom that she just stuck everything away on a shelf and never mentioned it. She knew that her sister wasn't religious anyway, so I wouldn't have been christened. There was no point in her handing over the dress."

"You might show this to Christine," I said, thinking of what the professor had said about the importance of ritual clothing. In this case, the dress was meant to be worn on a very special occasion: a baby's welcome—an initiation, really—into a family, a faith, a community. "She might be able to tell you something about the pattern in the lace."

"Good idea." Lori took her cell phone out of her tote. "I'll send her a photo and see what she says."

I stood up and picked up my carton. "Well, I guess I'd better get back downstairs."

Lori snapped the cell phone photo. "Aunt Jo also gave me a big brown envelope full of old family pictures. I haven't had time to look through them yet, but I'm hoping maybe I'll find some more clues there." She grinned. "I have the feeling I'm going to be busy for a while."

I grinned back, thinking that Lori looked happier than she'd been in quite some time. "Hope you find what you're looking for," I said, and took my load downstairs with the intention of sorting the photographs at the counter.

There was a constant stream of customer traffic in and out of the shop that afternoon—a good thing, really, because more traffic means more sales. But it also meant that I didn't get to the photos. And since I knew I had to work on my *Enterprise* article that evening, I decided that there was no point in taking them home with me. Caitie would be home, too, and I wanted to spend time with her. When I closed up at five, I stowed the carton under the counter, next to the box of magnetic letters I used on the bulletin board.

And as I did, I have to admit that I felt a certain amount of anticipation, of the goose-bumpy variety. If there really was a ghost, and if she really had decided to communicate with me via old photographs, maybe she'd be glad to have this batch to work with. When I stopped to think about it, I felt a certain sympathy with her. It would be pretty frustrating to go through eternity with something important on your mind and no way to express yourself except by humming or ringing a bell or fooling around with magnetic letters and an old photo on a bulletin board. She might welcome a little help.

Hey, China. It was my lawyerly self again, objecting. *Assumes facts not in evidence. What part of that don't you get?*

I got that. I got it *all*. Still, I couldn't help but wonder. What *was* it, exactly, that this ghost, if that's what she was, wanted to tell me? Why now, after all these years? And why me and not Ruby?

That's okay. I don't blame you if you don't believe it. I didn't, either—not really.

But still . . .

Chapter Eight

Pecan Springs, Texas
August–September 1888

In the few weeks after the storm, Annie was happier than she had been since Douglas died. Adam came often after dark, discreetly, by the path through the hedge. They loved, laughed, and talked together until the early hours of the morning. Her heart overflowed with the forgotten richness of loving and being loved, and she felt physically alive again, her skin tingling with an electric awareness, her senses alert to smell and taste and sound, her whole body singing and eager, anticipating Adam's arrival, his touch, his kiss. She couldn't stop thinking about him, loving him, *wanting* him with a passionate desire that she had not felt since the earliest days of her marriage to Douglas. It was as if she was under the spell of an irresistible power that was now in command of her heart, her body, her mind. She had no choice but to yield, and yield willingly, to anything it demanded.

Her happiness was not without its price, however. Annie had always thought of herself as a moral person, careful to respect the rights of other people. She tried never to lie and she was scrupulous in her dealings with her merchants and her girls. She would never take anything—not a skein of thread or a pair of scissors or even a needle—that belonged to anyone else.

But when she was with Adam, Annie's scruples took wing and flew right out the window. Love made its own rules, she told herself, and loving Adam felt utterly and beautifully *right*. She simply wouldn't allow herself to think that it was wrong to love another woman's husband.

When Adam wasn't with her, however, uncomfortable questions nudged themselves into her consciousness. Douglas, too, had always lived by a strict moral code, both in his personal life and in his business. What would he say about what she and Adam were doing? How had she gotten to a point in her life where she could justify sleeping with her neighbor's husband? Even if it was just a short-lived affair and Delia never found out about it, it was wrong.

But there was something even more disturbing. Annie already knew that she wanted Adam's baby, wanted it just as much as she had wanted her own first baby, Douglas' son. Her desire signaled—to her, at least—that this was not an ephemeral affair that would be concluded when her lover's wife came home. It could surely have no good consequences. Where was it going to end?

Annie pushed the questions as far to the back of her mind as possible, so they wouldn't dim the glimmering happiness that sent her spinning giddily through her days. Still, she was sensible enough to know that there were things that had to be done, and her happiness was no excuse for not doing them. She might want Adam's baby, but allowing herself to become pregnant was simply out of the question. She needed something to ensure against that happening, but she didn't dare buy one of the patent medicines at Mr. Carter's pharmacy. Mr. Carter was a dapper little man who prided himself on knowing everything that was going on in town and wasn't above passing the news along. As a widow, if she bought one of the patent medicines that women used as a contraceptive, it would be all over Pecan Springs in a day or two. She couldn't ask a friend to do it, either, for she would have to confess why she wanted it, and she couldn't do that.

So Annie mustered her courage and went to see Mrs. Crow, who had a reputation for keeping women's private matters to herself—and was much nicer than Mr. Carter. Mrs. Crow took her to a small room adjacent to the kitchen. There was a drying rack filled with bundles of herbs, a worktable fitted out with equipment for distilling essential oils and making tinctures and salves and lotions, and shelves of glass jars and boxes of dried herbs, small bottles of tinctures, and little pots of salves. Mrs. Crow knew that she was a widow, so Annie excused her request by saying that she was purchasing the herbs on behalf of a friend, a young, newly married woman who lacked instruction in the matter and was too shy to come herself. Oh, and she—Annie, that is—wanted some hibiscus tea, please.

Annie flushed uneasily when Mrs. Crow peered over her wire-rimmed spectacles and remarked in a knowing mutter, "You can tell your friend, my dear, that rue in thyme is a maiden's posy."

"I'm sorry," Annie said contritely. "What does that mean, exactly?"

Mrs. Crow raised her eyebrows. "It's an old Scottish proverb that means more than it seems to say. To be sure she's safe, your friend can drink a strong tea of rue and thyme as soon after the act as possible. On the other hand, she might find it better to repent of what she is about to do, in time to change her mind and not do it."

"Ah," Annie said, coloring. "I see."

Mrs. Crow chuckled wryly. "But we women do what we must, of course, when we must, since the matter is not often left to us, but to our husbands." She went to a shelf and took down two jars. "I will give you some rue and thyme to take to your friend for those times when she finds repentance beforehand inconvenient. Or impossible."

"Thank you," Annie stammered, wondering uncomfortably just how much this wise old lady guessed. "I would . . . I'm sure my friend will appreciate that."

Mrs. Crow gave her a shrewd look. "I tell all my ladies that it's best to take care of the matter immediately afterward, of course. It is all too easy to make a mistake. But if a second monthly is missed and it's a little too late for rue and thyme, there are other plants that can help." She gestured toward a shelf of glass jars. "Wild carrot seeds and cotton root are both known to be reliable."

"I've heard of wild carrot seeds," Annie murmured, remembering what Adam had told her. "Perhaps my friend should have a supply of those, as well."

Mrs. Crow nodded and began ticking items on her fingers in what sounded like a practiced recital. "Women used different plants back east, where I grew up. But in our part of Texas, there's epazote, tansy, pennyroyal, mugwort, and staghorn milkweed. In fact, I grow these right here in my garden—or I gather them myself, outside of town. Ladies ask for them quite often, as you can imagine, so I keep a good supply on hand for teas, and also as tinctures. The choice of plants and the dose depends on how far along a woman is, and her size and general health." She looked over her glasses again. "If your friend is in *that* case, Mrs. Duncan, it would be best if she could come herself. I might be of more help if I could have a look at her."

"Thank you," Annie said again, impressed by Mrs. Crow's knowledge. She had often heard her grandmother and her mother and her aunts talking about the plants they used, of course. Women didn't need to consult a doctor when it came to managing their families. They knew what had to be done when their husbands didn't want to make their beds in the loft and their health wouldn't permit them to bear another baby—or when they felt that eight or nine children were quite enough. They had grown most of the plants themselves, or they knew where to gather them, but in these modern times, with a pharmacy in town, many women found their answers in Lydia Pinkham's tonic or Madam LeRoy's pills. She added, "I'll let my friend know what you've said."

"Well, just tell her to keep me in mind," Mrs. Crow said with a benign smile. "I can give her tinctures or dried herbs and tell her how to use them. Some of the plants can be dangerous, if you don't know what you're doing." She took down a large glass jar and spooned out some prickly-looking brown seeds. "Now, these are wild carrots. Queen Anne's lace, they're sometimes called. Your friend should soak them in water to soften them a bit, then right afterward, chew a teaspoonful and wash them down with a glass of water. Not the tastiest things in this world, I'll grant you. But those who dance must pay the piper." She did a quick calculation. "That'll be forty-five cents for everything, please. That includes your hibiscus."

Annie paid for the herbs and went home with a packet of wild carrot seeds as well as envelopes of rue and thyme and a paper bag of ruby-red hibiscus flowers for tea. That night, as she and Adam lay together in her bed, naked under a single sheet, she told him what she had done. She wanted him to know that she was taking precautions so he wouldn't worry.

"Rue in time," he said soberly. "Truth be told, Annie my sweet, I rue it *all* the time. Not us, of course," he added hastily. "I don't regret us in the least. I'm just sorry it has to be this way. If we could . . . if we could only . . ." His voice died away.

She could tell by the shadow that crossed his face that he, too, was thinking of the irony. It was almost funny, although she didn't dare laugh. The two women in Adam's life—she and Delia, lover and wife— were using all the wiles they knew of to make sure that neither would bear his child. The difference was that his lover desperately wanted his baby but didn't dare become pregnant, while his wife just couldn't be bothered. But Annie didn't want to put the irony into words, for it would only remind them both of the painful truth: that she was not his wife and Delia was.

And then *he* put it into words. "I wish you and I could have a child together," he said, and traced the line of her jaw with his finger. "I want that more than anything."

His voice was low and gruff and she could hear the raw regret in it. She knew that he was asking himself the same questions she was. Where was this taking them? Where, where, *where* would it end? Surely tragedy loomed, one way or another. She turned away from him, shivering, suddenly possessed by the image of the two of them alone on an idyllic island surrounded by a threatening sea, with a hurricane of incalculable consequences looming over the horizon.

But he pulled her back and bent over her and kissed her, and she relaxed into his arms with a grateful sigh, willing herself to blot out the image, yielding herself to his protective strength. She shared his desire to have a child, but she knew he was relieved to hear about her precautions. She treasured this mark of their growing closeness, their deepening intimacy.

In other ways, too, things seemed to be looking up. Annie had scratched St. Louis off her list of future possibilities; to leave Pecan Springs now was unthinkable. She took the train to San Antonio, where she located two dress shops and a millinery shop on East

Commerce Street, each of which seemed to cater to the wealthiest women of the city. The proprietors were so impressed with her laces that they bought every scrap she had with her—bought it all *outright*, rather than taking it on consignment. And then they gave her orders for more, to be produced as quickly as possible.

"All I've been able to get is the cheap machine-made stuff," one shop owner told her. "Your work is beautiful, Mrs. Duncan. It will please my most demanding clients."

Back home, Annie and the girls, thrilled by their success, worked with an even greater dedication. They could meet the orders, she thought, but if they fell behind, she could look for other needlewomen to help. Annie's Laces had stepped back from the brink of disaster.

Between that daily excitement and the nightly delights with Adam, the weeks rocketed by, and if Annie felt any pangs of guilt, she simply refused to acknowledge them. She was no longer in control of events. She was simply moving as the feeling and the opportunity took her. She was comforted with the thought that if she couldn't help herself, she couldn't *blame* herself—not a very sophisticated argument, but the best she could come up with under the circumstances.

In one way, it was frightening to feel herself so entirely in the grip of circumstance.

In another, it felt utterly natural and right and good, and she simply refused to think of consequences, calamitous though they might be.

Chapter Nine

The carrot has a long and distinguished history. Wild carrot was cultivated in Northern Europe as early as 2000–3000 BCE, but not as an edible plant. Rather, it was grown for its flavorful, aromatic, and medicinal leaves, roots, and seeds. It was used to treat bladder and kidney ailments, and the seeds (in small doses) help to calm and settle the stomach and ease flatulence. The seeds were used as an aid to family planning.

Rich in phytonutrients and antioxidants, carrots have long been known to have cardiovascular and anticancer benefits. They're good for the eyes, too. Recently, researchers at the University of California at Los Angeles determined that women who ate carrots at least twice per week have significantly lower rates of glaucoma.

In modern times, carrot seed oil has become a popular wrinkle-fighting skin treatment. You can add a few drops to an ounce of olive or rosehip seed oil to use as a facial oil. If the carroty scent is strong and you find yourself being pursued by rabbits, you might try diluting it with a few drops of lavender oil.

"Anne's Flower"
China Bayles
Pecan Springs Enterprise

Caitie was up before dawn on Thursday morning. I could hear her singing happily to herself in her bedroom, and when she came downstairs, she was wearing her pink *Have You Hugged Your Chicken Today?* T-shirt. She skipped outdoors before breakfast to give her contestants some last-minute loving attention—cleaning their feet and polishing their toenails, removing all traces of poo, and fastening on the numbered plastic leg bands she had received with the entry form. Then she came back in the house and got her stuff together: the birds' feed and water dishes; the vet's Pullorum-Typhoid testing report, showing that the chickens were disease-free; and her emergency repair kit (baby wipes, olive oil, manicure scissors, nail clippers, and tweezers). She also unplugged her chicken cam from the bracket in the chicken yard and packed that, as well.

"You're taking your camera?" I asked doubtfully. "Why?"

The camera livestreamed a video feed to Caitie's Texas Chix blog, enabling people around the globe to see what her chickens were doing. It could also save sound and video to a flash drive and allow for cell phone monitoring, but I didn't think it was necessary for Caitie to keep an eye on her chickens while they were at the fair.

As usual, however, she had a logical answer. "I want to take the cam so I get a picture of the judges pinning a ribbon on the cage," she said reasonably. "Plus, I think people who visit my blog would like to see what goes on at a poultry show. I won't try to do a live feed, because I'd need Wi-Fi and that might get really complicated. But I can record the video to the flash drive and put it on the blog later, or upload it as a video." She slid me a glance. "I asked Dad and he said it was okay. He was going to help set it up in the poultry tent."

When you're surrounded and outnumbered, all you can do is give in as graciously as you can. "Well, okay, then," I said. "But here's the thing. Your dad's not here to help, and I'm clueless when it comes to electronics. Can you set it up yourself? And did you check to be sure that there are no rules against video cameras at the show?"

"I'm sure I can do it. I helped Dad when he installed it in the chicken yard." She frowned. "But I didn't think about rules. Why wouldn't they want people to put up cameras?"

I could come up with a half dozen reasons, but it would be quicker to check. "How about if I call Mr. Banner," I said. "He'll probably know."

As it happens, our nearest neighbor, Tom Banner, is a reserve deputy for the Adams County sheriff and also manages the security team at the county fair. I caught him on his way to the fairgrounds and asked my question. A few moments later, I was able to tell Caitie that there were no rules preventing her from keeping an electronic eye on her chickens—but only, Tom said, because nobody had ever thought to ask. Next year, they'd probably make a rule against it. In the meantime, he offered to help her set it up. He'd meet us at the poultry tent.

"Cool!" she said when I told her about the arrangements, and we finished packing. We ate breakfast, toted Caitie's gear and her chicken contestants (in Winchester's doggie carrier) out to my white Toyota, and we were off.

The Adams County Fair is the biggest event of the summer in Pecan Springs. It's held at the fairgrounds a couple of miles west of town, where nobody minds if the carnival stays open until midnight and the country music and old-time fiddlin' go on until the wee hours. The weather is always hotter than firecrackers, but folks don't seem to mind that, either. They look forward all year long to the carnival rides, the Cowboy Breakfast, the calf-roping and pig-wrangling contests, and the chance to win a blue ribbon for their canned peaches or strawberry jam or embroidered pillowcases. If you live in the city and are accustomed to sophisticated entertainment—off-Broadway shows, foreign-film festivals, opera and the ballet—you may find our downhome doings just a little too folksy for your taste. But for people who live in Pecan Springs, this old-fashioned country-style entertainment seems exactly right. It seems right to tourists, too, which is why the Chamber of Commerce gives it a double spread in the new four-color *Why You'll Love to Visit Pecan Springs* brochure.

The poultry tent is located between the 4-H tent and the food tent, on the west side of the fairgrounds, but close enough to the carnival that we could hear the cheerful hurdy-gurdy music as we waited in line at the poultry check-in booth. That's where every bird is carefully inspected for bugs, dirt, germs, and communicable unmentionables before being allowed into the company of other people's chickens. Although there have been no recent cases of avian influenza in Texas, it's still the eight-hundred-pound gorilla in the room. We're smack in the middle of the Central Flyway, the migratory route that wild birds take from Canada to the Rio Grande. Even the most diligently tended backyard flocks can catch the virus via direct or even indirect contact with infected migrants. Hence the careful checking.

The volunteer scrutinized Caitie's chickens from one end to the other, compared the numbers on their leg bands against the numbers on her entry forms, stamped her vet's P-T report, and gave her an exhibitor's badge.

"Section One," he said, and pointed toward a row of double-stacked cages arranged along both sides of the tent and down the middle, over a cedar-mulch floor. Section One was for chickens and ducks. Section Two was reserved for turkeys and geese, and Section Three for guineas, peacocks, quail, and pheasants. The air was filled with a raucous pandemonium of crows, cackles, clucks, quacks, honks, whistles, and shrieks. (The shrieks came from the peacocks on the other side of the tent. They sounded for all the world like a throng of women complaining about being murdered.) If you wanted to be heard, you had to raise your voice over the cacophony.

"Hey, China, over here!" Tom Banner saw us and waved. As security coordinator for the fair, he was uniformed and wore his duty belt, and since he's well over six feet and muscular, he cuts an impressive figure. "You're down at this end," he said over the hubbub, and walked us to the cages where Caitie's chickens would spend the next three days.

Tom and his wife, Sylvia, both experienced homesteaders, live just up the lane from us. As a volunteer reserve deputy sheriff, Tom—a former Delta Force officer in Iraq and Afghanistan—does weekly partner ride-alongs with the deputies, responds to emergencies, serves warrants, and generally helps to keep Adams County peaceful. At home, he raises chickens, geese, and ducks and is familiar with just about every homestead critter there is. Sylvia, a talented spinner and weaver, tends a flock of about a dozen Gulf Coast Native sheep. I wondered if she was showing her sheep in the livestock tent, and maybe some of her work in the Weaving Club's Sheep to Shawl exhibit.

When Extra Crispy and Dixie Chick were comfortably housed in their individual show cages, Tom and Caitie moved off to the side to attach the video camera high up on a nearby post. I stowed her gear under the cages and took a moment to glance around. And did a jaw-dropping double take.

In the cage next to Extra Crispy was the strangest rooster I had ever seen. He was totally black—black as coal, black as night, pitch-black, black as the inside of a black cat. From his black comb, wattles, and beak to his black legs, feet, and toenails, this rooster was amazingly, extraordinarily, exclusively black. Well, perhaps not quite. Among his high-arching black tail feathers and the plumy drape of feathers across his back, the blackness was highlighted with shimmers of iridescent purple and metallic green, like a sheen of oil on black water.

I was still staring at this incredible creature when Caitie and Tom got back. "What in the world is *that*?" I asked Tom, pointing. "He's spectacular! In a class by himself."

"I have no idea," he said, shaking his head. "I thought I knew chickens, but that one's a mystery."

But Caitie had an answer. "He's an Ayam Cemani rooster," she said. "I saw one on Animal Planet just last week." She went up to the chicken's cage and put her finger through the wire. The rooster came over and pecked it politely, saying hello. "And he's not just black on the outside, either," she added. "Under those black feathers, his skin is black. And under his skin, his muscles and bones are black. Even his heart and gizzard are black. It's called hyperpigmentation." She said it again, slowly, emphasizing the syllables. "Hy-per-pig-men-ta-tion. In Indonesia, where he comes from, he's considered magical. He's supposed to bring good fortune."

"Black heart and gizzard, too?" Tom asked, with interest. "So that accounts for his name." He pointed to the entry card pinned to the cage. It read *Blackheart*.

"Amazing," I said, still transfixed by his incredible blackness. "He must be very rare."

"Oh, he is," Caitie said authoritatively. "At least, he's rare here in America. And expensive. I've heard that roosters can cost twenty-five hundred dollars or more. And eight eggs were sold on eBay for fourteen hundred dollars. Not for eating," she added, "but for hatching. They were guaranteed to be fertile."

"Twenty-five hundred bucks for a *chicken*?" Tom whistled.

"And a hundred seventy-five dollars for an egg," I said incredulously.

Tom chuckled. "A little beyond my homestead budget, I'm afraid."

"Mine, too." Caitie made a wry face. "I'd love to have a breeding pair, but I can't even afford an *egg*." She paused, tilting her head. "But if you had a hen and a rooster, and the hen laid twenty eggs a month, you'd have—"

"A lucrative business," Tom said.

"Hi, guys," a woman called. She crossed the tent toward us, striding fast. She had a notebook in one hand and a camera around her neck.

"Hey, it's Slugger Nelson," Tom said. "Are you going to make us famous?"

"Sure thing," Jessica said cheerfully, raising her voice over the clamor. "What do you want to be famous *for*?"

Tom chuckled. "Not for being kidnapped, that's for sure."

I met Jessica Nelson a couple of years ago when she was a CTSU grad student, doing a journalism internship at the *Enterprise*. Now in her mid-twenties, she's a lively young woman with boy-cut blond hair and a generous sprinkle of freckles across her nose. A seasoned reporter with an observant eye and a curiosity that just won't quit, Jess proved herself by surviving a potentially deadly encounter with a kidnapper—which explains Tom's quip. I had a hand in her brave escape from the storage unit where she'd been held captive, and watched with pleasure when she was all over the news, telling her story. Anderson Cooper loved hearing her relate how she felt as she lay terrified in a parking garage storage unit, gagged and bound hand and foot. But he loved it even more when she told how she slipped out of her bonds, picked up a seven iron, and slugged her captor. Immediately, Anderson dubbed her the Seven-Iron Slugger. People who know the story still call her Slugger.

"I forgot to tell you," I said to Caitie. "Ms. Nelson would like to interview you and take a few pictures for the newspaper. Is that okay?"

"Oh, sure," Caitie said. She gestured proudly toward her chickens. "Meet Extra Crispy and Dixie Chick. They would love it if you made *them* famous." She turned to me. "Thirty-five hundred dollars," she said.

I blinked. "For what?"

"For twenty eggs, at a hundred seventy-five dollars an egg." She traced some numbers with one finger on the palm of her hand. "Thirty-five thousand dollars a year, assuming that she doesn't lay in the winter."

"Wow," I said, and regarded the rooster with a new admiration.

"And if you had *two* hens," Caitie began.

Tom held up his hand. "Excuse me, ladies, but I have to go. My security team is meeting this morning."

"You're in charge of security?" Jessica asked, scribbling in her notebook.

"Right," Tom replied. "I'm a reserve deputy sheriff. I help the sheriff's office with event security. The county fair, the rodeo, Fourth of July fireworks, that sort of thing."

"Tom served two deployments as a Delta Force officer in Iraq and Afghanistan," I put in. "He's not likely to tell you, but it's an important part of who he is. The sheriff's office is lucky to have him."

"Delta Force," Jessica repeated. She gave him an up-and-down glance. "Maybe I could interview you on the topic of terrorist threats here at the fair."

She was being snarky, but Tom didn't laugh. "It's something we take seriously, you know. Anywhere there are crowds, there's a certain risk. Open carry complicates the situation, too, which is why so many cops hate it. Could be a guy making a political point, or it could be—" He shrugged. "Sure. I'll be glad to talk to you." He gave her his cell number, said good-bye, and left.

"Sorry," Jessica said ruefully. "I ought to watch my tongue."

"That'll be the day." I chuckled. "Tom is one of the good guys. I'm glad to have him as a neighbor."

Jessica got busy with her interview and took a few photos of Caitie with her chickens. Then she noticed the black rooster.

"Jeez," she said breathlessly. "What is *that*? Is he yours, Caitie? He doesn't look real."

While Caitie explained and I contemplated the economics of rare chicken breeding, Jessica took several photos of the rooster. She had just finished when Caitie's best friend, Sharon Lincoln, came into the tent and joined us. Sharon is a freckled, feisty, red-haired tomboy. The girls were going to spend the rest of the morning at the fair. Sharon's mom, Sonia, who was working in the food tent, would be available if they needed a grown-up. After lunch, Sonia was driving them to the Depot to rehearse *Little Women*, and I would pick Caitie up there after work. Since McQuaid wasn't home, we were planning to treat ourselves. Girls' night out at Gino's Pizza.

I glanced at my watch. It was time I headed for the shop, but I hadn't forgotten the photo I wanted to show to Jessica. First, though, I gave Caitie a quick hug and told her to have fun at the fair.

"You can call me if you run into any problems," I told her. "The shop is only fifteen minutes away. You've got your phone? Leave it on. I'll check on you in a couple of hours. Oh, and don't eat too much junk food. Lay off the soda pop."

She gave me that long-suffering look that teenage girls bestow on fussy mothers. "I won't, Mom. We'll be fine. Don't worry."

The girls ran off, and I turned to Jessica. "If you've got a minute or two, would you take a look at this?" I opened my shoulder bag and pulled out the photo I'd taken from the bulletin board the day before—the one of the family sitting on the veranda of my building. "The date on the back of this says it was snapped in June 1890, but there are no names." I thought it might sound a little weird if I told her that I was trying to discover the name of the woman whose ghost was haunting my shop. So I just said, "Do you happen to know if these people are the original owners of my building? Mr. and Mrs. Duncan, I believe."

Jessica took the photo and studied it, her forehead wrinkling. "I remember seeing a picture of Mrs. Duncan, and I'm pretty sure this is her. She has that Gibson-girl look. The blouse with the big sleeves and all that hair pinned up on top of her head. But Mr. Duncan—Douglas Duncan, I think his name was—was a big guy with dark hair and a beard and mustache. It's hard to tell from the photo, but this man's hair looks sort of light colored, and he's clean shaven. I don't think he's the same guy." She held up the photo. "If you'll let me keep it, I could check on it for you. I have to go over to the Historical Society on another story. I could have a look through their archives if I don't find anything at the *Enterprise*." She gave me an inquiring look. "Why this sudden interest in ancient history?"

"Oh, just curious," I said vaguely. "Yes, you can keep it. I'd like to have it back, though." I glanced at my watch. "Ruby opened up for me this morning, but I've got some garden helpers coming in. I'd better get over to the shop."

"I'll let you know if I find anything," Jessica said, tucking the photo into her notebook. "I think I'll head over to the security office and talk to Tom. Maybe he can point me toward an exciting story or two here at the fair."

"He's seen quite a few adventures in his military career," I said. "But I'm afraid nothing very exciting is likely to happen here."

"I'm looking for another crime story." Jessica made a face. "I'm getting a little bored writing articles about historical buildings and covering the poultry tent at the fair."

"A crime story?" I laughed. "I think we can do without that kind of excitement, Slugger."

I was right. Oh, I was *so* right.

It was the first Thursday of the month, which meant that my team of volunteer helpers was already at work in the gardens around the shop. To beat the Texas heat, they start early on summer mornings. When I got to the shop, I would have preferred to go in and start digging through that box of photos. But I feel awkward if I let the volunteers work alone, so I ducked quickly inside, found my garden gloves, and went out to join them, leaving Ruby to monitor the shop.

It takes a lot of work to keep the herb gardens from looking raggedy, and I appreciate the women who are willing to lend a hand for a few hours every month. In return for their work, they receive free enrollment in one of our classes and are invited to take cuttings and snippets from the established stock plants. Usually, there are five or six volunteers, but summer is vacation time and this morning the crew was down to three. One was working in the apothecary garden, and the other two in the culinary garden outside the kitchen door. Cass uses herbs heavily in her dishes, and I try to ensure that there are always enough to meet her needs.

When I bought 304 Crockett Street, there were signs that some-body, decades ago, had had a large garden in the empty lot to the east, between my building and the yellow-painted frame house that is home to the Hobbit House Children's Bookstore. But by the time I moved in, the empty lot was covered with thirsty Bermuda grass that required frequent watering and mowing—in my opinion, a waste of space, wa-ter, and work. Why spend all that effort to grow grass when you can raise something that's both pretty *and* useful?

So, little by little, I took out the lawn and replaced it with small theme gardens, irregularly shaped and bordered by paths made of stepping-stones and bark mulch. The culinary garden has the usual mix of parsley, sage, thyme, mint, rosemary, bay, and as many different species of basil as I can fit into the space. The fragrance garden has a lovely stone fountain in the center, surrounded by heirloom roses prized for their scent and by nicotiana, lavender, rosemary, and scented geraniums—lemon, rose, orange, chocolate. Beside the tearoom deck, there's a dyer's garden, with coreopsis, yarrow, tansy, Turks' cap (which also makes a pretty ruby-red jelly), and a prickly pear cactus that is currently home to an industrious colony of cochineal bugs, the source of the famous red dye created by the Aztecs and Mayas of Central and North America. On the other side of the deck, there's an apothecary garden, with echinacea, St. John's wort, plantain, feverfew, sage, com-frey, lavender, garlic, and Queen Anne's lace.

And at the back of the lot, there's a zodiac garden, a large round space divided into twelve pie-shaped sections, representing the twelve astrological houses. Each of the house-sections is planted with herbs that are said to "belong," traditionally, to the sign that rules that house: Aries, the first house, with garlic, mustard, and horseradish; Taurus, the second, with thyme, mint, and catnip; Gemini, the third, with dill, parsley, and caraway. And so on around the circle. A large rosemary (Leo) rules the middle of the circle.

Ethel Barnett, one of my most regular volunteers, was on her knees beside the apothecary garden, pulling weeds. I set to work across from her, yanking out the surplus chickweed. Herbalists use chickweed in salves, lotions, teas, and tinctures to treat all manner of diseases, but the plant has bullying tendencies. It needs to be discouraged from taking over space that belongs to its neighbors. Lecturing doesn't work. You have to yank.

After a few moments, Ethel straightened her back and pulled off her gardening gloves. "I was noticing that plant," she said, pointing at the Queen Anne's lace. "I've been seeing it everywhere this summer, but I didn't expect to find it in your apothecary garden." She brushed a stray strand of gray hair from her sweaty forehead. "How is it used?"

I stood up, broke off a couple of leaves, and took them to her to sniff. "What do they smell like?"

"Why, carrots," she said in surprise.

I nodded. "Queen Anne's lace is wild carrot. The whole plant is edible—roots, leaves, stem, and all. We could just as easily have planted it in the culinary garden. But until modern medicine came along, this was one of the preferred treatments for stomach and digestive disorders, as well as kidney and bladder diseases. Nowadays, an essential oil made from the seeds is added to commercial antiaging skin creams. A very useful plant."

"Oh, really?" Ethel asked, interested. She put a hand up to her face. "Does it work? I spend a lot of time in the garden, and I certainly have my share of wrinkles."

"I've never tried to use it that way," I replied. "But some of my customers swear by it. There's some on the essential oil shelf in the shop. Help yourself to a bottle. Try adding a drop or two to your favorite moisturizer. Let me know if you like the way it works."

"I'll do it," she said. "Thanks."

"The seeds were used another way, too." I gave her a quick smile. "As a morning-after contraceptive. An herbal Plan B."

She looked surprised. "You're kidding."

"Nope." I shook my head. "I'm writing an article about the plant for my garden page in the *Enterprise*, so I've been doing some research." The plant in front of us had been blooming for several weeks, and one of the flowering umbrels had dried, pulling itself into the concave shape of a small bird's nest. I broke it off and shook some of the seeds into the palm of my hand. "It turns out that women used to chew a spoonful of these seeds after sex. They were considered the most reliable thing available." I had to laugh a little. "That's probably why this plant spread so fast after the founding mothers brought it to this continent. They needed it, so they took it with them wherever they settled."

"Well, my goodness," Ethel said. "There's something new to learn every day. Wild carrot seeds." She frowned. "And just think of the money we spend for birth control meds, when we could go out to the country and gather them." She pulled her gloves on again. "But I suppose the pill is more convenient," she added thoughtfully. "And the medication is standardized and labeled."

"That's all true," I said. I bent over and dropped the seeds onto the ground around the plant. "Wild plants don't wear labels. Which is another drawback where this plant is concerned." I straightened up. "Not long ago, a group of foragers out on a hunt for wild foods found what they thought was a patch of wild carrots. They harvested a big bag of leaves and put them in a salad, along with some other wild-gathered plants. They all got very sick. One person died."

"Uh-oh," Ethel said softly.

I nodded. "The killer was hemlock, the poisonous plant that is said to have killed Socrates. Its dominant chemical, coniine, is similar to nicotine, which is also a killer. Poison hemlock and wild carrot—Queen Anne's lace—are lookalikes. I've read that it only takes a handful of fresh poison hemlock leaves to kill somebody, and even less of the root or the seeds, where the plant chemical is more concentrated."

Ethel fingered the leaves of Queen Anne's lace. "Is it hard to tell the difference?" she asked. "Do they look much alike?"

"They're enough alike to confuse somebody who isn't careful," I replied. "The flower stalks are different, for one thing—poison hemlock is smooth, with dark spots or streaks. The wild carrot stalk is green and covered with little hairs. But there's another, more certain giveaway. Wild carrot smells like fresh carrot. Poison hemlock smells rank. It's really yucky."

"Good to know." Ethel laughed a little. "But I don't think I'll tempt fate. Better to be safe than sorry."

"I understand," I said, and went back to my weeding. In another twenty minutes, I had vanquished the rampant chickweed and Ethel had cleaned out the garlic chives that had sneaked over from the culinary garden. And the morning, already hot to begin with, hadn't gotten any cooler.

"I need to get back to the shop." I stood up and pulled off my gloves, wiping the sweat off my forehead with the back of my hand. "I think we've accomplished quite a bit, don't you?"

"We have," Ethel replied. She straightened up and gave me a hesitant smile. "I wanted to mention something odd that happened this morning, China."

"Odd?"

She nodded. "I got here early, because I wanted to work while it was still cool. I parked in the alley, and as I came around your stone cottage, I saw a woman dressed up like a Gibson girl—a white blouse and long dark skirt, with her hair piled up on top of her head. She was snipping lavender right over there, beside the fountain. She was carrying a basket, and she was filling it." She pointed. "She looked up at me and smiled."

My heart seemed to skip a beat or two. "Did you speak to her?"

She shook her head. "That's the strange part, really. I thought she was going to say something. She looked as if she *wanted* to. But then I heard Mr. Cowan's dog barking across the alley, and a cat squalled bloody murder and a garbage can went over. I turned around to see what was going on, and when I turned back, she was . . . well, she was gone." Ethel laughed a little uncomfortably.

"Gone?" My voice squeaked. I cleared my throat and tried again. "Gone, as in walked away?"

"Not exactly. I mean, one minute she was there and the next, she wasn't. It was like she just . . . vanished. If I believed in ghosts, I might have said I'd seen one. But I—" She ducked her head apologetically. "Sorry. I know that's silly. It was eerie, is all. Her disappearing like that. It kind of gave me the willies."

The Gibson girl. The woman in the swing with the baby in her arms. Who might have worn the white shirtwaist and gray skirt that Ruby and I had found in the storeroom. Who—

I shivered. Who might have pinned the photo and the fresh sprigs of lavender to my bulletin board. Had Ethel actually seen my ghost? If that was true, did it make her *real*?

"China?" Ethel was eyeing me curiously. "Do you recognize her? Maybe she's one of your neighbors?"

I shook my head numbly, then tried to laugh it off. "I'd prefer it if she asked before she helped herself to the lavender, but it doesn't matter. There's plenty for everybody." I bent over and brushed the dirt off the knees of my jeans. "Come on, let's see if anybody else is ready to call it quits."

I went with her to thank the others for their work, and to tell them that the fall classes were posted in the shop. If they wanted to enroll in their freebie course, it would be good if they could do that early, before the classes filled.

After the heat of the August morning, the shop was blessedly cool and quiet. A customer—Mrs. Birkett, who is ninety if she is a day but as sprightly as you or I—was browsing the bookshelves. I greeted her, then, trying to put the Gibson girl out of my mind, I stepped into the Crystal Cave to thank Ruby for opening the shop.

She was sitting on a stool behind her counter, checking stock orders. "No problem," she said. "I was glad to do it." She put down her pencil and adjusted the yellow headband that held back her frizzed carroty hair. "By the way, Christine Vickery called a little while ago. She said she's been trying to reach Lori, but nobody answers and Lori's voice mail doesn't pick up. Christine has to go out of town, so she asked us to give Lori a message."

I glanced back through the door to see if Mrs. Birkett was ready to check out, but she was still browsing. "What's the message?"

Ruby stood up and stretched her arms over her head, then bent to one side and then the other, pulling the kinks out of her back. She was wearing a yellow top and a pair of floral-print palazzo pants. She looked like a bright ray of sunshine in a flower garden. "It's about a photo Lori sent her. A baby's dress, I think she said."

"Oh, that one," I said. "It's a christening dress, very pretty, with a panel of embroidered lace down the front. Lori showed it to me yesterday." I paused, and something occurred to me. "Maybe Lori didn't get a chance to tell you. She located her adoptive aunt on Ancestry dot-com, and she drove up to Waco to meet her. The big news is that her aunt was actually able to give Lori the name of her birth mother."

Ruby grinned delightedly. "No, I didn't know!" She sat down on her stool again. "China, that's wonderful! She must be very happy."

I nodded. "Her aunt also gave her the christening dress that had been handed down in her birth mother's family. Lori was meant to wear it, apparently, but her adoptive aunt held on to it. Ask Lori to tell you the story. A classic family feud." I tilted my head on one side. "So what's the message?"

Ruby frowned. "Christine was in a hurry, and she was talking so fast that I'm not sure I understood everything." She paused. "If I got it right, it had to do with the baby's lace cap that was in the wooden chest we found in the storeroom. Remember it?"

I nodded. "I remember a baby's cap, a lady's cap, some collars—"

"Yes, all that lace stuff. Well, Christine said she couldn't be sure until she sees the actual baby's dress, but she thinks the pattern in the photo Lori sent yesterday might be the same as the pattern in the baby's lace cap. She thinks the two pieces might be a cap and gown set."

"The same pattern, maybe. But a set?" I said doubtfully. "That would be a long shot. The christening dress came from a small town north of Little Rock, which is a long way from Central Texas."

Ruby shrugged. "Sorry. I don't have a clue. You'll have to ask

Christine. Anyway, she wants us to tell Lori that she'll be back from her trip early next week. She hopes Lori will let her have the baby dress so she can do some testing."

I hesitated, wondering whether to tell Ruby what Ethel had seen in the garden that morning. But she had already gone back to her stock orders. Anyway, Ethel's now-you-see-her-now-you-don't Gibson girl was every bit as improbable as the ghostly rearrangement of my bulletin board—and I hadn't yet told Ruby about that. It was the kind of thing that should wait until we could sit down with a cup of tea and no distractions, when we could sort all this crazy stuff out.

So I went back to the shop, where Mrs. Birkett had found what she wanted, and rang up the book she was buying. A member of the Pecan Springs Herb Society and a lifelong Crockett Street resident, she is deeply interested in traditional medicine.

"I'm also looking for something about the history of women's personal uses of herbs," she said in her scratchy, high-pitched voice.

"Personal uses?" I asked.

"Yes." She took her checkbook out of her purse. "These days, we talk about family planning as if it's something new. But it's not, you know. Women planned their families back then—when to have babies, how many, how often. But they used the plants their mothers and grandmothers told them about, not some fancy prescription they got from a doctor. My grandmother knew a lot about that."

"It's interesting that you should ask," I said. "I'm writing an article for the newspaper about Queen Anne's lace—one of the herbs women used to manage their fertility. Along with tansy and rue and artemisia. It's a fascinating subject."

"Oh, good—I'll look for that." Mrs. Birkett smiled at me. "My grandmother would have loved you, China." With arthritic fingers, she finished writing out the check. "She would have loved your shop and especially your gardens." She tore out the check and handed it to me. "She had a big herb garden herself, you know, just a block or so down the street, at the very house where I live now. She sold herbs to the village ladies, and she kept the pharmacy supplied. She worked with herbs until she was well into her nineties. When I was just a little girl, she let me play in what she called her stillroom. She said the word comes down from the time when a room in a manor house was set aside for distilling cordials and brewing beer and making medicines— all that sort of thing."

"How marvelous," I said enviously. "It must have been fun, growing up with a grandmother who had an old-fashioned stillroom."

Mrs. Birkett's faded blue eyes grew a little misty. "Oh, my dear, it was! I lived in her house when I was a young girl, and moved back there again after my dear husband died. Come see me sometime and I'll show you her equipment. It's all antique now, of course." She giggled. "Like me. I'm another antique."

"I'd love to do that." I did a quick mental calculation. If old Mrs. Birkett had been a Crockett Street resident when she was a girl, she might be able to tell me something about the people who had lived in my building.

"I wonder if you remember the Duncans," I said. "They built this house in 1882 and lived here for many years."

"Duncan?" Mrs. Birkett frowned, thinking. "I noticed the plaque beside your door, but the name isn't familiar. I *do* remember the old woman who lived here when I was a girl, though." She looked around. "Actually, she told me once that her husband built this house for her. If I remember right, this room was her front parlor. Her workroom, too, she said. Her name was Hunt. Mrs. Hunt."

"Oh, really?" I felt a little thrill of excitement. Was it possible that Mrs. Birkett had actually met my ghost, back before she became a ghost? My lawyerly self got to her feet and said, with an air of bored and long-suffering tolerance, *Objection. Assumes facts not in evidence, Your Honor.*

"Hunt?" I rephrased. "But I thought her name was Duncan." I frowned. Had Jessica and the Historical Society made a mistake?

Mrs. Birkett shook her head firmly. "No, no, I was just a girl then, but I remember Mrs. Hunt very well. I knew her about the time FDR was first elected, you see. Her husband had been dead for five or six years, but she had several grown daughters, as I recall, and any number of grandchildren. She loved having children around." She smiled, showing a gold-capped tooth. "She taught me to crochet before I was old enough to go to school. Her hands were old and all gnarly with arthritis and she couldn't see very well. But she was still able to make beautiful things with her crochet hook and knitting needles. And bobbin lace, too. I was always fascinated by those bobbins."

I was instantly sorry that I hadn't held on to the photo I had taken from the bulletin board instead of letting Jessica have it. It had been taken long before Mrs. Birkett was born, but she might have been able to recognize the people and tell me who they were.

"I may have a photo of your Mrs. Hunt," I said, "but I've loaned it to someone. When she gives it back, I'll bring it over. You might be able to help me identify the people in the picture."

"Oh, do that," Mrs. Birkett said, picking up the book she'd bought. "And I'll show you my grandmother's old stillroom equipment." She smiled. "I love to talk about the old days—whenever I can find somebody who wants to listen. Not many do, you know. Most people seem to prefer the present to the past. Which is regrettable, I feel."

The bell rang twice, softly. Mrs. Birkett looked up, noticing that the door was still closed.

"Odd," she remarked. "Does it do that often?"

"Occasionally," I said. "I must have my husband take a look at it." Chatting, we walked together to the door, where we said good-bye.

I was turning back to the counter, still thinking about what Mrs. Birkett had said, when the bell began to ring impatiently, as if it were trying to tell me something. Then, as I turned, I caught sight of the bulletin board at the end of the counter, beside the door. I froze, staring, the gooseflesh rising on my arms.

In the empty space where the family photograph had been, there was a *different* photograph, stuck to the board with a smiley-face magnet, a fresh sprig of lavender tucked behind it. It was a sepia-toned studio photograph of a baby just a few months old, formally posed against a pillow on an old-fashioned parlor chair beside a table with a vase of white roses and an open book. The baby—I couldn't tell if it was a boy or a girl—was wearing a lacy white cap and a long white dress. The dress was carefully arranged to show the embroidered lace panel down the front. It was hard to tell from a photograph, but the dress looked a lot like the one Lori's aunt had given her.

I shook myself. Well, I had asked for it, hadn't I? I had felt some sympathy for a spirit who had to live through eternity with nobody to talk to. I had deliberately left the photographs under the counter, with the idea that the ghost—*my* ghost—might use them to communicate with me. And she had accepted my invitation.

So what was I supposed to make of the photograph she'd put up there? Was it the baby I was supposed to notice, or the baby's dress? What could a baby's dress have to do with anything, then or now? Who was the baby? Did that matter?

The more questions I thought of, the more impatient I felt. Finally, I muttered, "What do you want from me, anyway? I'm getting a little tired of being the one who keeps asking the questions. Maybe it's time you came with a few answers."

If you're thinking that I must have felt a little silly, talking to a ghost who doesn't exist, you're exactly right. But for once, my lawyerly self didn't jump up with an objection. And the words were barely out of my mouth when I heard, or thought I heard, the faintest sigh. A rueful sigh, as if my long-suffering resident ghost had decided, finally, that I was so utterly dense that it was impossible to communicate with me. She was giving up.

The bell over the door gave a halfhearted tinkle and fell silent.

Chapter Ten

Pecan Springs, Texas
September–October 1888

Annie might be able to comfort herself with the thought of the rightness of her love for Adam, but he could not so easily ignore the consciousness of his guilt. He might excuse himself by saying that if he hadn't been drunk that first time, he wouldn't have lost control, and he knew that was true. It was bottled bravery that had given him the nerve to step around that table and take his friend's widow in his arms, and heedless, reckless passion did the rest.

But while that might explain a first transgression and perhaps mitigate the guilt, it could not explain why he had gone to her the next night, and the nights after that. He might promise himself to end it when Delia came home. He might even try to excuse his actions by reminding himself (lamely) that what his wife didn't know couldn't hurt her. (How many errant husbands use *that* for an excuse? he wondered.) But he could not escape what he knew to be a fundamental truth: that he loved Annie and he needed to be with her.

In the beginning, of course, he had been simply powerless against the force of his need. Delia had long ago insisted on separate bedrooms, for she slept better, she claimed, when she slept alone. She had always made it clear that by allowing him in her bed, she was performing her marital duty, but after Caroline was born she had seemed to merely tolerate him, rather than welcome him. In fact, now that he thought about it, he realized that it had been quite some time since he and his wife had made love. It had been at least a month before she went off to Galveston, hadn't it? Or perhaps even six or seven weeks. She had pleaded headaches, and then a painful monthly, and after that a lingering summer cold. And every night, they continued to sleep apart.

In contrast, Annie's eager passion, her physical hunger for him—quite astonishing, he thought—was equal to his desire for her. When he was with her, he drowned in her physical presence. When they were apart, he was filled with the memory of holding her, kissing her, moving inside her. The feeling of her bare body beneath his hands and the urgency of her warm mouth under his had made an impression on his soul that would haunt him to the end of time. He remembered the song his friend Doug had often sung to her: *And for bonnie Annie Laurie, I would lay me down and die.* He understood that now, for he felt the same way. Rapt, entranced, enchanted, he couldn't stay away.

But as the days and nights went on, Adam began to understand—dimly at first, then more and more clearly—that what compelled him was not just simple physical need, powerful as that might be. Over the three years since Douglas' death, he had watched Annie become proudly, fiercely self-reliant. She had organized her business and pulled together a team of women to do the work. She knew what she wanted and had the courage to reach for it—and the determination to keep on reaching even when fate slapped her hands. He saw her as an incredibly brave woman, with a deep inner reserve of strength and resiliency. For all she was able to do under the most difficult circumstances, for all that she *was*, he loved her.

And when he knew this for certain, he told her so, holding her face between his hands, compelling her to look into his eyes when he said, "I love you, Annie." He wanted her to know that what he was telling her was God's truth. And when she whispered, "I love you, Adam," his heart sang out.

But he couldn't tell her what else he knew: that above all things, he wanted to spend the rest of his life with her, to give her a child, and children. He didn't tell her because he knew that this was impossible, and when he let himself think of it, the knowledge filled him with the blackest despair. For better or worse, he was married to Delia. People got divorced in these modern days, but they were fashionable people in big cities. And while his wife often chafed within the boundaries of their marriage, he knew she would never give up its comfort and security, nor tolerate the disgrace that would inevitably come with a divorce. And *he* could never bring himself to give up his daughter, whom he loved fiercely.

But he didn't know how he could give up Annie, either, and the thought of it made him cling to her now, while he could. He felt himself being torn apart, and he could see nothing but darkness and danger ahead.

And then things got worse.

QUITE suddenly, and a full week before she was expected, Delia came home.

Adam was glad to see Caroline, and he swept her up in his arms with a cry of delight. "How's Daddy's little princess?" He brushed her damp strawberry curls from her forehead. "Are you glad to be home?"

"Oh, yes, Daddy!" she said, and kissed him. "I've missed you so much, every day!"

But Delia was another story. When he touched his lips to her cheek in the usual welcome-home kiss, he felt her pull away from him, and her glance was sharp as she looked around the sitting room.

"I see you've let Greta skip the dusting," she said. "And the carpet needs to be taken out and beaten. What did that girl *do* while I was gone?"

At first he was relieved at Delia's distance from him, for a night with her could afford no great happiness beyond a certain physical release. He would have felt oddly unfaithful, as if Annie were his true wife and Delia a woman who shared his house. But when she pulled away from even the most casual touch again and then again, he was swept by a wave of guilty apprehension. Had his wife returned home early because she had learned about him and Annie? But how in the world could she have found out? Had the hired girl—Greta—somehow discovered what they were doing and written to tell her?

At first, he had dismissed that possibility, because he didn't think Greta could have found them out, or was likely to know Delia's Galveston address, or have the courage to write. She was a stolid, unattractive young woman with heavy breasts, a pockmarked complexion, and an ugly scar that gave her mouth a sinister look. She moved slowly and seemed, he thought, to be a bit simple-minded. In her late teens and clearly destined to be a spinster, Greta lived with her mother and aunt on the other side of town and went home every evening after she had finished serving dinner and tidying the kitchen. Adam had never left for Annie's until after the girl had gone for the evening, and he was back at home before she came to work in the morning. He even made sure that his sheets were rumpled, as if he had slept all night in his bed.

But in the past few days, Greta had seemed to regard him with a new and different expression that he couldn't read. He was afraid she had somehow discovered the truth. He was unnerved.

And then he happened on what he thought was an easy way to gain the girl's confidence and ensure her silence. Delia had never been a sympathetic mistress. None of the several girls who had worked for her had been able to please her, this one least of all—and least of all now, it seemed. Her leisurely weeks of parties and sophisticated social gatherings in glamorous Galveston had not sweetened Delia's disposition, and she made no secret of the fact that she wasn't happy about returning to Pecan Springs. She was curt with Adam and short-tempered even with Caroline.

But it was Greta who had become the chief target of Delia's ire. The girl could do nothing right. If it wasn't the cooking that Delia found fault with, it was the laundry, and the ironing, and the making of beds. Never the most compliant of workers, the young woman retaliated by becoming balky. She was silent and sullen, and there were mistakes at table. Salt for sugar, for instance, in the crystal bowl from which Delia sweetened her breakfast fruit, and sour cream instead of top cream for her coffee. Black ink was spilled on the rose-colored parlor carpet, and the next day, two glass lamp chimneys were found to be mysteriously broken.

Trying to keep the peace, Adam intervened. When Delia discovered the broken lamp chimneys, her hand flew out to slap Greta's face. But Adam seized her arm and made her step backward, and Greta threw him a look of astonished gratitude.

Something similar happened the following evening, when there was no hot water for Delia's bath and Adam stepped in to stop a tongue-lashing. In that instance, Greta's gratitude was even more obvious. She clearly viewed him as her protector, and he decided his strategy must be working. From then on (and never imagining that he might be misunderstood), he took Greta's part whenever he saw the opportunity and made a point of smiling sympathetically at her when Delia was looking the other way. Even if the young woman suspected him of *anything*, he felt confident that she wouldn't confide it in her mistress.

Now that Delia was home, of course, Adam could not see Annie. Because his wife's arrival was a surprise, he had not even been able to say a proper good-bye, and the sad loss of their hours together left him empty and hollow. Over the next few days, he saw her through the open windows of her workroom and kitchen and heard her singing as she tended her vegetables on the other side of the hedge. And once, when he saw her lifting her arms to smooth her auburn hair into its customary knot on the top of her head, he glimpsed the tantalizing curve of her breast and felt the hot desire knot in his belly. He thought longingly of waiting until Delia was asleep and then going next door, not to make love but just to talk with Annie, to hear her dear voice and touch her sweet face.

He didn't, of course, but not for fear of being discovered. His wife and daughter were in the house, and Adam had just enough integrity left to resist betraying them while they were both present. Given that he had already committed the ultimate betrayal, this was a quixotic distinction, and he knew it. But he needed to think of himself as an honorable man, and maintaining the fiction of his faithfulness while Delia and Caroline were at home seemed the honorable thing to do, the only thing he *could* do. So he resolutely turned away from any glimpse of Annie and tried to put her out of his thoughts.

The unceasing pain that this effort cost him, he thought with a rueful self-knowledge, was the punishment for his foolish wish to appear to be honorable when he wasn't.

ANNIE felt the same pain, and for very much the same reason. She had no regrets, for she knew that what she and Adam had was a deep, true love, the coming together of two people who had found in the other what each lacked, what each *needed*. Surely what they had shared couldn't just vanish, as if it had never happened.

But as the days went on, she had to ask herself what was to become of their relationship, now that Adam's wife had returned home. Delia herself was not to be seen, and when Annie spoke briefly with Greta, the Hunts' hired girl, she said that Mrs. Hunt was ill—not seriously, but enough to keep her at home. Their clotheslines were on either side of the low hedge between the two houses, which made it easy to talk as they hung up the laundry or took it down, and Annie cultivated their conversation.

In the beginning, the young woman wasn't very forthcoming. Annie often heard Delia shrieking at Greta and one morning after a particularly loud exchange, she had seen a darkening bruise on her cheek, as if from a slap or a blow. She felt a natural sympathy toward Greta, as she did toward the women she employed, and worried that the girl was being mistreated. She didn't intentionally press her for information and she never asked direct questions, but the two gradually developed an over-the-hedge friendship and bits of information emerged.

In Greta's view, Mrs. Hunt was clearly a witch, and completely irredeemable. But she spoke of Adam, "Mr. Hunt," with an eager lilt in her voice. Annie heard it and took note as well of the girl's bright eyes and ardent, even smitten expression, and she knew she had stumbled on a painful truth. Poor Greta was in love with her employer. Two or three months before, she might have smiled at the idea. Now, she couldn't. She knew what it was like to love someone she could never have. She knew how much it *hurt*.

Annie hadn't seen Adam—except for too-brief glimpses of him on his way out to the stable or on the street, walking to work or coming home. She hadn't heard from him, either, not even a note asking how she was or saying that he was thinking of her, or perhaps suggesting a time and place that they might meet, if he thought it was too dangerous to slip through the hedge.

But then she had to ask herself what she had expected. Adam said he loved her, and she believed he did. The passion they felt together, the meeting of minds and bodies in such a compelling union, could not be pretended—which made their separation all the more unendurable. If being together had been heaven, being separated was hell. Now that she was sleeping alone again, without the comfort of his body next to hers, she wasn't sleeping well. She wasn't eating well, either, and when she looked in the mirror over her dressing table, she saw a woman with a pale face, a taut mouth, and dark circles under her eyes—the face of a woman who had committed adultery with her neighbor's husband and was being punished for it.

But she would not, *could* not blame Adam. She had welcomed him eagerly, with her whole heart, without asking for any word of promise. If they had been characters in one of the dime novels that were so popular nowadays, he might have proposed that they run away to Mexico or to the South Seas and build a new life there, together. But that was not Adam's way. He was honorable. He took his obligations seriously. He had never said he intended to leave his wife or suggested that they might have a future together. And as for the possibility that Delia might leave *him*, Annie knew that would never happen. Adam's wife might love him or she might not, but love was simply irrelevant. Delia needed the marriage, and the house, and Adam's financial support. She would never give it up or allow it to be taken from her.

And now that she and Adam had been apart for a while, Annie had decided that even if he asked her to begin meeting him secretly, she could not do that. Their time together had been incomparably sweet, but it had been only an interlude. It would be foolish to think that they could resume their relationship where they'd left off, or that it could go on in some other form.

So Annie reached down deep inside herself and found a new resolve. She would simply ignore the pain and get on with her life. For her, Annie's Laces was a salvation. Now that she had located three San Antonio shops that were eager to buy her lace, there was plenty of demand to be met, and she worked every day with the girls and every evening by herself, often until late at night. She ordered more finely spun linen and cotton thread from the Corticelli Mills in Massachusetts. She advertised in the *Pecan Springs Weekly Enterprise* for another lacemaker and found two, one of whom had three children and could only work at home. There was no reason not to allow that, Annie decided, as long as the woman's lacework was acceptable.

And thus was born a new idea: women could choose to come to her workroom or work at home. When she offered the choice to her workers, two accepted immediately: old Mrs. Hathaway, who lived across town and had to walk quite a distance; and Miss Windsor, whose ill and elderly mother had just moved in with her and needed care and attention. They would work at home and deliver their work once a week. To Annie's surprise, that resulted in even more and better work and certainly more contented workers.

But there were still those who chose to spend their days in Annie's workroom, where their labor was lightened by laughter, camaraderie, and books. They finished *Huckleberry Finn* and began a detective novel by a new British writer named Arthur Conan Doyle. First published as a magazine serial in England the year before, the book was called *A Study in Scarlet* and featured a "consulting detective" named Sherlock Holmes and his friend and roommate, Dr. Watson. Annie and the girls agreed that it was an interesting and most unusual story, and very different from *Little Women* and *Huckleberry Finn*.

Annie had just finished reading aloud the last page of Mr. Doyle's book when she happened to glance out the window. That's when she saw him: a good-looking man with a dark pencil-thin mustache, springing almost eagerly up the steps of the Hunts' house next door. He was wearing a brown frock coat and a brown bowler hat, and he carried a gold-headed cane. Annie didn't recognize him as anyone she knew, and she knew almost everyone in Pecan Springs. He stood for a moment, knocking, and then the door opened. He took off his hat, bowed, and went inside.

It would be another day before she would learn the man's name. And it would be Delia who would tell her.

But Adam would learn it first.

That afternoon, Adam had business at the bank and came home to pick up some papers he had forgotten. As he turned the corner on Crockett Street, the front door of his house opened and a gentleman stepped out, clapping a brown bowler on his head. He was tall and slender, mustachioed and dressed for the city in a smart brown frock coat, with a cigar in his mouth and a gold-headed walking stick under one arm. He looked up, saw Adam, smiled and tipped his hat, and walked briskly in the opposite direction.

In the parlor, Delia was seated on the sofa, reading what looked like a letter on pale blue paper. Her blond hair was carefully dressed, and she was wearing her prettiest pink gown and amethyst earrings. She looked up, startled, when Adam stood in the doorway. Her eyes widened and she drew in her breath.

"Oh, you're home," she said, clearly flustered. "I . . . I wasn't expecting you."

So it would seem, he wanted to say, but didn't. He felt he should say something, though, so he remarked, "Looks like we've had a visitor." He sniffed the pungent odor of cigar smoke. "Smells like it, too."

She gave a nervous chuckle. "Oh, perhaps you met Mr. Simpson on his way out." She folded the letter (Adam was sure that's what it was) and tucked it into her sleeve. There was a guilty flush high on her cheekbones. He saw that the top button of her bodice was missing and the lace of her collar was disarranged. "I hope you were polite to him," she added.

"I would have been, but he didn't give me the chance," Adam said. "Who is Mr. Simpson?"

Delia lifted her head with the coquettish tilt that Adam had once found so attractive. "A friend of my sister's," she said lightly. "He was passing through on his way to Austin." She gestured toward an open box of foil-wrapped chocolate candies on the low table in front of the sofa. "He dropped in to bring me a gift and a letter . . . from her. From Clarissa."

Adam thought that a box of chocolates was an unlikely gift from Delia's sister, and that if Mr. Simpson were truly traveling from Galveston to Austin, Pecan Springs was considerably out of his way. Then his eye was caught by a pink button on the floor. He picked it up and handed it to his wife.

"I believe you've lost this," he said quietly, dropping his eyes to the obviously empty buttonhole on her bodice.

Delia's flush heightened. She looked uncomfortably apprehensive, and her wordless glance seemed to interrogate him: *How much do you guess? How much do you* know? But she only said, "Thank you, Adam," and took the button.

"I've come for some papers," Adam said quietly, "and then I'm on my way to the bank." He left the room, his feelings a jumble of suspicion mixed with guilt and—yes—an odd relief. What was sauce for the goose, his mother had often said, was sauce for the gander. If Delia had been on intimate terms with Mr. Simpson in Galveston, he could scarcely complain. What's more, he found that he didn't care. He had been with Annie while his wife was gone, and he longed to be with her at this very moment. But of course he was only guessing what might have happened—either in Galveston or this afternoon in the parlor. He might speculate, but he could not be sure.

Until he encountered Greta. As he went down the hall to the small room he used as an office, he saw her standing in the kitchen door, her feet planted wide apart, arms akimbo, eyes gleaming. She lifted her head and gazed at him boldly, and her look needed no interpretation. *I saw what your wife was doing with that man*, it said. *I know her secret.* She raised a hand to the shirtwaist that strained tightly across her heavy breasts, and her fingers played with the top button. She smiled— a smile that was clearly intended to be inviting, although the scar that pulled down her mouth gave the expression a starkly menacing cast.

If she can enjoy herself, the smile said, *so can we. I'm willing. Are you?*

Adam might be shocked at the open, undisguised invitation in the girl's eyes, but he was scarcely surprised. He had stood between Greta and his wife that very morning at breakfast, when the girl splashed hot coffee on the sleeve of Delia's blue silk dressing gown. Delia had shrieked and jerked her arm away, grabbing at a napkin to sop up the brown liquid.

"You did that on purpose!" she cried.

"Oh, *no*, ma'am," Greta had said. She'd glanced sideways at Adam. "I would never do that."

Adam had put down his newspaper. "I'm sure it was an accident," he'd said, and smiled briefly at Greta. "Get a towel and clean it up, Greta." Simpering at him, she'd done what she was told.

Now, seeing the invitation so plain on her face, he was suddenly unnerved. She must have misinterpreted his defense as a mark of personal interest. He remembered the way she had leaned against him as she set down a plate of fresh buttered toast, her full round breast brushing his shoulder. Had he inadvertently encouraged the girl to imagine that he had *romantic* intentions toward her—or worse, that he wanted to make love to her? The thought made him feel very small and cold inside.

He shook his head at her, turned, and went into his office, cursing himself. He was in a fix, and it was his own damned fault. He had never meant to give Greta any reason to think he might want to— *Sweet Jesus*, he thought. How could he have been so stupid? He stood for a moment, turning it over in his mind, aware now of his idiocy. But what could he do? The mistake had already been made. He'd been a fool.

After a few moments, Adam found the papers he was looking for and went back out into the hallway. Greta hadn't moved. She continued to stand in the kitchen doorway, her eyes fixed on his face, her fingers playing with the button on her shirtwaist, her mouth pulled into that oddly disturbing smile. Her expression was still inviting, but now it seemed to him to be menacing as well, and another alarming thought occurred to him.

Delia had given Greta every reason to hate her. It was likely that the girl had put an eye to a crack in the sitting room door a few moments ago and had seen something illicit going on between her and Mr. Simpson. The two of them on the sofa. Frantic embraces, ardent kisses, passionate caresses. The man's hand inside Delia's bodice, searching for her breast, or up her skirt. Armed with that kind of sensational report, what might a disgruntled, vindictive employee do? She might threaten to spread it all over town unless—

He shivered, and the word *blackmail* elbowed its brutal self into his consciousness. Unless what? Unless money changed hands? Unless . . . something else? But what?

At that moment, the parlor door opened, and Delia came down the hall toward them, her voluminous skirts swishing. Her eyes narrowed as she saw Greta in the kitchen door and Adam at the door to his office. To Adam, it felt as if the air had become electrically charged, and the hair stood up on the back of his neck.

"What's going on here?" Delia asked in a high, thin voice. "What are you two up to?"

"Nothin', ma'am," Greta said innocently. "Nothin' at all." Her glance went to Delia's bodice, where the button was noticeably missing, then— with an open impudence—to Delia's face. *I saw you*, it said. *I saw what you were doing.* She turned back to Adam, and her expression softened. He read in her eyes a plea—not a demand, but a mute entreaty—as if she were asking him to defend her once again. He opened his mouth to speak, but Delia intervened.

"Get back to your work, girl," she snapped. "This minute."

Greta's glance lingered on Adam's face for a moment. Then she turned and went back into the kitchen, her hips swaying. The kitchen door closed behind her.

Delia turned to Adam. "It certainly looked like something was going on." Her eyes were accusing. "The two of you were discussing *me*, weren't you? You were talking about me behind my back."

"Nonsense, Delia," Adam said evenly. "We weren't discussing anything at all. In fact, we hadn't exchanged a word. I was simply—"

But she didn't let him finish. "Did you get up to some monkey business with that girl while I was gone, Adam?" Delia's nostrils quivered, anger sparking in her eyes. "Ever since I got home, you've stopped me when I've been about to correct her. It is very clear that you are going out of your way to defend her." Her voice rose, strident and shrill. "Surely you've noticed the way she moons around you at the table, rubbing herself up against you every chance she gets. Why, the girl's in love with you, Adam. Don't tell *me* that there wasn't something between you while I was out of town! You've been in her bed!"

Adam stared at her. *Good God. Even his wife could see Greta's mistaken understanding. How had he been so stupidly blind?* But he couldn't explain it; all he could do was deny.

"Don't be ridiculous," he said evenly. "She's just grateful when somebody speaks up for her. All she gets from you is criticism—and worse. Lord only knows what you say to her when I'm not around to take her part."

"I'm dismissing her." Delia's voice was harsh. "Now. This afternoon. Before this thing—whatever it is between the two of you—goes any further." She put her hands on her hips and pulled her shoulders back. "There are plenty of capable young women who would be glad to have her job. We can't have a silly girl who keeps throwing herself at you and making you look like a damn fool—even if you *are* one."

Adam gave up trying to hold his temper. "And what if she saw what happened between you and Mr. Simpson in the parlor this afternoon?"

Delia's eyes widened and her face paled. She put her hand against the wall, steadying herself. "What makes you think she . . . Did she say something? Did she—" She lifted her chin. "Nothing happened. Nothing at all." But her face was ashen and her fingers felt for the empty buttonhole in her bodice. "I . . . I don't know what you're talking about."

He had been guessing before. He was sure now.

"Yes, you do. Think about it, Delia. If you dismiss this girl, there's no predicting how she'll retaliate. Maybe she'll tell me what she saw. Or maybe she'll tell the town. Do you want to take that chance?"

Delia's hand, trembling, flew to her mouth. "She . . . wouldn't!" She caught herself and tried to amend. "She couldn't have seen something that didn't happen."

If he needed another confirmation, this was it. But the knowledge didn't cheer him. It didn't anger him, either. *What's sauce for the gander is sauce for the goose*, he thought. He couldn't blame Delia—or Mr. Simpson. He was equally culpable, and his guilt robbed him of the right to complain or accuse. And he had behaved unconscionably toward Greta, encouraging her to think God knew what.

But one thing he did know. "Better leave well enough alone for now," he said. "And lay off the criticism. Things are bad enough as they are."

Without another word, Delia turned on her heel and flew up the stairs. In a moment, he heard her bedroom door slam hard enough to rattle the windows.

Adam found himself shivering as he went down the front steps and headed for the bank. He wasn't entirely sure what had happened in the last few moments, but he had the feeling that—whatever it was—it had altered his marriage forever. He walked faster and then even faster, feeling that he was pursued by something dark and ominous, that he was now enmeshed in a chain of events that could not be reversed and from which he could not escape. It felt as if a storm was on the way, or an earthquake, or a war. A cataclysm that would change everything.

Chapter Eleven

The Victorian "language of flowers" assigned meanings to many herbs and flowers. Those who were in on the secret language could exchange coded messages in nosegays. For instance, a white daisy ("innocence, simplicity"), a rosebud ("beauty"), a red carnation ("ardent love"), and fern ("deep sincerity") could be interpreted as "I love your beautiful innocence with a deep sincerity."

Some plants had double meanings. Lavender, for instance, signified both devotion and constancy *and* distrust and suspicion. The darker meaning arose from the ancient notion that asps (the deadly viper that killed Cleopatra) preferred to live beneath the lavender plant. An unwary admirer of the lavender might be bitten, so it was wise to approach the plant with a cautious distrust.

"The Victorian Language of Herbs and Flowers"
China Bayles
Pecan Springs Enterprise

Caitie and I didn't get our girls' night out, after all. She texted me to say that Sharon had invited her to stay all night, and since both girls were going to play rehearsal early morning, a sleepover made sense. I was glad to agree. There was something else, though, that Caitie didn't mention in her text: Sharon lives across the street from Kevin, Caitie's boyfriend, and I had the feeling that a get-together was in the works.

A few weeks before, Caitie and I had had the Boyfriend Conversation—not a talk about dos and don'ts, but about questions she needed to consider. We talked about what it means to have a boyfriend at fourteen, and how that might change at eighteen or twenty or twenty-three. (She's curious, naturally, about Brian and Casey.) About why she wants a boyfriend and why (in her opinion) Kevin wants a girlfriend. About respecting her body and saying no to sexual activity beyond holding hands and (maybe) kissing. Since I knew Kevin, I didn't think we had to go into the part about sexting or giving in to a boy who says if you don't, you're not cool.

But now there was a terribly unsettling complication: Kevin's illness. Helen had said that the family didn't plan to tell friends about it until after the surgery. But that didn't mean that Kevin wouldn't jump the gun and tell Caitie what was going on. In fact, I would be surprised if he didn't—and that worried me. I'm sure she remembers that her aunt died of cancer. How would she handle this?

But since Helen had asked me not to broadcast the news, there was nothing I could do to prepare her. So I simply texted her back: *Okay with me, sweetie. Be sure and thank Sharon's mom, have fun, and behave yourself. (Of course you will ☺)* This kind of Mom-talk is still new to me, and I'm not sure I always get it right, but I'm learning. Caitie is a good teacher.

With my husband and daughter both gone for the evening, I had a quiet evening alone, the first in a long time. That is, I was as alone as a person can be in the affectionate company of a basset with an agenda and a cat who adores laps. I ate my sandwich-and-soup supper with Mr. P lying across my knees and Winchester beside my chair, drooling over the possibility of a bite of sandwich and permission to lick my soup bowl. Winchester is devoted to food—any food, *all* food (but especially bagels and pizza). When we're eating, he offers up a plaintive, whining murmur and an imploring expression that will win even the hardest heart. I can't resist him, so he got the four crusty corners of my sandwich.

I was rinsing my few dishes when Blackie phoned with an update. Sheila was doing well, he said, but he was having a hard time keeping her out of uniform. With a chuckle, he added. "I may have to resort to sterner measures—locking up her badge and duty belt, maybe. She says to say hi, and thanks."

Blackie's call was followed by one from McQuaid, in Lubbock. He was in his element and loving it. As a former homicide detective, there's nothing he likes better than sorting through a mess of conflicting testimony—lies, half lies, deceptions, and dishonesties—and coming up with the truth, or the closest approximation thereof. I wondered what kind of questions he would pose to my ghost, but I wasn't about to ask him. He's snarky about Ruby's encounters with the Universe ("mystical claptrap," he calls it). I was sure he would say the same thing about whoever, or whatever, was haunting my shop—if that's what was going on.

So I skipped that subject entirely, and we talked about his investigation, about Sheila's health, and about Dixie Chick and Extra Crispy and the incredibly black rooster who was capable of producing his half of thirty-five thousand dollars a year just by doing what comes naturally.

And then I told him about Kevin's brain tumor, asking him to keep the news to himself. "Helen doesn't want us to tell Caitie until the family is ready to announce it," I said.

McQuaid was as shocked as I had been. "It's just not something you think about with kids," he said sadly. And I agreed. Surgery and radiation and chemotherapy don't belong in a kid's life. It was a somber end to our conversation.

After we hung up, I spent some time on my laptop, working on the article on Queen Anne's lace for the *Enterprise*. I went lightly on the traditional contraceptive and abortifacient uses of the plant (a touchy subject for some readers) and paid more attention to its use as a wild forage plant and its evolutionary role in the ancestry of today's garden carrot. Which led me to consider which of a half dozen recipes from my file I should include with the article. I settled on the Queen Anne's Lace Jelly and the Moroccan Chicken and Carrots I had made for our dinner with Brian and Casey. Then I ran across a recipe for carrot oil, added a couple of sentences about the cosmetic use of carrots, and called it done. I would email it to Hark tomorrow.

I had brought the carton of photographs home from the shop and was looking forward to digging into it. But when I opened the box, I discovered that there were only about a dozen photographs, when I had been expecting more. The rest of the box was filled with what looked like a random, haphazard collection of yellowed newspaper clippings from the early days of the *Enterprise*. I sorted the clips from the photos and put the clips back in the box. They would have to wait for another night.

I spread the photos on the kitchen table, under the bright overhead light. I added the one that had startled me with its appearance on the bulletin board at the shop earlier that day: the baby in the lace-paneled christening dress and cap. I propped the photo against the saltshaker and stared at it. The photo had showed up on my bulletin board for a reason—but darned if I knew what it was. If it was meant as a clue to a mystery, I didn't get it. Was it the baby who was important? Or the lacy dress? Did the dress in the photo have any connection with the dress Lori's aunt had given her? I shook my head at that, since any connection between them seemed wildly far-fetched.

Still, it would be good to rule out the possibility. So I took out my cell phone and snapped a photograph of the baby's picture, then texted the image to Lori, suggesting that she compare the lace insert in the photo to the lace in the baby's dress her aunt had given her. I didn't try to tell her why I was asking—the explanation was simply too implausible. After I'd done that, though, I remembered that Christine hadn't been able to reach Lori, so maybe this message wouldn't get through, either.

While I was looking at the baby's picture, I thought again of those mysterious sprigs of fresh lavender that had been left on the bulletin board with both photos. I remembered that nineteenth-century Victorians had invented a fanciful "language of flowers" that they used to send "secret" messages to one another. The Victorians—and my ghost seemed to belong to that era—viewed lavender with a certain ambivalent caution. The blossom signified devotion, loyalty, and fidelity, yes—and hence was often used in wedding bouquets, along with rosemary and baby's breath, which carried a similar message. But at the same time, lavender also signified suspicion and distrust. It seemed to suggest that beauty could not be trusted, for beneath it lay treachery, betrayal, danger, perhaps even death. Was that the meaning here?

All of which reminded me that Ethel had glimpsed a woman in a long dark skirt and white blouse in the garden, picking lavender. Had she actually *seen* my ghost? If so, who was—

Your Honor, please. My skeptical lawyer self again, leaping to her feet. *Assumes facts not—*

Yes, I know, I know. Facts not in evidence. And yes, there was a part of me that simply could not accept the idea that I was dealing with a ghost. But the real photographs I had found stuck to my bulletin board—they *were* a kind of evidence, weren't they? Of course they were, as were the others spread on the table, like exhibits ready to be put before a jury.

I gave the photos another, closer look. Four of them were taken inside my building, in its early years as a family residence, but none had names or dates on the front or back. The two most interesting pictured the room that was now my shop. In one photograph, five women of different ages, all wearing late-nineteenth-century dress, were seated in a semicircle with needlework in their laps, like a sewing club. While they worked, they seemed to be listening to a sixth woman, also seated, who was reading aloud from a book. I went to McQuaid's office, found his magnifying glass, and used it to study the photo, finally making out the book's title: *A Study in Scarlet*, which I knew was by Arthur Conan Doyle. I had to smile at that, remembering that it was the first piece of detective fiction in which a magnifying glass was used as a forensic tool.

In the other photo, the reader was on her feet, leaning over the shoulder of one of the needlewomen, pointing out something in the work she held. I studied the reader more closely, again with McQuaid's magnifying glass. I couldn't be sure, but I thought she might be the same woman with the Gibson-girl look who appeared in the veranda photograph, holding the baby. I was interested to see that there was a parlor stove in that room, as well as rugs on the floor, curtains at the windows, and some parlor furniture—a sofa and some overstuffed chairs—pushed back against the walls. Mrs. Birkett, earlier that day, had remembered the room as a "workroom." Why? Was it because the needlewomen gathered there for meetings of their sewing club? Since the Historical Society's plaque identified this as the Duncan House, perhaps the reader was Mrs. Duncan. But Mrs. Birkett, who knew the owner as an old lady, remembered her as Mrs. Hunt. Which was which?

There were two other photos of the interior. One pictured the room that was now Ruby's shop, a dining room, back in the day. There was a long dining table in the center, with chairs and place settings for six, two on each side and one at each end. In the middle of the table was a modest silver epergne filled with flowers and fruit. Off to one side stood a woman in a dark-colored dress and apron—a servant, perhaps—holding a tray. The photo might have been taken before a dinner party or a family celebration, I thought. Were there six members of the family? Two parents and four children? Was this the Duncan family—or the Hunt family?

I placed the dining room photo beside the two taken in the parlor-cum-workroom. To this group, I added a fourth photo, taken in a large bedroom, in the space that I recognized as our current tearoom. There was a Victorian double bed with an elaborate gold-colored spindled headboard and footboard. The bed itself was dressed in a white cro-cheted spread, flounced white skirt, and ruffled white pillow shams. There was a mirrored dressing table, a rocking chair, and a tall chest of drawers. On the chest was a framed photograph—a wedding photo, the magnifying glass told me. A stove stood against one wall and there was a white-painted commode in a corner. A commode? Of course. The bathroom under the stairs would not be installed for several more decades.

I stared at the photos for a long time. Of course, I had known that my building had a long history. These photographs, though, gave me the sense that it had a *personal* history, that it had once been a home where people lived, loved, worked, played, and died. In the pictures, the past and the present lay one on top of the other. It was an eerie feeling, as if I were peering through one of those old-fashioned stereo-scopes into a long-distant past—but a three-dimensional past in which real people were still living and moving and talking and working, just as they had lived *then*, when the photographs were taken.

There were also exterior scenes, and these included children. One was taken behind the house, where an old-fashioned rope swing hung from a large oak tree, now gone. There were four girls in the photograph, all with long hair and big hair bows, all dressed in white pinafores over cotton dresses, a kind of Alice-in-Wonderland look. A girl of nine or ten was pushing the two younger girls—twins, I thought, maybe four or five—in the swing, while the oldest one watched, clapping her hands. She might be eighteen. In another, the older two girls were hoeing weeds in a large vegetable garden, in the area where I now had my zodiac garden. And in a third, the twins were feeding carrots to a fat pony, beside the stable—which was now Thyme Cottage, my bed-and-breakfast. In the background, tall summer sunflowers grew up beside the stone walls.

The rest of the photographs were of the same couple I had seen sitting with the baby and the little girl on the veranda. One, a studio portrait, was clearly a wedding photo—Mr. and Mrs. Duncan? Yes, I thought, because it was the same photograph I had just seen (with the magnifying glass) on the chest in the bedroom of the Duncan house. The groom, seated, wore his Sunday-best suit with a stiff collar and tie and white rose boutonniere. The bride stood behind him, her hand on his shoulder, wearing a pale silk dress banded with embroidered lace. It was hard to tell colors in the sepia-tinted photo, but the dress might be taffy-colored. The woman's hair, dark brown or auburn, was partly covered by a lacy bridal veil caught under a floral crown. On a small table beside them lay her wedding bouquet of roses and ferns, tied with a cluster of ribbons. The groom—fair haired and clean shaven— wore a satisfied look, as if he had achieved something he had aimed for. The bride was attractive but not conventionally pretty. She had a firm chin, a full mouth, and large, dark eyes, deep-set and quite remarkable. As I moved from that photograph to the next, I had the uncanny feeling that her eyes were following me. She seemed to be actually *watching* me, and I shivered.

In another studio portrait, the same pair, in the same wedding garb, were posed with a young girl—the girl with banana curls from the picture on the veranda. She was wearing a flounced white dress, with white stockings and shoes and holding a small flowery nosegay. I turned it over and saw a penciled date on the back: *August 3, 1889.*

I held the photograph for a moment, studying it. Both the bride and groom looked to be past thirty, and the bride wasn't wearing a white dress. Was this a second marriage? Was the girl with the pretty curls the bride's daughter? And the baby, in the later photograph taken on the veranda, *their* child? The child of this second husband? Were the girls pictured around the swing in the oak tree their children, too? If so, then perhaps what I was looking at was a history of the Duncan family. Their story might not have been so different from many others: the bride, with a daughter from a previous marriage, marrying again in her thirties and giving birth to three more children.

But there was one other photo—also a wedding photo—which didn't seem to belong in this group at all. I regarded it, puzzled. The groom was clearly the same man in the other two wedding photos in front of me, although he seemed to be younger, perhaps by ten years. But the woman was different: quite young, in her late teens or early twenties, I guessed. She was blond and very pretty, smiling and with a flirtatious tilt of her head—the sort of girl who might be very much at home in a Miss Texas Teen beauty pageant today. The long satin train of her white lace-encrusted wedding dress was carefully arranged around her feet, and she wore a tulle veil and a tiara-like crown. A half dozen young bridesmaids, all beautifully gowned, stood beside the bride and groom, with tall candelabras and vases of flowers behind them. It had obviously been a lavish formal wedding. I turned the photo over. It was stamped *L. Vincent, Photographers. Galveston*. And two names, written in a girlish hand: *Adam and Delia*. A heart had been penciled around the names.

The story in front of me—the story told by the photographs—suddenly developed another chapter and a whole new set of questions. Two weddings—one in Galveston. One groom, two different brides. Judging from the man's apparent age, the Galveston wedding had come first, perhaps by ten years. Where was the pretty, vivacious blond bride? What had happened to her? Divorce was unlikely in those days, I supposed. Had she . . . died?

I was pulled away from my questions by another phone call—this one from Caitie, who wanted to remind me that I was supposed to stop at the fairground on my way into town in the morning and make sure that Dixie Chick and Extra Crispy had food and fresh water.

"I've already got it on my list." I had the feeling that this wasn't the reason for her call. Tentatively, I added, "Are you and Sharon having a good time?"

"Uh-huh," she said. I thought she didn't sound as chirpy as usual. And then I found out why. "Kevin came over after supper and we played video games. But he had to go home early."

I waited for a moment, then said, casually, "He's been sick, hasn't he? Is he feeling better?"

"Yes," she said slowly. Then, "No." Then there was a long pause, and she lowered her voice as if she didn't want Sharon to hear. "Actually, Mom, he told me why he's been sick." She took a deep breath. "I'm not supposed to tell anybody, but that doesn't mean you." Another breath. "He says he's got a brain tumor." Her voice wavered. "Cancer."

"Oh, Caitie." So that was why she had called. I clutched the phone, wanting to hold her close, feeling so far away. "I am so sorry to hear that, honey."

I could hear that she was doing her best to fight the tears. "It sounds sort of bad," she said, "but he says it's really not and I shouldn't be worried. He says the doctors know where it is and how to get it out and what to do after that. He's going to Houston next week. That's where the best doctors are, he says. But . . ." She stopped, gulping down the sobs.

I tried to sound confident. "I'm glad he has the best doctors. They'll do whatever they can to make him well. But he also needs good friends. You'll be that for him, I know, Caitlin."

"I *will*," she said fervently. "That's what I told him. But, Mom—" Another swallowed sob. "I can't help thinking about Aunt Marcia. She had cancer, too. And she died."

There were whole galaxies of grief in those three words. I pulled in my breath. "Yes, she did. But that was several years ago, sweetie. Doctors are learning more about cancer every day. Your aunt Marcia was older, too, and she'd been sick for a while. Kevin is young and strong."

"That's true," she said, reaching for hope.

"And he's a fighter." I managed a chuckle. "You remember how hard he fought to get that first chair away from you. I'll bet he'll fight this every bit as hard."

"I *hope* so," she said, clutching the word. I heard the slam of a door and a flurry of noise in the background. "I have to go. Sharon is saying it's my turn for the shower."

"Okay." I thought of something. "When Kevin gets back, and when his mom says we can, let's give him a party. Shall we?"

"Sure!" she said, brightening. "A party would be great. Everybody will want to come. All the kids from school and the orchestra. *Everybody.*"

"Good. Start thinking about that." It would give her something to look forward to. "Where we should have it. Who we should invite. What you'd like to have to eat."

"I will," she said. "Oh, and please don't forget about the chickens tomorrow morning."

"I won't," I said. "Good night, sweetie."

In the kitchen, I poured a glass of milk and carried it out on the back porch when I let Winchester out for his last call. As he loped down the path toward the woods, he surprised a large, fully armored armadillo digging for grubs and beetles and other gourmet delights among the peppermint and lemon balm in my flower bed. The armadillo, who might have been the same one that Howard Cosell—our previous basset—loved to chase every night about this time, understood what was coming and scrambled noisily for the safety of the trees.

Winchester let out a gleeful basset howl—*Ah-ha! Now I've got you, you scoundrel!*—and flew after the trespasser, paws pounding, ears flopping, tail flung up like a white torch in the darkness. The basset and his armadillo disappeared into the shadows of the woods. I could hear the two of them blundering through the underbrush like a pair of African rhinos, Winchester baying occasionally to let his prey know that he was still hot on the trail. Bassets aren't exactly built for speed, but then, neither are armadillos. We still laugh about the time Howard Cosell actually managed to catch one. He brought it to us clutched in his jaws like a partially deflated football. Released, the creature floundered drunkenly through the grass as Howard ran for his water bowl to rinse out his mouth. Armadillos apparently aren't very tasty.

I had the feeling that it might be a while before Winchester made his way back home, so I sat down on the porch steps to wait, admiring the sliver of silver moon that hung just above the trees and listening to the sounds of the nocturnal world. We tell people that we love living in the country because it's so quiet out here. But it isn't, really—and especially not at night, when the wild things come out to pursue their after-dark affairs. The shrill, strident thrum of the cicadas was counterpointed by the brisk chirping of crickets and the wheezy *wheep-wheep-wheep* of male green tree frogs eager for a close encounter with their female kind. Down at the creek, the nocturnal green heron gave a loud, squawking *kwok* and then another: *kwok-KWOK!* (If you didn't know this bird, you might think you were hearing the *honk-honk* of an old Ford flivver.) From across the meadow came the low, haunting call of the male poor-will—just two monotonous notes, *poor will*, over and over, a lone, lorn lover pining for an elusive sweetheart, somewhere out there in the dark. Up the lane toward Limekiln Road, the Banners' border collie, Blitzen, added a chorus of encouraging yips to Winchester's deep, melodic bay. And far, far across the cedar-clad hills, a clan of coyotes yodeled, as charmed as I by the silvery moon and the diamond stars spangled across a black velvet sky.

Yes, it was a noisy night. But these aren't man-made noises. They are the sweet sounds of nature's creatures going about their private business in the dark: earning a living, calling out to lovers and friends, singing to the moon, escaping a pursuer, surviving to fish another night along the creek or dig for grubs among my peppermint and lemon balm. Individual armadillos and tree frogs and poor-wills and coyotes may perish, but in all its vast and wonderful variety, life goes on.

And on and on. As it had for the family in the photographs on my kitchen table, who had spent their lives in the house where I now spend my working days. As it would, I passionately hoped, for a young boy with a brain tumor who—if life was fair—should be worried about nothing more important than getting an A in math and protecting his concertmaster chair from his talented girlfriend. Who, no matter how cheerful he might pretend to be, must be deeply worried about the fearful possibility of dying before he could graduate high school. So, too, his family and friends. One little friend in particular, Caitie, who was already far too well acquainted with death.

I thought about these things as the moon rose higher and the cicadas and the crickets and the coyotes and the poor-will continued to sing. I thought about houses that held the impressions of lives—happy, sad, long, short—that had been lived within their walls. About the bridges that the past sometimes builds to a distant future, embodied in photographs and pieces of antique lace and babies' dresses. And about eyes that seemed to follow me, to *watch* me, out of the past.

No wonder, then, that I dreamed about her again. About the woman in the pale taffy-colored wedding dress, who (in my dream) stepped out of the photograph and came toward me, holding out her hands, fixing me with those remarkable eyes that wouldn't let me go.

Who seemed to want, desperately, to tell me something, but couldn't speak, couldn't find the words.

Chapter Twelve

Pecan Springs, Texas
October 1888

Annie had been apprehensive about her first encounter with Adam's wife after her return from Galveston. Deeply conscious of what she and Adam had done, she felt as if her skin were as transparent as glass, and that Delia would see right through her to the truth of what had happened.

But Annie needn't have worried. Their meeting didn't occur until some two weeks after Delia's return home—on the day after Annie saw the mustached stranger in the brown frock coat climbing the porch steps next door. Delia breezed into the workroom with her usual haughty carelessness, moved a chair closer to Annie's, and began to chatter gaily about the glamorous parties she had attended in Galveston, about the cost of the two new dresses her sister's dressmaker ("the very best in the city") had made for her, the musical entertainments at the famed Beach Hotel, and the men who had asked her to dance at every party. Annie thought that there was something oddly high-pitched and brittle about her chatter, and she seemed more nervous than usual.

"Really, Annie, you should go to Galveston," Delia advised at the end of a long tale about a friend who had found an exciting new beau at a luncheon party at the Beach Hotel. "You'd be sure to snag a husband there, and one with a better future ahead of him than anyone here in Pecan Springs." She leaned forward, her expression avid. "Why, there are bankers and lawyers and doctors there, and ever so *many* of them! My sister Clarissa says that the men outnumber the women almost three to one, and I do believe it. Wherever I went, I found several of them just as *eager* as they could be for conversation with a woman they find attractive."

"It sounds like everyone has a great deal of leisure time," Annie said noncommittally. She understood that the society women might not have much to do at home, but didn't the men have to *work*?

"Well, of course," Delia said, as if it were a silly observation, and hurried on. "One of those gentlemen—a Mr. Simpson—even followed me here, to Pecan Springs. Why, he actually came to call!" She waved her hand in a dismissive gesture. "Of course, it was very silly of him. He came bringing a box of candy, but I didn't give him the time of day. I sent him on his way immediately. The poor fellow didn't even have a chance to set foot in the house." She leaned forward and added, in a confiding voice, "I just wanted you to know, in case you might have seen the gentleman at my front door and thought I might be entertaining him."

Well, that explains it, Annie thought, remembering the stranger she'd seen. She wondered why Delia was going to such lengths to make a point of how peremptorily she had treated the man—and why she cared about her neighbor's opinion anyway. But Annie wasn't going to flatter Delia by asking for details, even though the report contradicted what she had seen. The man *had* set foot in the house, although Annie had no idea how long he'd stayed.

Instead, she just laughed. "Why would I want to go looking for a husband in Galveston?" she asked lightly. "I've already had one husband—a very good one. I can support myself. I have everything I could possibly want." Which was a lie, of course, because she could not have Adam. "Would you like to work with us today, Delia?" she added. "If so, just pull up another chair while I get the lace that you started the last time you were here."

Delia rose hastily. "No, never mind, Annie. I just dropped in to say hello."

Annie's feelings toward her neighbor had changed over the summer, and quite remarkably. Before, she had envied Delia her marriage to Adam; now, she pitied her, for she knew that the marriage was an unhappy charade. Adam didn't love or desire his wife. He loved and desired *her*, and while they couldn't have each other, the awareness of that glorious truth was like a secret treasure chest spilling over with beautiful and valuable jewels that were hers alone. She had no idea what lay ahead, but she felt enormously confident about one important thing: that what she and Adam had shared together had changed them both in ways beyond measure. To go back to his wife's bed would be a betrayal.

But it wasn't long before she learned that her confidence might be misplaced.

Some weeks earlier, Mrs. Crow had given Annie some dried hibiscus blossoms, sent to her by a friend in South Texas, where the shrub blossomed reliably. Annie had used the flowers regularly to brew a pretty red hibiscus tea for her workers, and they liked it so much that she decided to get more. A day or two after Delia's visit, she left one of the girls in charge of the workroom and walked down the street to Mrs. Crow's boardinghouse. She had just turned off the dirt path along the street when the boardinghouse door slammed open and

Delia rushed out, clutching a handkerchief. Her face was pale and she seemed to have been crying. She brushed past Annie with a sweep of her wide skirts, scarcely saying hello.

Surprised, Annie watched her hurry down the street, then rang the bell. When Mrs. Crow appeared behind the screen door, she said, "Oh, hello, Mrs. Crow. I came because I wanted to get some more of what you gave me earlier, that wonderful—"

"I'm sorry, but I don't have any more wild carrot seeds at the moment," Mrs. Crow said firmly. "Another lady came for it, too, and I've just told her the same thing. I've been meaning to go out and gather more, but I won't have time to do that in the next few days. As I told that lady, if you really must have it now, you can easily get it for yourself. I saw a patch of it in the vacant lot behind Purley's General Store, between the store and that little strip of woods along the railroad track. The flowers are already dried out and the seed is ready to be harvested." She smiled and added, "But do be careful, my dear. There's hemlock growing there, as well, and you don't want to get the two confused. It's poisonous."

Wild carrot seeds? Annie stared at the woman as the truth began to sink in. If Delia had come to buy wild carrot seeds, it was for the same reason that she—and Annie, too—had purchased them some weeks before. Because she didn't want to have Adam's baby. Which meant . . . which meant that she and Adam were sleeping together again.

"I see," Annie said slowly, thinking that Delia wasn't exactly the kind of person to go out to a vacant lot to gather seeds. That might account for the distress she had seen on her face as she left the house. Or perhaps she was distressed because she needed the seeds *now*, to counter the possible result of something that had happened the night before. She took a deep breath, steadying her voice. "As it happens, I didn't come for wild carrot, Mrs. Crow. I'd like to buy some more hibiscus flowers. The girls who work with me love the tea."

"Oh, yes, indeed," Mrs. Crow said happily. She pushed the screen door open. "Well, then, come in, dear. I have plenty of hibiscus. Did you know it's medicinal, too? All the old books say that hibiscus is good for the heart. And if you have trouble falling asleep, just add a little lemon balm and St. John's wort and drink it at bedtime. You'll sleep like a baby."

"I'm glad to know that," Annie said, following the woman inside. As they walked down the hall toward Mrs. Crow's stillroom, she wondered whether, if hibiscus was good for the heart, it might help to heal a broken heart. She had been so foolishly confident in Adam, and the discovery that he and Delia were sleeping together again was more painful than she could ever have guessed.

Mrs. Crow opened a jar and began to fill a paper bag with dried red blossoms. "I hope your friend is doing well," she said. "I trust that the wild carrot seeds did their work."

"My friend?" Annie said blankly, and then remembered the little fiction she had contrived on her earlier visit. "Oh, yes, my friend! Yes, of course. She wanted me to be sure to thank you. The wild carrot seeds did just what they're supposed to do."

"I'm glad to hear that," Mrs. Crow said briskly. "I hope she'll remember that a little rue goes a long way, too." She gave Annie the paper bag. "That'll be twenty cents, dear."

Annie handed over the coins and took the bag. As she walked home with the hibiscus, she thought about Delia and Adam and what she had just learned. She was sure that Adam would never impose himself upon an unwilling woman. She knew—because he had told her—that he believed that intercourse was immoral without love.

But as she knew very well, Adam was a fervent lover whose need wasn't readily satisfied. Her cheeks colored as she remembered the nights they had spent together making love, falling asleep and waking to make love again. He and Delia were married in the eyes of man and God, and their lovemaking—unlike the lovemaking *she* had shared with him—was entirely lawful, even blessed. He might not love Delia the way he loved *her*. But she was his wife and an attractive woman who took care to make herself beautiful. And while it might be catty to think that Delia needed to hold Adam's love and attention because she had no resources of her own and could not survive as a single woman, it was also true. If she drew him to her bed, why should he say no?

And then she thought of something else. If Delia invited Adam to her bed, *could* he say no? Wouldn't she ask him why? Of course she would. And Adam—who was a cautious man by nature—would feel that he had to make love to his wife, if only to keep her from asking too many questions. He wouldn't want to do anything that made her suspicious.

These considerations made her feel a little better, but not much. One way or another, it was all the same in the end. Adam and Delia had made love, while she was alone and lonely. She tried to swallow down the hurt, but her heart really did feel as if it were breaking—in a way that Mrs. Crow's hibiscus tea could not cure.

ADAM had also a great deal to think about. Mr. Simpson's call and the encounter with Greta and Delia afterward had troubled him deeply, and the more he thought about it, the more uneasy he became. He had never been a man to take risks, but loving Annie had changed him— changed him inside and out, he thought. He fought with himself, but finally decided. Honorable, dishonorable, it didn't matter. He *had* to see Annie and talk with her about Mr. Simpson's visit and Greta's misunderstanding. He needed to know what she thought.

Since Douglas' death, he had been in the habit of doing the occasional chore for their widowed neighbor, as well as dropping off the stable rent once a month. So a day or two after Simpson's visit, he told Delia that he was taking the rent money to Annie.

"Unless you would rather do it," he offered, already knowing the answer.

Her reply was predictable. "I'm busy right now." She didn't look up from the magazine she was reading. "You do it, Adam. You're the one who's using the stable."

"I'll tell her you said hello," he said, adding, "She may have a few repairs that need doing." Delia nodded absently and he left.

The sky was still light when he took the path through the hedge. Now that Delia was home, he thought, Annie might not want to see him—she might even refuse. But when she answered his knock at the kitchen door, the expression on her face told him all that he needed to know. He shut the door behind him, glanced at the window to make sure the curtain was drawn, and gave up all pretense of being an honorable man. He pulled her against him, kissing her hungrily. For a moment, he gave himself over to the raw pleasure of holding her in his arms, of running his hands over her body, her face, her hair.

"I want you," he whispered urgently, his lips against her throat. "Oh, God, I want you, Annie. Please, let's—"

"No," she said. Flushed and breathless, she pushed him away. "I can't, Adam. I don't have any . . . that is, I can't take precautions right now. We wouldn't be . . . safe. I don't think we should risk it."

"Ah," he said. Regretfully, he dropped his hands, wondering if perhaps she had changed toward him, and this was a way to put him off—a way she knew he would understand and respect. But he discarded that thought immediately. Her kiss, her body against his, had told him she had not changed.

She went to the window and opened the curtains. "Will you have a cup of tea? It's already brewed."

"Thanks," he said, and pulled out a chair. "I've brought the money for the stable rent." He took the bills out of his pocket and laid them on the table. "I told Delia I was coming, and that I'd ask if you had any repairs that need doing."

"I don't, thank you," she said, and poured their tea. The silence that followed felt, to Adam, oddly uncomfortable. And then he found out why.

When she sat down, she added, "I saw Delia yesterday afternoon." She wasn't looking at him. "At Mrs. Crow's."

He frowned. "Who is Mrs. Crow?"

"The lady who runs the boardinghouse in the next block. She sells herbs. I went to get some of this lovely tea. Hibiscus. Do you like it?"

He picked up the cup and sipped. "It's very nice." He frowned again. "Delia was there? I wonder what she was—"

"Wild carrot seeds," Annie said, spooning honey into her tea. "Unfortunately, Mrs. Crow didn't have any. She told Delia where to find them, though. She said the plants are growing in the empty lot behind Purley's, right next door to your store. Now is a good time to—"

"Behind Purley's?" Adam asked, frowning. "I've never noticed. But I don't know anything about plants. I wouldn't know what I was looking at." His frown deepened. "Wait a minute. Wild carrot. That's the contraceptive, isn't it? I wonder what Delia wants *that* for. We're not—"

"Please, Adam." Annie lifted her cup in both hands, meeting his eyes over the rim. Her eyes were dark and troubled, her voice quiet, restrained. "You don't have to explain. I understand, certainly. After all, Delia is your wife. It's only natural for you to want to—"

"But I *don't*," he protested. "Even if she asked me, I wouldn't . . . That is, we haven't . . . Not since before she went to Galveston." He rubbed his jaw, not understanding. "Believe me, Annie, please. The subject hasn't even come up. If it did—if *she* brought it up—I wouldn't. I'd say no." He stopped, a thought coming to him, and then another. When he spoke again, there was a knot in his throat. He pushed the words past it with an effort. "If she's using that carrot seed, it's not on my account, Annie."

Clearly puzzled, she stared at him. "But I saw Delia when she left Mrs. Crow's. She seemed truly distressed. And Mrs. Crow told me what she asked for." She paused, frowning. "If you aren't . . . If the two of you haven't . . . then I wonder why—"

Adam didn't have to wonder. "I know why," he said. "I know *who*."

Annie's expression was blank. "Who? Adam, you can't possibly think—"

"Yes, I can," he said. "I met the man a couple of days ago, coming out of my house. In fact, that's what I came to talk to you about, Annie." He leaned back in his chair. "His name is Simpson. Delia said he was just 'passing through' on his way from Galveston to Austin. He brought her a box of candy and a letter. She said they were from her sister, but I don't believe it."

Annie put down her cup. "Candy and a letter? You mean, she actually had a conversation with him?"

He reached for her hand. "It wasn't just a conversation, Annie."

"Are you *sure*?" She hesitated. "I'm asking this, Adam, because

Delia made a big point of telling me about a man who came calling, a Mr. Simpson. She said he pursued her from Galveston, but she sent him away—him and his box of candy." She pulled her hand away. "She said something like, 'The poor man didn't even get to set foot in the house.'"

"He set *both* feet in the house," Adam said tersely. "He smoked his cigar in the parlor and—" He stopped. There was more, of course. "Her dress was . . . disarranged. And a button was missing. I found it on the floor."

"Disarranged?" Annie looked troubled. "Oh, surely not! I mean, what you're thinking—it's very serious, Adam. Perhaps you should give her the benefit of the doubt. After all . . ." Her voice trailed away.

He knew what Annie was thinking: that he imagined Delia guilty of doing something that he himself had done. And that she didn't want to charge Delia for a sin she herself had committed. But he shook his head again. "I might doubt it, if Greta—the hired girl—hadn't told me . . ."

He stopped. Greta hadn't actually told him anything. He had read her accusing expression, that was all, and interpreted it to mean that she had seen what went on in the parlor between Delia and that man. He cleared his throat. "Anyway, Simpson wasn't just 'passing through,' as Delia kept insisting. The man is still here. I saw him again this morning, having breakfast at the hotel."

"Oh," Annie said in a small voice. "Oh, Adam. You think she's . . . that they're . . ." She clasped her hands together tightly.

"I don't know what to think," he said. "What's fair for me is fair for my wife. If Delia and Simpson are engaging in a . . . liaison, I can scarcely complain."

"And I'm feeling terribly hypocritical, too." Annie ducked her head, the flush rising in her cheeks. Her voice was low. "This is so awkward, Adam. I can't feel sorry for what we've done, but I've put you in a difficult position."

"If I'm in a difficult position, it's not your doing, Annie," he said emphatically. "Anyway, when you get right down to it, I ought to be glad." He gave a wry chuckle. "Maybe she'll decide she loves him. Maybe she'll run off with him."

"What?" Annie's eyes were large. "Leave *you*? Leave Caroline? Oh, Adam, she could never do that! It's unthinkable."

Adam knew she was at least partly right. Delia might no longer love him—perhaps she never had. Perhaps she had only loved what she thought he could give her. But she truly loved their daughter. She would never leave Caroline—and a woman who abandoned her husband could not expect to keep her child. What's more, she valued her reputation as a dedicated mother and the charming wife of a respectable and well-off business owner. Running away with another man would create an enormous scandal, a public humiliation that she could not endure. Delia might like to imagine herself a femme fatale, he thought, especially when she went back to Galveston. But she was too conventional to abandon her marriage, no matter how sorely she was tempted.

Simpson complicated the situation, however. Why was the fellow still hanging around Pecan Springs? He didn't have business here, as far as Adam was able to discover. Was he watching for a chance to see and talk with Delia? Or was she leading him on, letting him hope that she might have some feeling for him? The titillating excitement of a flirtation was something she might very well relish, he thought—the thrill of being admired and perhaps even loved by a man who was not her husband.

As Adam thought of this, he felt a great gulf of despair open up inside him, all around him. He was condemned to spend his entire life with a woman he didn't love, a woman who might be foolish enough to engage in a dalliance that could injure all of them.

And then he came back, as he always did, to the terrible irony of his position. Here he was, in love with a wonderful woman who could be badly compromised—by visits like the very one they were having tonight.

If Delia could be said to be foolish, so, too, could Annie.

If Simpson was culpable, so, too, was he.

If Delia found out about Annie, she might use the knowledge against him—or worse, against *her*. And he couldn't, in good conscience, remonstrate. By his actions, he had yielded up the right to appeal to his wife, or to charge her or punish her. He had opened Annie—the woman he loved—to the same ugly charges that could be laid against Delia. He closed his eyes and passed his hand over his face. What a horrible mess he had made of things!

Now it was Annie's turn to reach for him. "I am so sorry," she said quietly, putting her hand on his. "I know how hard this must be for you, Adam. Delia is the mother of your daughter. In some ways, you must love her still. But are you *sure* you know what's going on? Perhaps . . . perhaps this thing with Mr. Simpson is just a casual friendship." She retrieved her hand and turned her head, but he had seen the tears brimming in her eyes. "And after all, you and I are hardly the pots to call the kettle black, are we?"

He heard her tender affection and knew that she was trying to make him feel better, which of course made him feel worse. "You're right," he confessed. "I don't know anything for certain. I'm only guessing. I'm not being fair to Delia. And I'm certainly not being fair to you." He pushed his chair back. "I'm sorry, Annie. I think I'd better go."

She nodded, silently. Her head was bent, her fingers twisted together.

He looked down at her, loving her, desiring her, but knowing what he had to do. "I can't come back, my love. From now on, I'll slip the stable rent under your door. If you need anything—repairs or the like—send me a note at the store. I'll arrange for someone to help you."

"Yes," she said. "I suppose that's best." She lifted her eyes to his and he saw that her cheeks were wet with tears. "Whatever happens, Adam, please know that I love you. Very much."

"I wish I deserved that," he said wretchedly, and left.

He stood outside for a long moment, hesitating. Then, rather than go home to Delia, he went into the stable. He was greeted by his horses and Caroline's fat pony, whickering softly in the dusky interior of the stable. He took a deep breath of sweet, newly cured hay and warm horseflesh. His throat burned with his own unshed tears as he thought of Annie and their impossible dilemma. He took the stable buckets out to the water pump to refill them, then brought them back to the stalls. As he set the last one down, he heard the low, husky voice.

"Hello."

He straightened, blinking into the dusty dimness. "Greta? Is that *you*?"

"Yes, it's me, sir," she said, stepping out of a shadowed corner. She was wearing a dark dress and a shawl flung over her head and shoulders. "I found somethin' I thought you might oughtta see. After what happened the other day, I didn't want to show it to you in the house."

"You found . . . something?" He was nervously aware that the two of them ought not to be alone here in the barn. If Delia should happen to come out, she would assume that they—

"Yessir." She cleared her throat. "It's the letter that feller gave Miz Delia the other day. The feller who brought the candy. He's got a room at the hotel an'—"

"I know the man you mean," Adam broke in gruffly, remembering the blue letter Delia had been quick to tuck in her sleeve. "But it's Mrs. Hunt's letter. How did you come by it?"

The girl came toward him. Her shawl fell back and he noticed that she was wearing a red ribbon and some sort of cheap flowery perfume, so strong that it overwhelmed the other scents in the stable. "I found it," she said. "In the wastebasket in her bedroom. She must not've wanted it no more, so she was throwin' it away." She took another step closer, and there was a provocative note in her voice. "You've been so nice to me, Mr. Hunt, and I appreciate it. I figgered you might want to have it."

Whatever was in the letter, Adam didn't believe for a minute that Delia had thrown it away. The girl must have stolen it out of a drawer or a jewelry box. He had no right to his wife's private correspondence, but he had to make sure Greta didn't keep it. There was no predicting how she might use it. With an effort, he managed what he hoped she would see as a conspiratorial smile.

"Very good, Greta." He held out his hand. "I'll take it, then, with my thanks."

"Just thanks?" Greta smiled coyly, both hands behind her back, her head tilted on one side. In the dusky half light, Adam saw that her posture was obviously meant to be tempting. Her shawl had fallen away and he could see that several buttons of her bodice were undone, revealing mounds of swelling white flesh. "Don't you think you ought to give me somethin' more than words for it?" She came a little closer, her voice seductive, and held up the letter. "What'll it be, sir?"

He took a breath, understanding that she was offering what he could not, *would* not take. But he wasn't sure how to reject her obvious proposal without making her angry—and he could hardly wrestle the letter from her.

"I believe you have my best interests at heart, Greta." He gave her a long, grave look. "You do, don't you?"

She seemed to take that seriously. "Oh, yes, sir," she said, with a quick nod. "I *do*, sir. With all my heart, I promise you."

"And I have yours, believe me." He swallowed uncomfortably. "My dear."

She gave him a smile and he thought she was touched by the endearment. "Well, then," she said suggestively, but she kept her hands—and the letter—behind her back.

"How can I know what you have unless you let me see it? Give it to me, and then we can talk about when and what else we might . . ." He let his voice trail off in what he hoped was a tantalizing way.

Later, he was ashamed to think that the girl—who couldn't be much more than nineteen—was taken in by his half promise. She brought one hand slowly out from behind her back and held out a folded piece of blue stationery, the very same blue, he thought, as the letter he had seen Delia reading on the afternoon of Mr. Simpson's visit.

"Here 'tis," she said, handing it to him. There was a soft smile on her lips, and as he took it, she seized his hand, her fingers gripping his. She leaned toward him, her voice low. "So now can we talk about what else—and when?"

Her perfume was almost stifling. He returned the pressure of her fingers, then dropped her hand and stepped back. "This isn't a good time, I'm afraid." He pocketed the letter.

"I'll have it back, then," she said, her mouth tightening in reproach.

He pretended not to notice. "We'll talk later," he said, and once again added, "my dear." Hearing the hollowness of it, he was ashamed but could not take it back. "It's late, and my wife is expecting me back at the house. I don't want her to think that we—"

She pouted. "It's late because you was so long at Annie Duncan's house—again." Her eyes were on his, and her startling directness was as sharp as a slap to his face.

"I was paying the stable rent," he said.

"You an' me, sir, we know all about Annie, don't we?" Greta's voice was sly, half-mocking, and Adam felt chilled. How much did she know? How *could* she?

She lifted her chin. "But Annie Duncan's been a friend to me and I won't say nothin' against her. It's your *wife* I've got my eye on." Her mouth set crookedly. "She sure rules the roost in your house, don't she? Gets everything her little heart wants and then some. Thinks she can boss everybody around, make 'em do all she wants done, just by snappin' her fingers. Orders me to do the wash, scrub the floor, clean up after her sick in the morning, cook the meals, wash the dishes, go out and collect them seeds she wants." She peered at him through the gathering darkness, her voice tightening. "But maybe not no more. Not after you read what's in that letter—what never should oughtta been written to another man's wife."

Thinking just how dangerous she might be, Adam flinched against the acid venom in the girl's flood of vindictive words. He had the letter, yes—but she knew what was in it. How would she use that knowledge? And what might she do when he, or Delia, didn't give her what she wanted?

He knew he had to find a way to deal with her, but he had no idea of what that might be. He was suddenly bone-weary and quite aware that he was a coward. Whatever he had to do could wait until tomorrow.

"I'll wish you good night, then," he said stiffly. And in a lower, half-guilty voice, added again, "My dear Greta."

That pleased her. Her face lightened and she leaned toward him. "Let's have a little kiss, then," she said. "To seal our bargain." She closed her eyes and puckered her lips.

A bargain with the devil, he thought. He bent toward her, brushed his lips against her forehead, and stepped back quickly, out of her reach. "Go home now, Greta," he said.

She gave him a hooded look. "You read that letter," she commanded. She pulled her shawl up over her head, turned, and left.

He stood for a moment uncertainly, the letter in his hand, apprehension in his heart. An honorable man might return it, unread, to the person to whom it belonged—his wife. But Adam already knew that he was not an honorable man. And besides, Greta had read it. To deal with the girl, he had to know what *she* knew.

Full dark had fallen since he had come into the stable, and he fumbled his way to the lantern he knew to be hanging on a hook by the door. He scratched a match against his thumbnail and lit it.

By its flickering light, he unfolded the letter and began to read.

Chapter Thirteen

Queen Anne's lace is a favorite of people who like to forage for edible foods. As a biennial, this wild ancestor of the garden carrot produces leaves and roots in the first year; in the second year, it produces flowers and seeds. You can mince the fresh leaves and add them to salad or soups. The roots are best harvested in the spring or fall of the first year when they are tender; second-year roots become woody. The peeled flower stalk has a carroty flavor and may be eaten raw or cooked. The flower itself makes a flavorful jelly or a pretty garnish. The ground seeds are spicy. However, pregnant women should avoid eating this plant; the root and seeds can produce uterine contractions and cause a miscarriage.

And, foragers, please beware! You must take extra care to be sure that what you are harvesting is wild carrot—not its deadly lookalike, poison hemlock. Crush a few leaves. If they smell like fresh carrot, you're safe. If they have a foul odor, leave it alone. This is serious stuff, folks, so pay attention. Mistakes with this plant have cost lives.

"Anne's Flower"
China Bayles
Pecan Springs Enterprise

The telephone beside the bed was ringing. I climbed toward it out of a dream where I was lying flat on my back, smothered under a mound of musty old newspapers, antique photographs, and vintage clothing and furs—which turned out to be Winchester, stretched out beside me, nose to my feet, his tail in my face. Caitie's cat, Mr. P, was curled up cozily on the other side. I opened one eye wide enough to see the phone, fumbled for the receiver, and lifted it.

"H'lo," I mumbled between thick lips. "Who'z it?"

But I was hearing the dial tone and it wasn't the phone that was ringing, anyway. It was the alarm clock, again. I had set it a half hour early, so I would have time to swing past the fairground and tend to Caitie's chickens before I went to the shop.

"Rats," I muttered, and killed the alarm. Mr. P jumped down from the bed and went to take care of his morning business. Winchester stirred, sighed, decided that there was nothing in the world that required a basset's attention at *this* hour, and went back to sleep.

I fumbled into my clothes, splashed water on my face, combed my hair, and went downstairs to rustle up some breakfast. I had fed the cat and was finishing my breakfast burrito when Winchester made his way downstairs—backward, as is his habit, and slowly, one step at a time, feeling his way with his hind paws. Bassets live life close to the ground and stairs seem to make Winnie feel acrophobic. He was obviously hoping that somebody had already put something in his bowl, and when he saw that it was empty, he collapsed with a despairing sigh, belly and tail flat on the floor, front and rear legs splayed, head down, nose touching his empty bowl. You can be in a hurry, but no matter. When a basset goes flat, no force on earth can budge him until *he* decides he's ready to get up.

A cup of strong coffee (yes, coffee is an herb, too) had already set the world more or less right for me. While Winchester's world is never altogether right, he brightened considerably when I filled his bowl, and even more when I offered him the last bite of my burrito. But when I began to load my laptop and the carton of photographs and clippings into the car, he once again became despondent. He hates facing a long, boring day alone, with nothing to do but nap in Mc-Quaid's leather recliner and nobody to talk to except that stupid cat.

The sky was overcast as I drove into town, with that pearly half-light that blesses the landscape in the cool hour just after dawn. The summer sun wasn't scorching everything yet, the air was still sweet and clean, and the morning traffic on Limekiln Road was fairly reasonable. As I drove, I thought about the photographs I had studied the night before and the story they seemed to tell—a tale of two families, although I still wasn't sure I had sorted them correctly. I wondered what Lori would tell me about the christening dress in the photo I had texted her. And I wondered, half-apprehensively, what the ghost had left on my bulletin board this morning—and then rolled my eyes at my apprehension.

Assumes facts not in evidence, Your Honor.

Sustained. There *had* to be a rational explanation for the inexplicable goings-on. I just hadn't found it yet. I needed to dig a little deeper. Now, in the clear light of day, I was doubly glad I hadn't mentioned any of this ghost nonsense to McQuaid. He would never let me live it down.

I was so deep in thought that I missed the road to the fairgrounds and had to make a U-turn and go back. It was still early enough that the day's activities hadn't gotten under way and the parking lot was almost empty. I was able to park right behind the poultry tent, next to Tom Banner's burly Dodge RAM pickup. The truck is Aggie maroon (because Tom is a Texas A&M grad and maroon is the Aggies' team color), with a gun rack and shotgun in the rear window. At first I was surprised to see the truck, but then I wasn't: as security coordinator for the fair, Tom was probably clocking plenty of overtime.

The check-in booth outside the poultry tent was unmanned,

except by a team of hungry crows cleaning up a spill of popcorn, and the carnival's hurdy-gurdy music hadn't started up yet, although somewhere, somebody was hammering something, loudly. Somebody else was frying breakfast bacon, and the mouthwatering scent of it was sharp on the morning air. The flaps on the canvas poultry tent were closed, and I raised one to duck inside. It would have been totally dark in the tent, but a thin string of overhead bulbs cast puddles of pallid light across the cages. Sensing that a new day was dawning, the birds were beginning to wake up, and the air was filled with the subdued dissonance of poultry voices—chickens, ducks, geese, guineas, with a couple of peacocks adding an occasional screech.

Caitie's birds were at the far end of Section One, past a long row of chickens that were stretching their wings and wondering where they were and what they were doing there. But when I finally reached Caitie's two cages, I was stopped, almost in mid-stride.

Dixie Chick was settled in her cage, preening her yellow-gold feathers and clucking contentedly to herself.

The door of Extra Crispy's cage was open. The cage was empty. Caitie's rooster was *gone*. Just . . . gone.

The black rooster—Blackheart—was gone, too.

My heart did a flip-flop. Incredulously, I stared at the two empty cages, then turned and looked wildly around, searching. But that was ridiculous. Chickens don't unlock their cages and take off for a night on the town.

No. Somebody had wanted those birds—or more likely, that rare rooster. Somebody had stolen Blackheart, and in the process, noticed Caitie's Cubalaya (he's an unusually classy-looking bird) and thought he might be worth money, too. I swung around, looking for other empty cages, and saw none. It appeared that the chicken thief had made off with just two birds—the *best* two. Caitie would be devastated, and it was a sure bet that Blackheart's owner would be pretty upset, too. After all, that rooster had the potential to produce tens of thousands of dollars a year, doing what he liked to do best.

I stood there for a moment, trying to think. Then I remembered Tom Banner's truck. I took out my cell phone, pulled up the recent calls, and clicked on Tom's number, praying for him to pick up fast. He did.

"Yo, China. What's up?"

"I'm here at the fairgrounds, Tom. In the poultry tent. Where are you? Can you get over here, fast? There's something you need to see."

"Something—"

"Chicken theft," I said tersely. As I clicked off, I noticed a drift of red-orange breast feathers among the cedar-shaving mulch that covered the tent floor. Caitie's rooster had not been taken without a fight. He had struggled bravely against his kidnapper. And then something else caught my eye, a square of shiny plastic on the shadowy ground under the cages, half hidden under the mulch. I picked it up by one corner, carefully, and was examining it when Tom appeared. He was in uniform with his badge and sidearm, so I knew he was on the job.

He stood beside me, staring at the empty cages. "Damn," he muttered. "Hell's bells." A Delta Force veteran has a more colorful vocabulary, I'm sure. He must have been editing it for me.

"There's no nighttime security in these tents?" I asked.

But that was a dumb question. I already knew the answer. What's more, I had read the fine print in the Exhibitor Agreement that I had cosigned with Caitie (a minor, of course), in which we released the management of the Adams County Fair from any and all known damages, injuries, and losses from theft, fire, water, wind, storm, acts of a third party, or for any other cause known to man. Which pretty much covers it. If Caitie and the owner of that valuable black rooster wanted to be reimbursed for their loss, they wouldn't have a legal leg to stand on. For Caitie, of course, that wasn't the issue. She loved Extra Crispy with all her heart. Right now, she was dealing with one big threat: Kevin's cancer. I hated the thought that she might have to face another.

"We do our best," Tom said, sounding resigned. "We hire guys to patrol at night, but they can't be everywhere. Some of the other tents—the livestock tents, for instance—get more attention, since the animals are more valuable." He pulled down his mouth. "Guess we didn't count on somebody exhibiting a rooster that costs as much as a registered heifer."

I handed him the item I'd found, using just the tips of my fingers, in case the thief might have left prints. "I found this under the cages," I said. "I'm guessing that Caitie's rooster gave the guy a hard time." I bent over and picked up a few of the feathers scattered through the mulch. "I hope he wasn't too badly damaged—the rooster, I mean." I hoped the thief got a rooster claw in his eye. He had it coming to him.

"An exhibitor's badge!" Tom exclaimed. "Looks like this jerk is such an amateur that he left us his business card." He read the name on the clip-on badge. "Dana Gibbons. Exhibitor 20245. Must have dropped this when the rooster objected to being abducted. Damn lucky, huh, China? We've got a name—I can get the address from the fair's database."

"Hang on a sec." I pursed my lips. "I'm not saying it's not evidential, but that badge could have been dropped anytime yesterday." Even the dumbest defense lawyer would pop up with that claim in a New York minute, unless— And then I thought of something. "However, we may have a witness."

Tom frowned. "A witness?"

"Up there." I pointed at Caitie's chicken cam, mounted about six feet up on the nearest tent pole, aimed down at the cages.

"Shit," Tom said reverently. "Forgot all about that. I never thought, when we put it up there—"

"Neither did I," I replied. "But I'm glad it's there. With any luck, we may get a glimpse of Dana Gibbons, whoever she is."

"She?" Tom said, startled. "I thought Dana was a guy's name."

"She, he, whoever." I headed for the camera. "Maybe this will tell us." A minute or two later, I had taken it down and retrieved the thumb drive. But Tom and Caitie hadn't tested the camera when they put it up. It's finicky sometimes. Maybe it hadn't been working.

Tom frowned. "We're going to need a computer to read that."

"My laptop is in my car. And let's take this." I reached under the cages for the carrier we'd brought the chickens in.

"Why the carrier?" Tom asked.

"Because I want to get those roosters back," I said. "And they don't automatically perch on your shoulder, like a trained parrot." Actually, Extra Crispy would, but I didn't know about Blackheart. If we managed to retrieve the roosters, I didn't want to be the one to lose a twenty-five-hundred-dollar bird.

"Sorry, wasn't thinking," Tom acknowledged ruefully. "Come on, let's go. I'd sure as hell like to catch this guy before that reporter friend of yours gets wind of this story."

I raised my eyebrows, but I understood his concern. A theft like this could get the fair a very public black eye. We went out to the parking lot and I opened the laptop on the hood of my Toyota, where we could both get a good look. I held my breath for the few moments it took to boot the machine and bring up the thumb drive. I was relieved when a surprisingly clear color image of Caitie's two cages appeared, with Blackheart's cage just visible to the left. We could see Jessica and me, and Caitie running off with Sharon, and Tom leaving, then Jessica and me leaving. And so it went all day: the motion-sensor image turned on as people walked past the cages or when the birds themselves moved, eating, drinking, preening themselves, or stretching their wings. It turned off when there was no movement.

Tom and Caitie had installed the camera early the previous morning. The tent had been closed for the night at seven p.m., so the camera had recorded some ten hours of movement. I fast-forwarded through it, watching as the day ended, the tent was closed, the overhead lights dimmed (but didn't go out), and the birds settled down for the night. I kept on fast-forwarding, until just after midnight a blurry, bulky figure appeared out of the darkness. I froze the image, and we peered at it.

"Can't see the face under the bill of the cap," Tom said, squinting. "From the hair, though, looks like a woman."

"Doesn't look like a woman to me," I said. "See those broad shoulders? Could be a long-haired guy." But what I could clearly see was that the person was wearing a black T-shirt with white lettering: *This Ain't My First Rodeo*. I noticed that an exhibitor's badge was clipped to the shirt—important detail. I glanced at the cages. The roosters appeared to be snoozing.

The thief had come prepared. Carrying a small plastic crate with a wire door, *Ain't My First Rodeo* stopped in front of Blackheart's cage, unlatched the door, and swiftly reached inside. In one motion, he grabbed the sleeping bird by the feet, dragged him out, thrust him into the carrier, and fastened the door. He was turning to leave when he paused in front of Extra Crispy's cage, bent over for a closer look, and then decided to take him, too.

The second snatch didn't come off as easily as the first. Extra Crispy had been awakened when *Rodeo* boosted Blackheart. When the thief reached for him, he hopped away, aiming a barrage of furious pecks at the guy's bare hand and wrist. *Rodeo* jerked his hand back, then—angrily—cornered the rooster and grabbed him by his tail. He was successful this time, although feathers flew as Extra Crispy, wings flapping wildly, struggled with all his might against his abductor. That was when *Rodeo* lost his exhibitor's badge, although he didn't appear to notice. He was busy shoving the second rooster into the crate with the first. A moment later, he was out of the picture, and the camera clicked off.

But it had given us what we needed: proof that the badge belonged to the jerk who stole those chickens. "How fast can we get Gibbons' address from your database?" I asked. "It won't take him long to discover that Caitie's rooster isn't all that valuable—except to her, of course. I don't want to find my daughter's chicken in the frying pan when we get there."

Tom narrowed his eyes. "When *we* get there?" he asked warily.

"Damn straight," I said. "That's Caitie's pet rooster. I have to make sure she gets him back, alive. Let's find that address, Tom. Maude Porterfield lives about six blocks from here." Maude is a justice of the peace, and in Texas, justices have the authority to issue search warrants. "On the way to Gibbons' place, we can stop at her house and get a warrant. The exhibitor's badge and this video give us plenty of probable cause." I scowled at him. "And if you think you're doing this on your own, think again. You're not leaving me behind. Now, hurry up. With any luck, we can catch Maude before she heads for court."

"Mmm," Tom said, frowning. "Well, in the interest of quick action—" He took out his cell phone and called the main office at the fairgrounds. "It's early. Let's hope Susanna is at her desk." After a moment, he said, "Hey, Suze. I need a quick address check on an exhibitor. Can you pull up that file for me, fast?" After a moment, he said, "Name, Dana Gibbons. Exhibitor ID: 20245." He pulled a small notebook out of his pocket. There was a pause, then he said, "1116 County Road 12. Got it. Phone number?"

Another pause, while he scribbled quickly. He flipped the notebook closed and tucked it back in his pocket. Into the phone he added, "Thanks. Yes, actually there is a problem. Gibbons made off with a couple of birds from the poultry tent last night. One of them is a rooster that's apparently pretty valuable. You might let Charlie know that I have an ID and a video on the thief and am on my way to get a search warrant for the address you just gave me. I'll check back with him later." He clicked off the phone.

"Charlie?" I asked. Obviously, fair security was very well organized.

"Charlie Powell. He's in charge when I'm out." He took his vehicle keys out of his pocket. "Put that carrier in the bed of my truck. And bring your computer. Porterfield may want to look at that video before she issues the warrant."

I moved fast. Of course, we had no way of knowing whether Gibbons had taken the chickens to his house or somewhere else. But we had to start somewhere. And there was no point in going anywhere without a warrant.

Maude Porterfield, who presided over my marriage to McQuaid, may well be the longest-serving justice of the peace in Texas. She has been on the bench for over fifty years and knows everything there is to know about her job. This morning, we caught her sitting down to a plate of pancakes, wearing a red tracksuit with black racing stripes, her white hair still in curlers and her cane hooked over the back of her chair. She hadn't put her hearing aid in yet, so we had to ring the doorbell several times before she came to the door.

But while Maude may be one of Pecan Springs' older citizens, she is one of the sharpest. She put in her hearing aid, listened to Tom's story, looked at the exhibitor's badge, and watched the video on my laptop.

"What do you reckon this feller wants with those chickens?" she asked, peering at the screen over the tops of her glasses.

"He might want that black rooster for breeding," I said. "Caitie said somebody on eBay was asking a hundred and seventy-five dollars an egg. This guy may already have a black hen—or know where he can get one."

"Or *steal* one," Tom muttered.

"Jiminy crickets," Maude muttered. "I've been on this earth longer than Noah, but I'm always surprised by the things some folks will get up to." She reached for her pen. "Better include 'vehicles, premises, and all buildings' in the warrant. The birds could be in the chicken coop. Or the toolshed."

"Maybe make it a search-and-seizure warrant," I suggested. "We've got a carrier in the truck. If we find those chickens, we ought to confiscate them. To ensure their safe return," I added. "That black bird is wearing a hefty price tag." And the other was priceless, at least where Caitie was concerned.

"Right," Maude said, and began filling in the warrant. "You'll want to get them back to the fair before the judges get around to the chicken section." She gave me a sympathetic glance. "Wouldn't be right for that daughter of yours to miss out on a chance at a blue ribbon because some jerk made off with her chicken."

"Thank you," I said, although I wasn't sure that Extra Crispy would be in blue-ribbon shape. He'd lost quite a few feathers in the tussle.

Maude paused, looking at Tom. "This isn't a no-knock warrant, is it?"

"Nope. No need. I'm not looking for drugs." The Fourth Amendment—and Texas law—requires that even if the police have a search or arrest warrant that justifies entering a property, they must knock and announce themselves and their purpose before they enter. One important exception: the cops don't have to knock and announce if doing so would give suspects the opportunity to destroy the evidence by flushing the drugs down the toilet. If an officer thinks he'll need to enter unannounced, he can request a no-knock warrant that gives him authority to barge right in without so much as a hey-there. I go into full defense-lawyer mode when I hear this, of course. It can make for a lively discussion in the courtroom.

"Makes sense," Maude said. Finished, she signed her name with a flourish and handed the warrant to Tom. "China riding shotgun on this one?"

"I don't think—" Tom began.

"You bet I am," I broke in emphatically. "That's *Caitie's* rooster." I frowned at Tom. "And when we get those birds, they need to go straight back to the fair. I don't want them shut up in the sheriff's evidence locker for who knows how long." Or taken to a shelter, as are animals seized in cruelty cases.

"I agree with China," Maude said. "Special case. The chickens go back where they came from. The poultry tent." She frowned at Tom. "And if I were you, I'd take her, Tom—unless, that is, you're sure you can personally identify both of these stolen birds. You figure you can do that?"

Tom muttered something under his breath, but Maude only smiled.

"I thought so," she said briskly. "You two better be on your way, then. It would be a damned shame if that jerk decided to barbecue the evidence."

COUNTY Road 12 took us out into the wooded hills south of Pecan Springs, along the Pecan River. A narrow, asphalted two-lane with no shoulders, the road hugged the twisting river for five or six miles, then crossed it on a rusty iron bridge and headed west into the Hill Country. I called Ruby to ask her to open the shop for me.

"Tom Banner and I are pursuing a pair of stolen roosters," I said. "One of them is Extra Crispy."

"Somebody stole Caitie's *chicken*?" she exclaimed incredulously. "Who would want to do a thing like that? Why?"

"It's complicated," I said. "I'll fill you in later. Anything going on there?"

"Lori came in a few minutes ago. Her phone quit working, which is why nobody could reach her. She got it fixed, but in the process, she thinks she lost a text from you. She says maybe it had an attachment?"

"Oh, right," I said. That would be the picture I had texted Lori of the baby in the white christening dress. I wanted her to tell me whether it was anything like the christening dress her aunt had given her. "Tell her I'll resend it when I get a minute. Not right now."

"I'll do it. When do you think you'll be in?"

"As soon as we've got the chickens back. I hope it won't be too long." I clicked off and brought up the map on my cell phone. "Looks like it might be seven or eight miles," I told Tom, calculating. "Maybe twelve minutes?"

"Working on it," Tom said.

The houses along the road were mostly double-wides and small frame dwellings surrounded by poorly tended yards and patches of uncut weeds, with junky cars parked in the driveways or propped up, without tires, on concrete blocks. Once, we passed what looked like an auto junkyard shielded from public view by a screen of Ashe junipers, and Tom made a note to check for the permit. The county licenses junkyards, but unless the neighbors report violators, they can fly under the radar for years. Meanwhile, all those abandoned vehicles are leaking noxious fluids into the groundwater, potentially poisoning the neighbors' wells.

As we drove, I kept an eye on the painted numbers on the mailboxes. We were making good time until we got behind a tractor pulling a trailer loaded with hay bales. We crawled along behind it on the narrow road until Tom finally got to a place where he could pass. We got around it and sped up.

I slanted a glance at Tom. I was impatient to get where we were going and nervous about retrieving those roosters, but he was confident and relaxed, his big hands light on the steering wheel of the heavy truck. He has the look of somebody who knows what he's doing, with a firm jaw and eyes that seem to see things the rest of us can't. There's a wariness in him, too, that I suppose comes from his Delta Force deployments, when he had to be constantly on the lookout for invisible threats to his buddies and himself. His wife, Sylvia, told me once that his war experiences, which must have been horrific, still trouble him. He has violent nightmares—dreams that sometimes scare her as much as they disturb him. I know that he keeps his marksmanship skills up; he has a gun range at his house, and on weekends when I'm home, I can hear him target shooting.

I glanced over my shoulder at the gun in the window rack—a Remington twelve-gauge pump-action shotgun with a pistol grip, like the one McQuaid had taught me to use. Tom was also wearing his sidearm holstered on his right hip. He was ready for whatever came next, I thought, but he wouldn't get to use his weapons today. Nobody was going to the mat over a pair of roosters, so we could both relax.

Tom's truck was equipped with a two-way radio. When we left Maude's house, he had asked the dispatcher to run a make on Gibbons. Now, she radioed back. The man had two priors: a misdemeanor domestic violence and a Class C misdemeanor for shooting a deer from a public road. "What have you got on him today?" she asked.

"He stole two chickens," he said, in answer to the dispatcher's question, then: "C-h-i-c-k-e-n-s. As in Kentucky Fried." He glanced at me. "Sorry," he said, cutting the mic. "Poor choice of words."

I could hear the dispatcher laughing.

Tom clicked the mic again and said: "No joke, Phyllis. One of them is supposed to be worth twenty-five hundred dollars, maybe more if he gets to be a regular daddy. The other one is a little girl's show rooster. They were lifted from the poultry tent at the county fair last night." He gave our location and asked, "Who's patrolling out here today? Where is he?" Then: "Good. Give Roy my destination. ETA: five minutes."

"Do you always check on the backup?" I asked as he keyed off the mic and replaced it.

"I'm cautious," he said, "especially this far out in the country." He didn't say, *And especially when I have a civilian riding along*, but I knew he thought it. I was a liability.

"Where is he?" I asked. "Roy, I mean."

"About fifteen minutes away from our location," he said. "Available if we need him." He jerked a thumb to the left, where a gravel road dead-ended into the county road. "Out here, you never know what you're going to bump into. A couple of months ago, Roy and I closed down a meth cooker at the end of that road. Arrested two guys and a woman, all three of them armed. There's more of that going on in these hills than people think."

"How'd you happen to find them?" I asked curiously.

"A tip. A neighbor's bull got out and he was repairing his fence. He just happened to smell the acetone they were using to polish the red coloring out of their product, and recognized it. The meth heads had moved their mobile lab to the back of the property to get it as far from the road as they could, thinking that would be safe. But they backed it right up against the neighbor's fence line." He grinned. "This ain't the Wild West some folks think it is."

"Wild enough," I said, glancing back down at my cell phone, where I had brought up Google Earth. The image showed dark green wooded hills and ravines cut into the limestone, with a few patches of open meadow, the road twisting like a narrow white ribbon through the valleys and along the crests. The houses were scattered like miniature Monopoly pieces across the rugged terrain. Seen from the satellite, this part of the Hill Country was a wilderness, only thinly populated.

"The place is about two miles ahead," I added. "On the right." It was nearly nine now. The sun had risen high enough to feel warm through the window, and Tom turned up the truck's air-conditioning. It was going to be another bright, hot day, with humid air streaming up from the Gulf. By noon, the temperature could easily be in the upper nineties. I hoped we'd have those chickens in custody by then— or that they were in a place with good ventilation. Chickens die of heat stroke even easier than people.

In a few minutes, Tom slowed. The numbers on the rusted, tilting mailbox—1116—told us that we had arrived, and he made a sharp right turn. The house itself was at the end of half a mile of rutted caliche lane, marked by several large No Trespassing signs. The lane wound through a section of overgrazed pastureland, heavily infested with broomweed and prickly pear cactus and dotted with mesquite trees. The house at the end was small, with weathered siding, a narrow porch across the front, and a rusty metal roof. Off to the left was a pen enclosing a mama goat and several kid goats, a couple of black Barred Rock hens scratching around them. In the yard, I saw a compact tractor with a hydraulic loader on the front end and a cultivator on the rear. An older-model black Chevy pickup was parked in the driveway—a ranch truck, judging from the mud on the rear tailgate and the bales of hay and sacks of feed in the bed. Gibbons, I thought, was a homesteader.

Tom pulled up and stopped close behind the Chevy. "Stay with the truck," he said, "unless I tell you different." He shut off the ignition and pocketed the keys.

"But, Tom—" I began.

"That's an order, China." His face was stern. "I doubt that there'll be trouble over a couple of chickens, but there's no predicting. I don't want to have to explain to my friend McQuaid how I managed to get his wife shot up."

"Ridiculous," I muttered, but I didn't press the point. Tom knows his business, and anyway, he's the law. I just wanted to get this over with and get Caitie's rooster back—and the black rooster, too, of course. And Tom was right. This wasn't a drug bust or a high-profile arrest. Gibbons was just a guy who had a yen for an expensive all-black rooster and thought he could get one for free. I had my fingers crossed that retrieving the chickens was going to be a relatively simple matter.

But despite the evidence of the truck parked in the driveway, nobody answered Tom's repeated knocking at the front door. He knocked and called, waited a reasonable time, and called and knocked again. Then he left the front porch and walked around the back, out of sight.

I sat there, waiting, listening to the mutter of the police dispatcher on Tom's radio as deputies around the county checked in. I noticed a red-blue strobe flasher light on the dash, and to the right of the steering wheel a box of digital switches that monitored lights and siren. Tom was well equipped. He must be more involved with the reserve deputy program than I had thought. He had turned off the AC with the ignition and the truck was hot, so I opened my door and got out. He had told me to stay with the truck—he hadn't said "Stay *in* it."

I stood there, letting the cool breeze wash over me and taking a look around. Off to the right was a thick cedar brake, and between it and the driveway a rocky, unmowed strip of native goldenrod, hemlock, poverty weed, and buffalo gourd. Ahead of us in the driveway was the Chevy ranch truck. And lying at the edge of the driveway a couple of feet from the Chevy's passenger side door was a wilted green plant stalk, a couple of feet long. I frowned. Ragweed? Hemlock? Or—

"Hey, China." Tom had come around the back of the house and was beckoning to me to bring the carrier and join him. He must have seen the chickens, I figured, or someone in the house had told him where they were. I hauled it out of the back of the truck and took it to him.

"You've found the roosters?" I asked eagerly. "Where are they?"

"Haven't found them yet," he said, taking the carrier from me. "But I heard one crowing. And there doesn't appear to be anybody at home, so you might as well help me round up our missing chickens. *If* they're here, that is. You'll know them when you see them, I hope?"

"I'll certainly recognize Caitie's rooster. That black one shouldn't be too hard to pick out, either. And they should both be wearing leg bands, unless Gibbons has removed them." I heard a rooster crow, too, then. "Sounds like it's over there," I said, nodding toward a rickety wood-frame barn on the far side of a fenced vegetable garden and an empty corral.

The crowing was followed by a loud cackling. "Well, *that's* not our rooster," Tom said dryly. We walked up to the barn. He stopped, put down the carrier, and rapped on the door frame. "Sheriff's deputy," he shouted, his right hand on his holster. "I have a search warrant. Anybody here?"

Nobody answered. The cackling paused briefly, then began again.

"I'll go first," Tom said, and went in. After a moment, he returned. "Nobody here," he said, and picked up the carrier.

I followed him into the barn. After the bright sunshine outdoors, I had to blink to adjust to the shadowy darkness inside. The air was sweet with the scent of fresh hay. Along one wall was a row of several rabbit hutches. Along another wall, a half dozen metal chicken nest boxes. A large black hen was perched on one, cheerfully celebrating a freshly laid egg. I couldn't be a hundred percent positive in the dimness, but I was pretty sure that she had a black comb and black legs, like Blackheart.

So that's it, I thought. Dana Gibbons already had an Ayam Cemani hen. He had stolen the Ayam Cemani rooster to sire a flock of Ayam Cemani chicks. He was hoping they would bring him good fortune—and at a hundred and seventy-five dollars an egg, he could be right. But that wasn't going to happen, because we had a warrant to seize the rooster. And on the barn floor in front of the nest boxes was the small plastic crate we had seen in the video from Caitie's camera.

I ran to the crate, Tom at my heels, and peered in. I saw two disconsolate roosters, their tails dragging, crouched together for comfort—Extra Crispy and Blackheart.

"Hello, baby," I crooned, opening the crate's wire door and reaching for Extra Crispy. "It's okay. We're taking you home now. Caitie will be so glad to see you." Silly talk, yes, but there it is. I was relieved to see both birds, and I could almost believe, from the glint in his eye, that Extra Crispy was glad to see me.

"Hold on a minute, China," Tom said, and took out his cell phone. He snapped several pictures of the crate, the two bedraggled birds in the crate, and the black hen on the perch, and emailed the photos to the sheriff's office while I transferred the roosters into the carrier. Blackheart was docile enough to come without a struggle and Extra Crispy knew me, so I got the job done without too much wing-flapping.

The birds, though, were not nearly as sleek and pretty as they'd been when they were checked in at the fair. They were dusty and disheveled, they had both lost feathers (perhaps in a brief dispute over who was boss of the crate), and their rear ends were covered in poopee. In their present condition, neither would win a ribbon. That would be a huge disappointment for Caitie, but I knew she'd be thrilled that Extra Crispy had been rescued.

"We're done here," Tom said, glancing around the barn. "We'll take these birds back where they came from, and I'll talk to the sheriff about the charges."

"Felony theft," I said grimly. "Maybe throw in a couple of counts of animal cruelty for good measure. There's no food or water in this crate. And the birds may have some injuries we can't see."

"Sounds right." Tom picked up the carrier. "Come on. Let's boogie."

Tom was carrying the roosters and I was a step or two behind him. When we got to the Chevy, he walked along the driver's side, but I detoured to the passenger's side, wanting to get a better look at that long green stalk of wilted, crumpled plant material I had spotted earlier. I paused, looking down at it. The stalk had been cut at its base, and my first thought was that this was a tall ragweed—an allergen—that somebody wanted to get rid of.

And then I looked again. This was definitely not ragweed. The top end of the stalk was thickly studded with fist-sized clumps of fuzzy, purply-green-brown buds. Lots of buds. Lots and lots of buds. I bent over and took another look.

Was it? Yes, it was. Unmistakably.

"Tom?" Clearing my throat, I straightened. "Tom, come here."

He finished loading the roosters into the back of his pickup and came around the truck toward me. "What's up, China?"

"Weed," I said, pointing to it.

"Yeah? Well, what of it? What's to get excited about a stalk of rag—" He bent over and looked. "By damn," he said softly. "It really is. Weed."

Pot, in other words.

Marijuana.

Which opened a whole other can of worms. The Fourth Amendment gives every citizen protection against unreasonable and unwarranted searches. Tom's search-and-seize warrant allowed him to look for the stolen chickens, and that was it. Anything else—say, stolen stereo equipment in the house, or a cache of money hidden in a tin can in the barn—was off limits, legally speaking. In other words, we didn't have a license to hunt.

But the courts have recognized some searches as valid without warrants—for example, under what's called the "plain view doctrine."

To apply "plain view" to this case, Tom had to be lawfully present here on the driveway (he was); he had to have a lawful right of access to the evidence in question (he did); and the incriminating character of the evidence had to be immediately apparent (it darn sure was). The guy who stole two chickens was all of a sudden in a heckuva lot more trouble.

Tom was taking a photo and I was bending over again to get another look when from somewhere near the barn, I heard somebody whistling. Tom straightened, grabbed my arm, and jerked me around.

"Leave it," he said roughly. "Get in the truck and duck down under the dash." He was already unsnapping his holster. "Do it *now*, China."

I scrambled for the truck. Stolen chickens are one thing. Back-country marijuana grows are something else. While Texas is preparing to license growers to produce low-THC medical cannabis, growing grass for the ordinary consumer is extremely illegal. If you're caught in possession of anything between four ounces and five pounds—the goodies on that one plant lying on the driveway, for instance—you're facing a fine of up to ten thousand dollars and six months to two years in prison. Plus additional charges if you're marketing your crop.

But this little deterrent doesn't stop the pot farmers. Just the month before, a hundred miles west of Pecan Springs, deputies on aerial patrol had looked down to see the mother of all marijuana farms: some forty thousand plants, growing in lovely green rows in a four-acre field. At the time I read the story, I had done the math. One outdoor plant, grown under good conditions, could yield a pound of salable cannabis. Street prices vary, but a quick Internet search told me that the average asking price for an ounce of medium-quality pot, at the time, was two hundred and eighty dollars. Which put the street value of that crop of cannabis at eleven million and change. The sheriff was still looking for the farmers, who (he believed) were members of a Mexican cartel, growing weed on our side of the border to save on trucking and avoid detection at the checkpoint.

Tom was right. What we had stumbled onto was bigger than a pair of stolen roosters. Bigger, potentially, than an amateur meth kitchen. It was time to get out of Dodge, and fast.

I was already in the truck when it happened. A man stepped out from behind the barn and yelled, "Who the hell are you? Get off my property!"

He was some thirty yards away from the truck, but even at that distance I could see that he had long hair and the general configuration of our chicken thief. Dana Gibbons, aka *This Ain't My First Rodeo.* He was carrying a rifle.

Using the open truck door as a shield, Tom unholstered his side-arm and shouted, "Sheriff's deputy. You're under arrest for suspicion of cultivating marijuana. Drop that weapon and—"

Gibbons raised his rifle and squeezed off three shots, fast. One zinged off the hood. One smashed the windshield above the steering wheel. The glass exploded in flying splinters and I felt a sharp, burning pain above my left ear. One hit Tom. He went down.

I didn't stop to think—you don't, in a situation like this. Adrenaline takes over and you just do what you have to do, fast. I turned in the seat and jerked Tom's Remington out of the gun rack. I shoved my door open and jumped out, crouching low. I snapped off the safety and levered a shell into the chamber. Using the Chevy as cover, I crept forward until I could see Gibbons, now advancing cautiously, raising the rifle to fire again, his gaze fixed on his target: the cop on the ground.

I stood up, locked the shotgun tight against my shoulder, and aimed, just as Gibbons caught sight of me and swung his gun around.

Without a word, I pulled the trigger. The Remington blasted, and Gibbons flew backward.

Ears ringing, I chambered another shell, hard and fast, and aimed again. Gibbons was flat on his back. He was moving, so I knew he wasn't dead—but he wasn't going anywhere anytime soon. Watching to see if anybody else would appear around the barn, I ran to him and retrieved his rifle, then back to Tom.

He had propped himself against the truck and was clutching his left upper arm. His uniform sleeve was bloody.

I knelt down. "Where did he hit you?"

"Upper arm," he said, between clenched teeth. "Did you get the son of a bitch?"

"He's down," I said. "He'll stay down for a while. Here's his rifle." I dropped the rifle on the ground and retrieved Tom's gun, which was several yards away. "I didn't see anybody else back there."

"Good girl," he grunted. He looked up at me. "Where's that blood coming from?"

"Blood? What blood?"

"All over your face."

"Ah." I put my left hand to my head, over my ear, and when I pulled it away, my fingers were dripping blood. I could feel the blood running down the side of my neck. My T-shirt was wet. Biting my lip, I felt again and found the shard of glass under my scalp. My hair was on fire.

I dropped my hand. "Not important," I said.

"Good." Tom closed his eyes. "Get on the radio. Roy's not far away. He can be here in two shakes."

No, not two shakes. And I didn't need to get on the radio. Roy was already pulling into the drive. In a moment, he was out of his squad car and bending over Tom.

"Somebody shot you over a damn *chicken*?" he asked incredulously.

"There's a pot grow out back somewhere," Tom said. "Check the shooter. He's on the ground by the barn."

Roy pulled his gun. "Did you get anybody else, or is he the only one?"

"I didn't get him," Tom growled through clenched teeth. "China did." He nodded at me. "If she hadn't shot him, he could have finished me off."

Roy looked at me. "You're bleeding," he said unnecessarily. He pulled his shoulder radio mic forward.

"Officer down," he said into it. "Three casualties. Medics and backup. *Now.*"

Chapter Fourteen

Pecan Springs, Texas
October 1888

 It was just before four when Annie saw Dr. Grogan stop his buggy in front of the Hunts' house next door.

The October afternoon was unusually warm, even for Texas. The sky was dark and a fitful wind was blowing. Storm clouds had piled up on the horizon to the north, and the taste of rain was in the air. The first cold front of autumn often announced itself with a storm.

Annie had not spoken to Adam since the evening he had brought her the rent. She had taken the train to San Antonio the day before and collected the money for her sales, so this morning she paid her girls and laid out the new orders. The San Antonio shop owners were eager for lace, and the orders ranged from six yards of narrow crocheted lace for chemises in a young lady's trousseau to a yard of Mrs. Jenson's fine bobbin lace for a collar—altogether, nearly twice as many orders as she'd ever gotten from the Austin shops.

Annie was glad to have so much good work to do. It took her mind off her last, heart-wrenching conversation with Adam, when they had agreed by mutual consent to end their affair. She knew it was best. Adam's obligations to his family, and especially to little Caroline, came first, ahead of everything else. She respected that. But the days since had been bleak and the nights black and empty, and she found herself often on the verge of tears. What's more, she couldn't help also hoping—perhaps more than just a little—that Delia might decide that she loved Mr. Simpson and wanted to make a home with him in Galveston, setting Adam free. But that was a cruel hope, and unworthy, and she suppressed it.

The matter of Mr. Simpson and Delia's visit to Mrs. Crow had been much on Annie's mind, however, especially after a brief over-the-hedge conversation with the Hunts' hired girl. As they were hanging out the wash a day or two after Adam's evening visit, Greta had remarked that Mrs. Hunt had sent her to pick up some ribbon at Purley's General Store, and she had discovered a pecan tree growing at the edge of the strip of woods behind the store, along the railroad track.

"The nuts ain't ready just yet," she said, pinning up a towel. "But I aim to be there with my bucket when they start to fall." She bent over the basket and took out a child's white cotton chemise, bordered with lace. Annie recognized it as the one she had made for Caroline's birthday. "My mama makes the best pecan pies," Greta added. "Better'n anybody."

Behind Purley's? Annie thought of the wild carrots that Mrs. Crow had told her about. Had Delia asked Greta to gather some seeds after she picked up the ribbon? Was that how the girl had chanced to discover the pecan tree? But Annie didn't want to know the answer to that question. She refused to think about *why* Delia might want the seeds.

So she only smiled and said, "Cooking for myself, I don't bake many pies. But I'd love to have your mama's recipe. Does she use molasses?"

Now, it was late afternoon, and the girls had finished their lacework and gone home, ahead of the threatening storm. Annie was tidying the workroom when she looked out the window and saw Dr. Grogan climbing out of his buggy and hurriedly tying his horse to a small tree in front of the house next door. Carrying his old black leather doctor's bag, he hastened up the walk.

Dr. Grogan was a fixture in Pecan Springs, and deeply respected. He had been practicing medicine there since the year Franklin Pierce was elected president, and everyone recognized him, even at a distance, by his lean, upright figure and his unruly mane of white hair. He had tended to Annie when she lost Douglas' baby, and he'd been sympathetic and kind. Usually, he moved at a deliberate speed that reflected his seventy-some years, but as she watched, he took the steps two at a time, obviously in a hurry.

Annie's first thought was of Caroline, and her mouth felt suddenly dry. Measles, chicken pox, scarlet fever—there were so many childhood diseases and they were always a dire threat. Perhaps she should go next door and offer to help. There might be something she could do, even if she only sat with the child and allowed Delia to get some rest.

But as she watched, apprehensive, Adam appeared from the direction of his store, striding fast toward the house. He, too, took the steps two at a time, his face a mask of deep concern. Deciding that she could not go next door now that Adam was there, Annie pulled up a chair near the window and sat down with her bobbin pillow, keeping an eye on the Hunts' house. When Adam left, she would go. A sick child was such a worry—Delia would need support.

The clock on the wall ticked monotonously, the sky grew even more menacing, and the wind stopped. It was almost as if the world were holding its breath, Annie thought. Then, finally, the front door opened and Dr. Grogan reappeared. He was walking slowly now, his

229

head bowed, his shoulders slumped. Without a thought, Annie dropped her work in the chair and ran out to the street, catching him as he was putting his doctor's bag into his buggy.

"Dr. Grogan," she said breathlessly, "I saw you and Adam—Mr. Hunt—going into the house a little while ago. How is she? Is there any way I can help?"

The doctor turned. "Oh, it's you, is it, Mrs. Duncan?" He peered at her over his gold-rimmed spectacles. "Haven't seen you for quite some time, have I? Since the baby, was it? I trust you're keeping well."

The wind was picking up again, and Annie's skirts whipped around her ankles. "Well enough, thank you," she said. The doctor was a talkative old man; he would run on forever if she didn't prompt him to the subject. "Please—how can I help?"

Dr. Grogan's mare nickered and shifted her weight, impatient to be home before the rain came. The old man patted her nose affectionately. "We'll be off in a minute, Gracie. We have another couple of stops before you can go to your barn." To Annie, he said, "Yes, yes, of course. Good of you to ask, my dear. You might take little Caroline to your house and give her some supper—perhaps keep her overnight, if that seems right to you. The hired girl has been sent home and I doubt whether Mr. Hunt will think of it. He's distraught. Quite naturally, of course, as anyone would be. And the child is old enough to know what's happened. She is very upset."

"Take . . . Caroline?" Annie faltered. "Then, it's not Caroline who is ill?"

"No, not the child. It's the mother." The old man fixed her with mild blue eyes. His tone was deeply sympathetic. "She's gone, my dear. Quite unexpectedly, I'm afraid. You've been neighbors for some years—I suppose you were close friends?"

Annie gaped at him stupidly, feeling her heart pounding in her chest. A few raindrops splattered on the shiny roof of Dr. Grogan's buggy, and she felt them wet against her face. "Delia is *gone*?" she asked, her voice rising. Had she gone off with Mr. Simpson? "Gone . . . where?"

"I don't wonder you ask, it's so surprising." The doctor began untying his horse. "Mrs. Hunt died a half hour ago. I should have been sent for earlier, but Mr. Hunt was at work the whole day and the stupid hired girl didn't have the brains to think of it." He tut-tutted. "Really, these girls are so careless. One would expect—" He broke off, frowning at her. "Are you all right, Mrs. Duncan?"

"Dead?" Annie whispered. She felt as if she had just been hit hard in the stomach. The world was whirling around her as if it were propelled by the rising wind. She grasped the buggy wheel to steady herself. "But that's not possible! We spoke just yesterday—" She stopped, trying to remember the last time she had seen Delia. Had it been at Mrs. Crow's? "No, not yesterday. Two days ago, perhaps." She put up a hand to push the hair out of her face.

"Mrs. Hunt had been ill since last night, I'm told," the doctor said. "But she'd had gastric problems earlier in the year, and that's what she thought it was at first. Nausea, vomiting, the usual abdominal pain. This morning she experienced cardiac symptoms. And then convulsions, seizures, coma." He shook his head. "All very typical, I'm afraid. Even if I'd been called earlier, I couldn't have done much to help. Of course, under the circumstances, there'll be an autopsy. We'll know more when that's done." There was a flicker of lightning to the east.

Convulsions, seizures, coma. Annie couldn't quite make sense of what the doctor was saying, but she managed to gasp, "Typical . . . of what?"

231

"Why, of hemlock poisoning," the doctor said, over the growl of thunder. "I've seen it before, you know. Probably every doctor in this country has seen it, one time or another. But I didn't have to guess. There was the evidence, right there in the drawer of Mrs. Hunt's bed-side table. An envelope with some of the seeds still in it. *Both* seeds. All I had to do was look at them and I knew what had happened."

"Both . . . seeds?" Annie whispered, trying to understand.

"Yes, both. But after all these years, I should have thought Mrs. Crow would be more careful." He was still frowning at Annie. "You're pale. Before you take little Caroline, I advise you to go home and pour yourself a stiff drink. You look like you can use it." He looked up at the sky as if he were surprised. "Why, bless me, I believe it's going to rain."

"Wait, please," Annie said, putting out her hand. "I don't under-stand. Hemlock poisoning? How is that possible? And what does Mrs. Crow have to do with it?"

The doctor climbed into the buggy and picked up the reins. "Be-cause Mrs. Crow is the one who supplies the local ladies with wild carrot seeds—as a contraceptive, you know." He frowned. "The enve-lope in Mrs. Hunt's drawer had Mrs. Crow's name on it. The old lady must have somehow gathered poison hemlock seeds by mistake. They look quite similar to the untrained eye, although if you know what you're doing, it's not hard to tell the two apart. Mrs. Crow is quite experienced. She should *not* have confused the plants."

"Wild carrot?" Annie whispered. And then, suddenly, she under-stood. She had heard the tales: poison hemlock was sometimes mis-taken for wild carrot, with fatal results. But it was usually the leaves and the roots that people ate. In fact, she had read of it not long before, in the *Austin Weekly Statesman*. A lady in East Texas had found wild hemlock growing in her yard and served up the frilly green leaves as a salad. Her error had killed her, and her husband had barely survived.

"Yes, wild carrot." Dr. Grogan lifted the reins. "I need to fetch Sheriff Atkins. And then we'll go see Mrs. Crow." He frowned darkly. "I really would not have thought that the old lady could be so careless. Perhaps she needs new spectacles."

"Please *wait!*" Annie cried breathlessly. "It wasn't Mrs. Crow's mistake, Dr. Grogan! She didn't give Delia those seeds. She didn't *have* any! Delia sent—"

But her words were lost in a sharp crack of lightning, followed by a sudden loud thunderclap. Startled, Gracie jerked and began to move forward. The doctor raised his voice. "You be sure and get that little girl, Mrs. Duncan. I don't think her father is in any shape to handle the child tonight."

As the wind whipped her hair and her skirts, Annie stood watching the old man drive away, her heart thudding hard in her chest. She was thinking that she knew two things with certainty. First, that Mrs. Crow had *not* given Delia the seeds that killed her. And second, that Delia had sent her hired girl on an errand to Purley's, where the wild carrots—and the wild hemlock—were growing in the same empty lot.

And there was a third thing, although Annie shuddered when she thought of it. Mr. Simpson had been in Pecan Springs for several days. Men often boasted about their conquests, especially when they had too much to drink. What if he had inadvertently let it slip in one of the many saloons in Pecan Springs that he had come to town to see Delia Hunt? What if he had bragged that they were engaged in a dalliance? Hearing that, would people think that Adam—

The wind was suddenly cold and the rain began to pelt down. As

Annie ran for the shelter of the house, a swirl of questions whirled like dry leaves through her mind.

What if word got around that Simpson and Adam's wife had been having an affair? Wouldn't they believe that Adam was *jealous*? Would they whisper that jealousy was a powerful motive for murder?

And that those fatal seeds were the perfect murder weapon?

WHEN the doctor and Sheriff Atkins drove up in front of Mrs. Crow's a half hour later, Annie was standing beneath her umbrella, waiting for them. The rain had diminished to a fine drizzle, and by this time, she had recovered her breath and was filled with a steely determination. She was going to tell them what she knew. And they were going to listen—*before* they accused Mrs. Crow, or Adam, of poisoning Delia Hunt.

And listen they did, perhaps persuaded by the look on Annie's face and the combative set to her shoulders. Doctor Grogan and the sheriff, a man in his late forties, with a badge pinned to his vest and a gun on his hip, stepped down from the doctor's buggy and heard her out. It took Annie only a few minutes to relate what Greta had told her about finding the pecan tree behind Purley's, where the wild carrot and the poison hemlock were said to grow in the same vacant lot.

At the end, she said, "I think this was a terrible accident. I believe Mrs. Hunt sent Greta to get those seeds. And I doubt if she cautioned Greta about those plants—or that if she did, Greta could tell them apart. Apparently even experienced people can be fooled."

The sheriff considered this for a moment. "Thank you, Mrs. Duncan. That casts a somewhat different light on the matter." He turned to the doctor, who was tying up his horse. "Agree, Grogan?"

"It's entirely possible," the doctor said. "I would be frankly relieved to discover that Mrs. Crow isn't responsible for Mrs. Hunt's death. But let's hear what she has to say before we talk to the hired girl."

"Yes, the girl." The sheriff tipped up the brim of his Stetson. "What did you say her name was, Mrs. Duncan?"

"Greta is the only name I know," Annie said.

"Greta Higgens," the doctor said. "Tom Higgens' oldest daughter. Lives with her mother on the other side of the tracks." He drew his brows together. "I did think it was a bit odd that she didn't send for me right away when Mrs. Hunt began having convulsions. Not that I could have done the poor lady much good," he added thoughtfully. "But I wondered why she delayed. The girl, I mean."

Annie took a deep breath. Yes, Greta could have accidentally confused the two plants. But what if it wasn't an accident? What if she had done it *deliberately*? She hated the thought, but Delia was dead and a little girl was left without a mother. Out of fairness, the whole story had to be told, no matter how unpleasant it was.

"There's something else," she said, choosing her words carefully. "I think Greta found Mrs. Hunt to be a demanding mistress. I sometimes heard her—Mrs. Hunt, that is—voicing her displeasure with the girl's work. Other neighbors might have heard it, too," she said, not wanting to be the only one raising the issue.

"I see." The sheriff gave her a searching look. "Were there any physical blows that you know of?"

"It's possible," Annie said. By now, she was feeling quite wretched. What if poor Greta was blameless, and she was casting suspicion on an innocent young woman? "I saw a fresh bruise on her face once. I didn't ask her what caused it."

The sheriff tipped his hat. "Thank you, Mrs. Duncan. You've been helpful. We'll talk to the girl as soon as we've heard what Mrs. Crow has to say."

"You're welcome," Annie said. "Now, if you'll excuse me, I'm going to see if Caroline will come home with me for supper, and spend the night."

The doctor nodded, pleased. "You do that, Mrs. Duncan. I'll be performing the autopsy in the morning, so the undertaker's helpers will come for Mrs. Hunt's body shortly. It would be good if the child wasn't there to see her mother being taken away."

As it turned out, Annie made supper for both Caroline and Adam—gingerbread pancakes, shaped like gingerbread men, because that's what the little girl asked for. Caroline was pale and spent from crying. But she brightened up over supper and was pleased when her father sat down in Annie's rocking chair, took her in his lap, and told her a story about his growing-up years out on Limekiln Road, just west of Pecan Springs. When she fell asleep, he kissed her and put her down in a little bed of soft quilts that Annie made on the floor, next to her own bed.

Afterward, Adam came into the kitchen, and Annie poured him a cup of strong coffee. "Please, sit down," she said. With Caroline there, they hadn't had a chance to talk at supper and there were things she needed to know.

He pulled out a chair. "I can't stay long. I have to go to the depot and telegraph Delia's sister. It's going to be a terrible shock to her. I'm sure she'll want to help arrange the . . ." His voice faltered. "The funeral." His face was drawn and his eyes seemed sunken in his face. "I'm going to stop at the hotel, too."

Annie stared at him. "Mr. Simpson isn't still in town, is he?"

"I don't think so. But there should be an address for him in the hotel register. I think he ought to know that Delia has died." He spoke somberly. "Their relationship was more than just friendly, Annie."

Annie stared at him. "How can you know? Did Delia tell you so?"

"I have the letter he wrote to her the day he brought the chocolates." Adam clasped his hands around his coffee cup. "Greta said she found it in a wastebasket, although I'm sure she stole it." He looked away. "She gave it to me."

"*Gave* it to you?" Annie bit her lip, thinking that Greta must have hated her mistress even more than she had guessed. "What does it say?"

"Enough so that I can piece together the rest of the story. They were seeing each other regularly whenever Delia went to Galveston. They had obviously been intimate for some time. What's more, Delia's sister knew it, and helped Simpson." He shook his head. "Clarissa never thought I was good enough for Delia."

"Intimate!" Annie stared at him, her eyes wide. But she couldn't blame Delia and Mr. Simpson for doing the same thing that she and Adam had done. Perhaps they had been deeply in love—and now Delia was dead. What would Mr. Simpson say when he got the news? How would he *feel*?

She looked back down at her cup. "Did Dr. Grogan tell you how Delia died?"

Adam nodded. "Poison hemlock seeds. The doctor thinks Mrs. Crow gave them to her accidentally, instead of wild carrot. He blames the old lady for carelessness." His eyes met hers. "Delia wasn't using those seeds on my account, I promise you, Annie. But of course, I couldn't tell that to the doctor. I'm sure he assumes that Delia and I were sleeping together. I didn't want him to think that she might be—" He broke off, shaking his head. "Everything is all mixed up. It's a mess."

There were so many things that needed to be said that Annie almost didn't know where to start. She took a deep breath. "Mrs. Crow had nothing to do with it, Adam. She didn't *have* any seeds, remember? She told Delia where to find them, in the empty lot behind Purley's. Delia sent Greta to Purley's for ribbons, and I think she ordered her to gather the seeds while she was there." Quickly, she reported her over-the-hedge conversation with Greta, ending with, "Mrs. Crow told me that wild hemlock was growing in that area as well, and warned me to be careful. She said she told Delia the same thing. But Delia may not have cautioned Greta, or Greta may not have known how to tell the difference between the two plants. She might have made a mistake."

And then Adam asked the same question Annie had asked herself. "But what if it wasn't an accident? What if she did it on purpose?"

There was a long silence. The kerosene lamp over the kitchen table burned with a steady flame. In the distance, Annie heard the mournful wail of the steam whistle as the railroad train neared the depot on its late-night run south to San Antonio.

"I've thought about that, too." Annie bit her lip. "I know that Delia wasn't very kind to her. I once saw a bruise on the girl's face after an especially loud exchange."

"Delia outright abused her," Adam said flatly. He rubbed his hand along his jaw. After a moment, he added, "If Greta mixed up those seeds deliberately, she might have had another motive."

"*Another* motive?"

Adam nodded. "If my wife was cruel to her when I was around, I stepped in. Once, I kept Delia from slapping her." He slid Annie a guilty look. "Greta misinterpreted that. She thought I had a more personal reason. That I . . . that I liked her. More than that, maybe."

With a start, Annie remembered the girl's bright eyes and eager expression when she talked about Adam. "Did she tell you that? How do you know?"

"She made her feelings clear the night she gave me the letter. She was . . . well, *seductive* is the only word I can think of. I was caught off guard. I wanted to get that letter away from her because I couldn't be sure how she might use it. I didn't want to reject her outright and send her away in a huff. So I . . . well, I played along." He gave Annie a straight, hard look. "But I was only trying to make Delia lay off the girl, Annie—I swear it. I have no romantic feelings toward Greta. Anything else is a product of her imagination."

"I believe you," Annie assured him. "I told both the doctor and the sheriff that Mrs. Crow had nothing to do with it, and that Delia may have sent Greta to collect the seeds. I also told them that Greta wasn't happy with the way Delia was treating her." She took a breath. "You need to tell the sheriff that Greta imagined that you were attracted to her, Adam. That could be another reason for her doing it."

"No!" Adam shook his head firmly. "If I tell him that, I'll have to tell him about the letter Greta gave me—and what's in it. Don't you see how complicated this is, Annie? If the sheriff decides that my wife was murdered, Greta isn't the only one who will be under suspicion."

"Don't, Adam." Annie put her hands over her ears. "Please, please don't."

He leaned forward, his eyes on hers. "I had an opportunity, too, you know. My store is next door to Purley's. I could simply step out my back door, gather some of those poison hemlock seeds, and put them in the envelope in the drawer of the table beside Delia's bed. The letter from Simpson—and the fact that I have it—gives me plenty of reason to poison my wife."

"I don't see how," Annie protested helplessly. "You didn't know anything about the hemlock seeds—about how Delia died, I mean—until the doctor told you."

"That's only my say-so," Adam said. "I could just as easily be lying." His voice was flat, expressionless. "What's more, our relationship may come out. Yours and mine. The other night in the stable, Greta gave me to understand that she knows about us—at least, that she knows I'd been coming to see you. She wasn't going to say anything to Delia because you've been a friend to her. But if she's pushed, maybe she'll change her mind. If she tells them about Simpson's letter . . ." He shoved his chair back and stood up. "I have to go to the telegraph office, Annie. Clarissa needs to know what's happened. I'm sure she'll get on the first train out of Galveston tomorrow."

Annie stood, too, and went to the kitchen door with him. "I'll be glad to keep Caroline here, Adam. She's no bother at all, and she likes to play at making lace with the girls in the workroom." She managed a smile. "Actually, she's quite good. Her little fingers are nimble, and she understands the patterns."

"Could you?" He sounded relieved. "That would be a big help. I'm going to give Greta a couple of weeks' salary and let her go. Now that I'm alone in the house, it's not a good idea to have her around." He put his hands on her shoulders. "The next few weeks are going to be hell, Annie. But we'll come through it somehow, I promise you. Don't give up heart."

He bent and kissed her quickly and left.

* * *

ADAM thought he was prepared for what was to come, but he could not have been more wrong.

Caroline was staying with Annie, and Adam had closed his tack and feed store until after Delia's funeral. Clarissa was to arrive on the evening train, and he would meet her at the station. He had already made the necessary arrangements with Lloyd Butler, the local under-taker, and Reverend Childers, the pastor at the Congregational church Delia had sometimes attended. But the funeral couldn't take place until Dr. Grogan completed the autopsy and released Delia's body for burial. And he still hadn't been able to get in touch with Simpson. The man seemed to have disappeared.

Burial. Adam still couldn't quite believe what had happened. He and Delia had not made each other happy in recent years, but she was still his wife, and the thought that he was about to bury a beautiful young woman whom he had once loved filled him with a deep, dark ache that seemed to invade his very bones. Why had this happened? *How* had it happened?

This afternoon, he was wandering aimlessly around the house, looking sadly at Delia's decorative touches—doilies, embroidered pil-lows, pictures on the walls—remembering the happy times of their marriage, and regretting his many shortcomings as a husband. Per-haps, if he had paid her the attention she needed, she wouldn't have fallen for Simpson. If he had loved her more, spent more time with—

His guilty reflections were interrupted by a knock at the front door, and he opened it to Dr. Grogan.

"Good afternoon, Adam," the doctor said. "If you have a moment..."

"By all means," Adam replied. "Come in, Grogan. There's coffee in the kitchen." He and the doctor had a friendly acquaintance that went back to Adam's mother's last illness some ten years before, when the doctor had come to see her almost every day for a month.

The old man followed Adam to the kitchen, where he sat down at the oilcloth-covered kitchen table and hung his brown derby hat on the back of his chair. He was silent while Adam filled their cups and took the chair across the table from him. Finally, he spoke.

"I finished your wife's autopsy a little while ago, Adam." There was a deep sympathy in his faded blue eyes. "Given the physical evidence and the seeds I found in the drawer beside her bed, I've listed the cause of death as hemlock poisoning." He paused and added, "In my opinion, the poisoning was accidental. That's what I put on the death certificate."

Adam tried to hide the flood of relief he felt at the word *accidental*. "Hemlock," he muttered. "Of all the crazy things in this world . . ."

"I understand," the doctor said. "It's a rather unusual situation. But I found something else, too, and I thought you'd want to know about it—if you don't already." He cocked his head, studying Adam. "Your wife was pregnant."

"Pregnant!" Adam stared at him. "But that's impossible! We hadn't . . . I mean, she—" He stopped. Of course it was possible.

"I take it you didn't know, then," the doctor said softly, pityingly. "Well, I'm sorry to be the one to tell you. It's a sad thing to lose a wife and a child, both at the same time. But it happens, you know. Your neighbor, Mrs. Duncan, lost her husband and baby son on a single day and has managed to cope. You must be as brave as she."

"How far—" Adam cleared his throat and tried again. "How far along was she?"

"It's a little hard to be sure, but I'd say, oh, about nine or ten weeks."

Adam pulled in his breath. "Nine or ten weeks?"

"Ten at the outside." The old man picked up his coffee cup and took a drink, then set it down. His voice was measured. "According to Mrs. Crow, Mrs. Hunt wasn't eager to have another child and was in the regular habit of taking wild carrot seeds. They're a fairly reliable contraceptive, and many women depend on them. But nothing is a hundred percent. Mistakes happen all the time. I know," he added wryly. "I deliver the results."

Nine or ten weeks. Adam scarcely heard what the doctor was saying. He was flipping rapidly through a mental calendar. He and Delia hadn't slept together for a couple of weeks before she left for Galveston. That was the middle of July, and she had been gone for seven weeks—no, eight, wasn't it? It was now early October, which made it . . . thirteen weeks, he thought. Well, that made it certain, although he didn't intend to let Dr. Grogan in on the secret. He wasn't the father of Delia's baby.

But the calendar in his mind raised another question. "Ten weeks," he said. "I'm certainly no expert on women, Dr. Grogan. Delia and I . . . we didn't talk much about such things. But in ten weeks, she would have missed two of her monthlies, wouldn't she? Shouldn't she have known—or at least suspected—that she was pregnant?" He paused, then spit out the rest of his question. "And if she knew, why in the hell was she bothering with a contraceptive?"

The doctor looked troubled. "That was my thought, too, Adam. In my experience, a married woman—especially a woman who doesn't want another child—keeps her eye on the calendar. She might not notice when she misses one monthly, but missing the second gets her attention." He pulled a cigar out of his breast pocket and studied the end of it critically. "I've given some thought to this in the past hour or two. I'm sorry to say that it's my opinion that Mrs. Hunt took those seeds, not as a contraceptive, but as an abortifacient."

Adam blinked. "Abort—"

"Yes. Abortifacient, or abortivant, if you prefer. An agent used to intentionally cause an abortion." Grogan lit his cigar. "It appears that your wife realized she was pregnant and felt the need to end it. For the purpose, she used what she thought was wild carrot, but she could have used other herbs, as well. Tansy, rue, thyme, pennyroyal, cotton root, epazote. In these modern days, there are also quite a few so-called patent medicines that may serve the purpose, if a woman doesn't have access to herbs. Lydia Pinkham's, for instance. But also Portuguese Female Pills, Hardy's Woman's Friend, Pennyroyal Pills, and a dozen others."

"Lydia Pinkham's." Adam tapped a finger on the table, remembering. "I've seen bottles of this in Delia's medicine cupboard, but I thought it was just a sort of general tonic. You're telling me that it's . . . it's used to cause abortions?" He shook his head, wondering. How many times had his wife conceived—and managed to end it—over the years since Caroline's birth? And he'd been completely in the dark.

"Yes," Grogan replied, a cloud of blue smoke wreathing his gray hair. "And the others, too. I'm sure you've seen the advertisements. They're in every newspaper, and the medicines are remarkably popular. Some are more effective than others, of course. And some—like the Cherokee Pills for Females—include the specific direction that, for greater effectiveness, the pills should be taken together with an herbal tea, such as tansy, rue, or thyme. They seldom say explicitly that these are abortifacients—although I recently saw one that warned pregnant women against taking it, for a 'miscarriage will certainly ensue.'" He smiled. "The message is clear, isn't it? If you want to miscarry, take this pill."

Adam stared at him, thinking that women shared a whole world of information from which—as a man—he was excluded. "These . . . medicines actually *work*? And the plants?"

"They can, when they're taken early. That's why they are so popular. Women talk among themselves, you know. They share information about what's effective and what isn't." The doctor paused and looked at Adam, one eyebrow raised. When Adam did not reply, he went on. "In this case, I believe your wife intended to use wild carrot to abort her pregnancy, so she took quite a large dose. It would most likely have been effective, too. Unfortunately . . ." He pulled on his cigar. "She got hold of the wrong plant."

Adam thought of Simpson. While the letter made it clear that he and Delia had been lovers, Simpson hadn't mentioned the pregnancy in his letter, so he must not have known about it. Delia probably had no more wish to bear her lover's child than her husband's, so she had decided to abort it. Or maybe— He swallowed. Maybe Simpson had told her to get rid of the baby. Either way, it was unconscionable. Under his breath, he said, "How she thought she could live with herself—"

"Don't take it that way, my boy." The old man gave him a deeply sympathetic look. "Don't blame her, please. We have it easy, we men. We take our pleasure, but we don't have to endure the consequences. Giving birth is called 'labor' for a reason, you know. You might find it easier to forgive your wife if you could see what I see every day— women having babies, one after another, and having the worst hard time you can imagine." He scratched his head. "I've heard it said that if men had babies, there wouldn't *be* any babies. I can't quarrel with that. It's not an experience I would voluntarily undergo. Nor would you, I wager."

Adam let the silence lengthen. At last he said, "So we know *why* Delia took the seeds that killed her. Has anybody figured out where she got them? Mrs. Duncan, next door, said she didn't believe they came from Mrs. Crow." He got up to get a saucer for Grogan's cigar ash, hoping the doctor hadn't noticed the softening in his voice when he spoke Annie's name.

If Grogan heard, he gave no evidence. He tapped his ash into the saucer Adam set in front of him. "Your neighbor is correct, as I understand it," he said. "I believe I should let the sheriff fill you in on that, though. I'm not sure—"

"Don't make me wait, Grogan," Adam said gruffly. "You said it was an accident. So tell me the rest of it."

For a moment, he thought the old man wasn't going to answer. Then he let out a long breath and said, "It appears that your hired girl was the one who made the mistake. The girl told Sheriff Atkins that your wife sent her to the empty lot behind Purley's, where she would find a stand of wild carrot, with seeds ready to gather. Unfortunately, there was also some poison hemlock growing nearby. I know, for I've just come from there. I saw the plants myself. To the unskilled eye, the two species look very much alike, as do the dry seeds. And once they've been gathered, it's hard to see the difference without a magnifying glass." In a different tone, he added, "I've told the sheriff to send someone out there to destroy the hemlock. I don't want to see any more such accidental deaths."

But Adam persisted. "Greta, as she was gathering the seeds, did she know what to look for? Was she aware that this other plant, this poison hemlock, was growing there, too?"

The doctor puffed on his cigar in silence for a moment. "She says not, Adam. She told the sheriff that Mrs. Hunt said nothing about there being any 'bad' plants there. Your wife told Greta to buy two yards of pink ribbon for her at Purley's, then go to the vacant lot behind the store and gather some seeds from the plants there. She showed the girl the few seeds she had, as an example, and gave her a paper bag to put them in. Greta simply followed instructions, she says. She gave the seeds to Mrs. Hunt. And that's all she knows—or will say. She's distraught, of course."

Suddenly aware that he was holding his breath, Adam let it out. "And you believe her?"

The doctor met his eyes. "I don't know. I don't profess to understand all that goes on in the human heart. But whether I believe her or not is irrelevant. The girl may not have liked her mistress very much. She may even have resented her and wished to do her harm. But to arrest and charge her, Sheriff Atkins must have evidence that she deliberately gathered the wrong seeds and gave them to your wife with the *intention* of poisoning her. There simply is no such evidence."

"So she's not going to be charged," Adam said, trying to hide the new surge of relief he felt. And it appeared that there was no indication that *he* was suspected of having something to do with his wife's death.

"As I understand it, no," the doctor said. He reached into his waistcoat pocket and took out his watch. "It's late," he said. "Mrs. Harrison is expected to deliver this evening. I must be on my way." He finished his coffee and stood up, holding out his hand. "I'm sorry to have been the bearer of such terrible news, Adam."

Adam shook his hand, managing a crooked smile. "I suppose it's part of your job, isn't it, Grogan?"

"Too often, I'm afraid," the doctor said ruefully. He put on his hat. "Far too often."

Adam walked with the doctor to the front door and stood on the porch, his hands in his pockets, watching the old man trudge out to his buggy. When he had driven off down Crockett Street, Adam turned toward the house next door. Across the garden and through the workroom window, he could see Annie moving around, see his daughter, seated, with a piece of needlework in her lap. Annie was bending over her chair, one hand on the child's shoulder, showing her how to do something. Caroline looked up at her and smiled, and Annie smoothed her hair.

Adam watched silently. Caroline would miss her mother. Yes, that was natural and right. But time would dull that loss, and Annie would love the little girl and care for her as if she were her very own. He, too, would miss Delia—or rather, would miss the Delia he had imagined was true and faithful to him, and try to forget that she had ever been anything other. He could never forget that he had betrayed her, and never forgive himself. But he had to carry on, for Caroline's sake. And there was something to hope for.

After a respectable period of mourning, he would ask Annie to marry him, and they would have a new life together. Given all that had happened, it couldn't be as simple as that, could it?

Could it?

Chapter Fifteen

Botanists tell us that the tiny red flower in the center of the blossom of Queen Anne's lace (*Daucus carota*, aka wild carrot) is there to attract pollinators. But storytellers have other explanations. Some say it is a drop of blood from the royal finger, pricked when the queen was making lace. Others say it represents a sapphire from Queen Anne's crown, lost when she was walking in her garden.

But still others (and more ominously) say that this tiny red floret is the devil's spit and that the blossom carries a curse. If you pick it and take it indoors, your mother will die. This dire warning explains two of the plant's folk names: Mother-May-Die and Stepmother's Blessing. These names may also be the remnants of an oral tradition that cautioned women against the careless use of seeds thought to be wild carrot and taken as a contraceptive or an abortifacient, because they could be confused with the deadly seeds of poison hemlock.

"Anne's Flower"
China Bayles
Pecan Springs Enterprise

"Omigod," Ruby breathed, when I called her from the hospital to tell her that I wouldn't be able to get to the shop until later in the day. "You really *shot* somebody, China? Over a couple of *chickens*?" She sucked in her breath and rattled on. "You're okay? You're not hurt?" Another breath, then, anxious: "They're not going to throw you in jail, are they?"

"Yes, I'm okay," I said, omitting the bloody details. "Yes, I shot somebody, but I didn't kill him. No, it wasn't over chickens. And no, they're not going to throw me in jail—at least, not if I've got anything to say about it. But I have to meet with the sheriff's officer-involved-shooting team. And that may take a while."

A twelve-gauge shotgun packs a wallop, even at fifteen yards, so my victim's wounds were not inconsequential. After the surgeon finished digging nine double-ought buckshot pellets out of his belly and patching the holes, Gibbons would be charged with aggravated assault of a police officer, assault with a deadly weapon, possession and cultivation of marijuana, and the felony theft of two roosters. There would probably be more charges after the deputies finished searching the premises. A man who steals chickens probably has a few other violations under his belt. They would throw the book at him.

Thankfully, the officer involved in the shooting—Tom Banner—was alive to back up my account of what had happened. The bullet had torn through his upper arm, shredding the muscle and just missing an artery. In fact, he was in the curtained ER cubicle next to me, where the doctors were working on him while I (less seriously injured) waited in the adjoining cubicle. Somebody had given me a couple of thick gauze pads and I was holding them to my head, trying to stop the bleeding—without much success. My blood-soaked T-shirt was already ruined, of course.

Finally, a young doctor came in. "Looks like you've got a gusher," he said, sounding mildly interested.

"Glass splinter," I said.

The doctor parted my hair and took a look. "Glass *spike*," he said. "How do you feel about brain surgery?"

"Just take it out, Hawkeye," I gritted.

"You need to work on your sense of humor," the doctor said cheerfully, and patted my arm.

My scalp didn't hurt as much after the local went to work, but it took a while to pull out the shard (about the size of a shark's tooth), disinfect the wound, and sew it shut. The whole operation cost me twelve stitches and an earmuff-sized patch of hair on the side of my head, covered by an earmuff-sized bandage, held on by wraparound gauze. I didn't ask for a mirror.

When the doctor was finished, two sheriff's deputies from the officer-involved team escorted me to a small conference room where somebody fetched me a cup of cafeteria coffee and the three of us sat around a table. The Adams County sheriff, Curt Chambers, is one of McQuaid's fishing buddies—law enforcement types tend to stick together—but these two were men I didn't know.

The situation required some explaining, because this particular officer-involved shooting involved a civilian: me. Tom hadn't had time to get a shot off. The deputies were carefully polite and coolly professional, one asking questions and recording the interview, the other taking notes. I mentally lawyered up and walked them through the somewhat bizarre steps that had led to the exchange of gunfire: discovering the chicken theft at the fairgrounds and identifying the thief by the dropped badge and the images on the thumb drive from Caitie's camera; getting the address from the fairground office and the warrant from JP Maude Porterfield; finding and repossessing the roosters and discovering the marijuana; and being fired on. The interview felt rather déjà vu, although when I had sat in on similar interrogations, I had been the shooter's counsel, not the shooter. I knew it was routine, of course—it had to be done, even though I had a pounding headache, the local was beginning to wear off, and I might not be entirely coherent.

But I also knew that I had to make the case that I had fired on Dana Gibbons in order to protect the officer Gibbons had fired on—and that my action had been necessary and unavoidable. The team would interview Tom, then compare our stories and weigh both against the forensic and ballistic reports and the accounts of the other officers on the scene. The full report would go to the Adams County district attorney for review and possibly—since I was a civilian ride-along with a reserve deputy on a criminal investigation—to a grand jury. I expected that, in the end, the shooting would be ruled justified and I could get on with my life. Until then . . . well, I was just a little nervous. Understandably nervous.

Roy, Tom's partner, was waiting outside the conference room when the deputies were finished grilling me, and he filled me in on what they had found at the pot farm.

"Pretty impressive operation," he said. "A half acre at least, of high-yield plants. This isn't something Gibbons was doing on his own. We've got the place staked out, so we can pick up the others who were helping him tend the crop as they show up. And in the house, we found a laptop and some emails that may take us to the distribution network Gibbons was plugged into. So you and Tom didn't just find the farm. You opened a path for hitting the hub. The sheriff is calling in the Rangers and the feds to move the investigation forward. He needs to get a lid on it fast, before word gets out about this morning's bust. The media will be on this like ducks on a June bug."

I didn't doubt that. "Have you seen Tom?" I asked urgently. "Is he going to be okay?"

Ray nodded toward the nurses' station. "Yeah. He's tough. That red-haired nurse will tell you where he is. His wife's with him, but I'm sure he'll want to see you."

Sylvia was sitting beside Tom's bed when I went into the room. She launched herself out of her chair and wrapped her arms around me in a fervent embrace.

"I can't imagine what would have happened if you hadn't been there, China," she said. "That man could have killed Tom."

"Nah," I said. "Not a chance."

"Believe it." Tom's voice was slurred—painkillers, I thought—and I had to lean close to make out the words. "Gibbons knocked me down and my gun flew out of my hand, out of reach. He would have finished me off if you hadn't taken him out."

"If you say so. I give up." I held up both hands in a gesture of surrender. "I never argue with a cop. Even one who is flat on his back."

AND then there was Jessica. She was waiting for me in the hall when I left Tom's room.

"Holy cow," she said, eyeing my bandage and my T-shirt, soaked with blood and plastered to me. "What the hell happened to *you*?"

"Old war wound," I said. "Say, could you give me a ride back to the fairgrounds? I need to pick up my car. And check in on some chickens."

"I'll give you a ride if you'll give me the story," Jessica said.

"I don't know what Sheriff Chambers is ready to release," I said, frowning. "I understand he wants to keep a lid on this."

"I've already talked to the sheriff," she said. "He's laid down the law about what goes into print until their investigation is further along. But he's cleared your part of the story, as long as I don't get into who and where, and Hark wants it for the next edition. So what's this business about Caitie's rooster getting kidnapped?"

I grunted. "Word gets around fast."

Jessica shook her head. "Superior investigative reporting. Dug it out all by myself, clue by clue. And I heard that you shot a guy to keep him from killing a cop. True?"

"You don't need my story," I said. "You've already got it."

"Yeah, the outline. Now I need the gory details." She took my arm. "Come on. I'll drive you to the fairgrounds while you fill in the gaps."

ONE of the deputies had returned the roosters to their cages in the poultry tent, so they were safe—but a sorry sight. Extra Crispy had sustained a nasty cut to his comb and was missing a patch of breast feathers the size of a half-dollar. Blackheart's tail looked as if it had been chewed on by a raccoon and one foot was bloody. Both were dusty and smeared with poopee. And the judges were just entering the tent to begin their rounds.

"Poor things," Jessica murmured, snapping their pictures. "They look like they've been through the wars."

"Give me your pen and a page of your notebook," I said. I wrote down a two-sentence summary of the morning's extracurricular activities and clipped it to Extra Crispy's cage. I wanted the judges to know why the two roosters were not in the tip-top form they'd been in when they were entered. "Let's get out of here," I said. "I can't go to the shop in this bloody T-shirt. I've got to go home and shower and change into clean clothes."

"Not just yet," Jessica said. "Stand right there, beside those roosters. I want to get a photo of you."

"Hey, no!" I protested. I put my hand up to the bandage over my ear, where my hair was caked with blood. "I'm a complete mess."

"Of course you're a mess," Jessica said gleefully. "That's what makes this such a terrific story. Say *Extra Crispy.*"

"You are a mess, China." Ruby patted my arm sympathetically. "With that gauze wrapped around your head, you look like a mummy. Sort of."

"If you think this is bad, you should have seen me before I showered and changed. And put on fresh gauze." I smothered a giddy giggle. "The bad guy looks a heckuva lot worse, though. And Tom Banner isn't all that great, either. Not to mention the roosters. It was a rough morning for all concerned."

"Tell me," Ruby commanded. "From the beginning."

It was nearly two o'clock. The lunch crowd was gone, and Ruby and I were having a very late lunch in the tearoom—grilled cheese sandwiches, a couple of dill spears, a scoop of chicken salad, and iced hibiscus tea—while Cass finished up in the kitchen and Jenna tended to the shops. It had been a long and strenuous morning, and breakfast was ancient history. I was hungry.

I had told the story several times already, so it went pretty fast, even pausing for one or two applause lines. "If I hadn't shot Gibbons," I concluded, "he might have killed Tom. And once he'd done that, he had every reason to kill me, too." I could still hear the *crack!* of the bullet that had shattered Tom's windshield and feel the sharp splinters of flying glass. "I've never been crazy about guns. But McQuaid thinks

I should know how to handle a shotgun, so I owe him for making me practice."

"Did you . . ." Ruby swallowed. "Did you *mean* to kill him?"

She had asked one of the most important questions a defense attorney would ask a client he had allowed to take the stand. "I meant to put him out of operation," I said. "If I had meant to kill him, I would have aimed higher." Which suggested, of course, that I had controlled my aim. Which was not necessarily the case. I'd been pretty nervous when I fired that gun.

Ruby picked up her iced tea. "And all this happened because of a couple of roosters," she said wonderingly.

"Not really." I put down my fork and pushed my plate away. "Tom and I were there because of the theft of the chickens, of course—which turned out to be a good thing."

"Really? A good thing?"

"Well, sure. I hate to say this, because I know how upset Caitie will be when she hears what happened to Extra Crispy. Both he and the black rooster are out of the running for a blue ribbon now, I'm afraid." I picked up the pitcher and poured myself another glass of icy hibiscus tea. "But if Gibbons hadn't stolen those roosters, Tom and I would never have followed the trail out to his place. He could still be contentedly tending his half acre of weed."

Ruby pursed her lips. "That sounds like a lot of marijuana. How much is it worth?"

"It's a sizable crop. I've read that an outdoor grower can put some five thousand plants on a half acre, with an average yield of a pound of saleable pot from each plant. If it's selling for two hundred and eighty dollars an ounce, that's a street value of twenty-two million dollars. The grower doesn't get all of that, of course. He's working for somebody. And there's a markup along the distribution chain."

"But still," Ruby said. "That's a *bushel* of money."

"And that's just one season," I said. "Next spring, he could start all over again." In fact, he probably would have, reasoning that if his little farm hadn't been discovered this year, it would be safe next year, too. And he already had the space and the equipment—that tractor, for instance.

"But you put him out of business."

"His farming days are over." I said it with special relish and leaned back in my chair. "The state of Texas has zero patience with guys who try to kill cops."

Ruby was shaking her head. "I still don't understand why he stole the chickens. Isn't that a little out of character for somebody who's into drugs?"

"He might not have been personally into drugs, Ruby. He obviously had homestead interests on the side. It's my guess that he stole the black rooster so he could produce and sell those rare Ayam Cemani chickens—which are going for exorbitant prices. He raises Angora rabbits, as well. He had several hutches in the barn, and it turns out that he entered two French Angoras at the fair. One of them got a blue ribbon." That information had come to me from Jessica, who thought it was a nicely ironic touch for her rooster-napping story, which would run in the next day's paper (minus the name and address of the offender, of course). "I think he's a homesteader who was looking for a quick cash crop. An easy way to make money."

"Well, it's good that you got the chickens back," Ruby said.

"Yeah. They're back in the poultry tent. I left a note on the cages to explain what happened, but that won't make any difference to the judges." I chuckled wryly. "I don't think they have a prize category for roosters that were taken hostage."

"Caitie will be disappointed," Ruby said. "But not as much as she'd be if Extra Crispy had been . . . well, fried."

"Please." I shuddered. "Let's not go there."

"Does she know what happened?"

"Not yet. She's at play rehearsal today. I'm picking her up after work and we'll drive out to the fairgrounds then." I changed the subject. "Anything interesting happen here?"

"Mostly just the usual." Ruby frowned. "But that doorbell of yours has been a problem ever since we opened this morning. I've gone to your shop several times when I thought you had a customer, but nobody was there." She folded her forearms on the table, looking perturbed. "China, I don't like to harp on this subject because I know you don't believe in ghosts. But I think you really ought to consider the possibility that—"

"I've already considered it."

"You *have*?" Ruby was taken aback. "You mean, you might agree that what we have here is a *ghost*?"

Instead of answering, I looked around. Our tearoom is a lovely, inviting place. We've installed hunter-green wainscoting partway up the old square-cut limestone walls, painted our tables and chairs green, and set the tables with floral chintz napkins (yes, real cloth!) and small crystal vases of fresh flowers and herbs. Baskets of ferns hang in narrow, deep-set windows that look out onto the gardens. But for just a second, I was in an entirely different place. And time.

"This used to be a bedroom," I said.

"Really?" Ruby tilted her head. "Well, I know that you had an apartment here, but I remember this as your living room."

"It was. But back in the day, way back, this was a bedroom. The bed was over there." I pointed. "It had an elaborate spindled headboard and footboard and a white crocheted spread with a white skirt, and ruffled white pillow shams. All very Victorian. There was a dressing table over there, with one of those three-paneled mirrors, and a commode there." I pointed toward the corner where we park our serving trolley, which was already stocked with cutlery, pitchers, and stacks of plates for tomorrow's lunch.

"A commode? Oh, right. No bathroom back then, I guess." Ruby frowned. "Hey, wait a minute. How do you know all this stuff?"

"There were some photos in that carton we found in the storeroom upstairs. Shots of the garden, plus several of the interior. This room was a bedroom. Your shop was the dining room, with a long table and six chairs. My shop was the parlor, where the neighborhood ladies got together to do fancy needlework and listen to Mrs. Duncan read to them—sort of like a sewing circle, I guess."

Back in the shop, the bell began to ring fast and hard, as if it were disagreeing with me. Jenna came to the door and said helplessly, "Sorry. It's just *doing* that. All by itself. I don't know how to make it stop."

"We know, dear," Ruby said. "Thank you."

"If that's our ghost," I said crossly, "I wish she'd find another way to communicate." And then I had another thought.

"Excuse me," I said. I got up, stepped into the shop, and looked at the bulletin board. FALL CLASSES had been pushed up to the top of the board, and a whole new arrangement was in place: HELLO ☺.

259

Tucked behind the smiley-face magnet was a sprig of fresh lavender.

I went back to the tearoom and sat down at the table again. "She did," I said flatly.

Ruby raised both eyebrows. "Who did? What did she do?"

"The ghost," I said. "She has found another way to communicate. She's left me a message on the bulletin board."

Ruby got up, went to look at the bulletin board, and sat back down. "I noticed that this morning. I thought you put it there. It's cute. The smiley face, I mean. Cheery."

"Oh, it's cheery all right," I said. "But I didn't do it."

And then I told her the whole thing, start to finish. The humming I'd heard in the storeroom, the photos and lavender and letters rearranged on the bulletin board, Ethel's sighting of the woman in a long skirt in the garden. And of course the bell over the door, which Ruby already knew about. I left out the scary dreams, feeling that they were probably a product of my overanxious imagination. In fact, it seemed easy now to think of all this as the work of a ghost. But even without the dreams, there was plenty to tell, and the story took a while.

"Well, good," Ruby said with satisfaction, when I had finished. "I guess we do have us a ghost, huh?"

My lawyerly self leapt to her feet. *Facts not in evidence, Your Honor!* But she knew when she was defeated. She sat down and put her head in her hands.

"I suppose we do," I said, feeling a deep sympathy for the lawyerly part of me. It's hard to give up treasured assumptions. "The question I've been trying to answer is *why?* Why now? And why me?" I pointed at Ruby. "You're usually the one who attracts ghosties and conjures up supernatural doings. But these messages seem to be directed at *me*."

"Maybe because this is *your* building?" Ruby asked reasonably. "You're the owner."

"I suppose," I said with a shrug. "Makes sense, since our ghost must be Mrs. Duncan, the first owner."

In the shop, the bell gave a series of irritated peals.

I crossed my arms on the table and raised my voice. "Well, then, if you're not Mrs. Duncan, just who the devil *are* you? The Historical Society says this is the Duncan family house."

Ruby and I stared at each other while the bell fired off another loud volley of exasperated dings.

"Sounds like she's expecting you to figure out what her name is," Ruby said. "Would the Historical Society have any clues?"

"I don't know," I said. "But I can take another look in that carton of photographs. There are some newspaper clippings."

Ruby cocked her head, listening, but the bell was silent. "She has no objection to that, I guess." She gave me a small smile and pushed back her chair. "I have to go. I'm teaching a meditation class this afternoon."

I began picking up our dishes. "Tell Jenna I'll be back in a few minutes. I have to check things out at the cottage. We have a new guest arriving tomorrow."

"Oh, really? Who is she?" Ruby always makes a point of stopping to say hello to our bed-and-breakfast guests.

"I don't know much about her," I said over my shoulder, on my way to the kitchen. "She filled in the rental form online. She's from out of state."

As I rinsed the dishes and headed out to the cottage, I thought about the photos I had studied the night before. One of the out-of-doors shots had shown two little girls—twins, I thought—standing beside the stable on a long-ago summer day of sunshine and sunflowers, feeding a carrot to a fat pony. Were the girls my ghost's daughters? And if she wasn't Mrs. Duncan, who *was* she? I was itching to know. Maybe the answer was in those newspaper clippings. I would go through the carton tonight.

THE stone stable is long gone, of course. In the years after World War I, most people gave up horses in favor of automobiles, and it was turned into a large garage. Later, when the architect bought and remodeled my building, he reincarnated the stable-cum-garage as a lovely one-bedroom guesthouse with a fireplace in the living room, a small built-in kitchen, and a hot tub on its own private deck. I list it as a rental in the Pecan Springs Bed-and-Breakfast Guide and on the Internet. It comes with linens, towels, and a ready-to-eat breakfast that Cass assembles each afternoon and stashes in the cottage refrigerator, so our guest can pop it in the microwave while she's brewing her morning coffee.

There's extra work connected with the cottage, of course—a bit of light housekeeping, laundry, bed-making, and so on. But it's proving to be a welcome source of income, so I don't mind the chores. I had already cleaned and straightened after the last guest, but I wanted to go through my checklist and make sure that everything was in order for the next guest.

I was in the bedroom, polishing a few fingerprints from a glass pane in one of the double French doors, when I heard Lori's light voice.

"China? Are you here, China?"

"In the bedroom," I called. "Come on back."

A moment later, Lori was standing in the doorway. She was wearing blue pedal pushers and a white T-shirt with the words *Keep Calm and Carry YARN* in bright red letters. Her brown hair was loose around her shoulders, giving her a little-girl look.

"Uh-oh," she said, staring wide-eyed at me through her tortoise-shell glasses. "What in the world happened to *you*?"

I had forgotten about the gauze bandage over my ear. I gave her the heavily edited version. "A deputy sheriff and I were repossessing a pair of stolen roosters when we ran into an armed farmer who thought he had to defend his pot crop."

"Honest?" Her mouth fell open. "You're kidding!"

"Nope. Swear to God. True story. But keep it under your hat. Charges pending."

Lori shook her head, chuckling. "China, you lead an *eventful* life."

"I left out the part where I returned fire," I said helpfully.

"Oh, dear." Lori sobered. "Nobody's dead, I hope."

"Nobody's dead, just banged up a little. We got the roosters back, the pot farmer is headed for the county jail, and his half acre of marijuana will soon be a cloud of smoke."

"A happy ending."

"Mostly," I agreed. "For the roosters, not so much." I sighed. "Extra Crispy is okay, but he won't be bringing home a blue ribbon."

"That's too bad. But Caitie entered two chickens, didn't she? Maybe the other one will come through." Lori looked around. "This is *lovely*!" she said. "I've been in the cottage, but never back here." She went over to the bed to examine the log-cabin quilt, pieced in shades of browns and oranges. "What a stunning quilt! Who made it?"

"A friend," I said. "It's hand-pieced and hand-quilted."

"It's beautiful work," she said admiringly. "And I love the crocheted lace on your pillow shams."

I nodded. "Sometimes I think I could just move right in here myself. I wouldn't have to drive to work, either. I could just walk across the garden." And then I remembered. "I tried to text you a photo last night, but Ruby said you didn't get it."

Lori nodded. "My phone's been out of commission. Big nuisance, really. But it's working now. You can send the photo anytime."

"Actually, I don't need to send it," I said. "Give me another minute to check out the bathroom and kitchen, then let's go out to my car. I'll show you the original."

Ruby and I park our cars beside Big Red Mama (our shop van) in the graveled parking area just off the alley, at one end of the cottage. I had taken the carton of photos with me when I left the house this morning. *Was it just this morning?* I wondered, as Lori and I walked out to the car. It felt like a couple of centuries ago.

My Toyota was parked in the sun, so it was blistering hot when I unlocked the door. I took out the carton of photographs and rummaged through it until I found what I was looking for: the studio portrait of the baby in the christening dress and cap, posed in a parlor chair beside a small table with an open book and a crystal vase of white cabbage roses. It was the second photo to mysteriously appear on my bulletin board, and I still didn't understand why.

"Here it is," I said, handing it to her. "That dress reminded me of the christening dress your aunt gave you when you went to Waco a few days ago. That's why I thought of sending the photo to you."

Lori looked at it and blinked. "China," she whispered. "China, I already *have* this photograph!"

"You already have it?" I frowned. "I thought you didn't get my text."

"I didn't. But when Aunt Jo gave me my birth mother's christening dress, she gave me several photographs. This—" She held it up. "This was one of them. She said that the dress and the photos had been in the family for generations, so I was assuming that the baby—it's a little girl—could be one of my long-ago relatives." She turned the photo over. It was blank. "The one I have has a date written on the back, though. I don't remember the day, but it was June 1890."

"You're saying it's the very *same* photo?" The hair was standing up on the back of my neck. "Are you sure?"

"Positive." Her voice was awed. "What's more, China, Aunt Jo gave me the dress that this baby is wearing! I've compared the two. The pattern on the lace panel on the front of the dress is distinctive. No mistake. They're the same." She bit her lip. "So I guess I have to ask—where did *you* find my family photo?"

"It was in the carton we took out of the storeroom." I omitted the thing about the ghost posting it to the bulletin board. That would only confuse an already mystifying situation. "Do you have your photos with you? The ones your aunt gave you? I'm wondering if there are any other matches."

Lori shook her head. "They're at home." She checked her phone. "Gosh, look at the time. I've got a class to teach."

"Why don't you come over to my house this evening and bring your stuff," I suggested. "I would offer to come to you, but I don't want to leave Caitie alone. We can spread out the photos and see what we have. Maybe we can come up with an explanation."

Lori brightened. "I'd love to," she said. "I'll bring the christening dress, too, so you can compare it to the one in the photo."

"Will eight be too late?" I asked. "I'm taking Caitie to the fairgrounds, and then I thought we'd go out for pizza."

"Eight is perfect," Lori said. "See you then!"

* * *

CAITIE's eyes grew as big as saucers when she hopped into the car in front of the Depot and saw me. "Mom!" she cried. "Your head! What happened? Are you . . . are you okay?"

"It's a long story, honey," I said. "I'll tell you as we drive."

By this time, I had told the story so often that I could rattle it off. For Caitie, I left out the grisly parts. I told her that the roosters had been chicken-napped, and that Mr. Banner and I had gone after the thief, who was now under arrest. And during that process, we had discovered that the crook was growing marijuana, so he would be going to jail for a good long time.

"Extra Crispy is just fine," I added, reaching over to pat her bare leg. "He's not as pretty as he was, but he didn't suffer any injuries. When you get him cleaned up, he'll be good as new."

For a moment, I thought she was going to cry, but she didn't. She pressed her lips together, straightened her shoulders, and said, "So I guess he didn't get a blue ribbon."

"I'm sorry," I said.

She sighed. "So am I." She brightened. "But there's always next year."

"Right," I agreed. "There's always next year." I turned off San Antonio Avenue toward the fairgrounds. "Let's go see if Dixie Chick won a ribbon, shall we?"

The parking lot was full and we had to walk a good half mile to the poultry tent. The afternoon sun was still high, and the air hadn't grown any cooler. By the time we got where we were going, I was hot and sweaty, and under my wraparound gauze headband, my bandage itched.

It was even hotter inside the poultry tent—and noisy, of course. Crowded, too, because the judging was completed and people were gathering in front of the cages to gawk at the winners. There were blue ribbons on some cages, red and yellow and no ribbons at all on others—happy chicken fanciers and unhappy ones.

Caitie's chickens were at the far end. When we got there, the first thing she saw was the blue ribbon attached to Dixie Chick's cage. She'd won a first in the "Heavy Breeds" class.

"Oh, Mom!" she cried, dancing up and down. "I knew Dixie Chick could do it! I just *knew* it!" And then we turned to look at Extra Crispy and got a big surprise.

When I left the rooster that morning, I had jotted down a few sentences of explanation and hung it on his cage. And now, the cage was covered with dozens of little notes, saying things like *Sorry this happened!* and *You're a fighter!* and *So glad you didn't get barbecued!* Some people had even pinned up little trinkets—a tiny plastic chicken, a plush chicken doll, a little gold-colored heart, a purple smiley face, a green rubber frog.

And at the top right corner of the cage hung a large purple bow with ribbon streamers and a handwritten tag in the shape of a heart, colored purple. *This valiant rooster is hereby granted the Brave Rooster Award for courage on the field of battle!* And on Blackheart's cage, next to Extra Crispy, was the same thing.

Caitie burst into happy tears. "Oh, Mom," she cried, "he's won a *purple* ribbon!"

And at that perfect moment, Jessica showed up with her camera.

AFTER supper, Caitie went upstairs to talk to Kevin on her cell phone, taking Mr. P with her. I settled down at the kitchen table with the contents of the Corticelli carton in front of me, and Winchester at my feet.

There were well over a dozen clippings and pieces of paper, and when I finally got them laid out on the table in chronological order, I could see that they told a story—my ghost's story, as nearly as I could make out. There were gaps, of course, and while I could see what had happened, the whys were not at all obvious. But in the end, I was able to reconstruct the major events, more or less.

The first clipping in the storyline was dated May 17, 1882, and announced the wedding of Miss Annie Laurie Scott, 21, to Mr. Douglas Duncan, 28. (*Annie Laurie*, she of the Scottish folk song I had heard hummed in the storeroom. This must be my ghost's name!) According to the clipping, the newly married couple had moved into the house Duncan had built at 304 Crockett in Pecan Springs—*my* building, which now bore the Historical Society's plaque with the Duncan name on it. A "prominent local blacksmith," Duncan operated a smithy on the alley behind the house, where "those requiring his services" could easily find him.

But the Duncan story had a tragic ending. The next clipping was dated some three years after the wedding, on September 21, 1885. The headline—"Douglas Duncan Killed by Train at the Houston Street Crossing"—was bordered in black, with a subhead: "Horse Also Killed, Buggy Wrecked." Apparently, Duncan was in the habit of racing across the railroad track ahead of the train, and this time, he lost. He was survived by his widow, Annie Laurie, who (according to the article) had been so distressed by the terrible news that she gave premature birth to a stillborn infant son. I sat for a moment, struck by the enormity of her loss: her husband and her little boy, on the same bleak day. And the awfulness didn't end there, I realized, for in that day and age, a young woman—at that point, Annie was only twenty-four—couldn't have had many options after she became a widow. She might go home to her parents, if they were alive. She might marry again, and hope for better luck the next time. Or she might work—but at what? Domestic labor?

And then I found an answer to my question. Among the clippings, I uncovered a pretty calling card with *Annie's Laces* printed on it in fancy calligraphy, and a date in pencil, 1888, written on the back. The card had a scalloped, lacelike edge and bore Annie Duncan's name and address, and a pastel drawing of a blossom of Queen Anne's lace. There were also several clippings of newspaper advertisements for lacemakers, with Annie's name and address, all dated in 1888 and 1889.

Ah-ha! I thought, feeling like Sherlock Holmes. At some point after her husband died, Annie must have gone into the lacemaking business, with several local ladies she had located through ads she had placed in the newspapers. Why lacemaking? I wondered. Was it something she had learned as a girl and liked to do? Or had it been a desperation move, when she had no other resources to fall back on?

Whatever prompted her to create her business, it apparently became a success. One clipping, dated later in 1888, was headlined, "Mrs. Annie Duncan Secures New Accounts in San Antonio, Austin." The story described her affiliation with women's dress shops and millinery shops in the two cities and noted that the handcrafted laces produced by her lacemakers were prized for their delicate patterns and graceful execution. "Mrs. Duncan is to be commended for her artistry and her business acuity," the reporter noted enthusiastically. "She is an outstanding example of Pecan Springs' entrepreneurial spirit!"

So the women in the photograph weren't a neighborhood sewing circle—they were part of Annie's lacemaking business! Some of the laces we had found in the wooden chest must be theirs. Christine would be interested to learn about this, I thought excitedly. She could add Annie's Laces to her research on women's late-nineteenth-century needlework businesses in Texas—and it had happened in what was now my shop!

But the clippings in the box told a second, separate story, as well. An 1881 piece from the Galveston *Daily News* announced the marriage of Miss Delia Louise Crawford, 19, of Galveston, Texas, to Mr. Adam Hunt, 29, of Pecan Springs, Texas. This reminded me of the photo I had seen of the formal wedding. I took it out, turned it over, and saw the two names, handwritten on the back: *Adam* and *Delia*, with the little heart drawn around the names. According to the clipping, the Hunts were at home in a house Mr. Hunt had recently built at 306 Crockett in Pecan Springs. *They were Annie's neighbors*, I thought, with some surprise, living in the yellow-painted frame house that is now the Hobbit House Children's Bookstore, on the other side of my garden. I would have to show their picture to Molly McGregor, who owns the bookstore. She'd be interested in this bit of history.

The Hunts seemed to flourish. In 1882, they announced the birth of a daughter, Caroline. Several clippings over the next few years reported the expansion of Mr. Hunt's business, Hunt's Feed and Tack, which was located beside the railroad track, next to Purley's (now Beans' Bar and Grill, our favorite eating place). Other clippings noted that Mrs. Hunt and her daughter, Caroline—she appeared to be an only child—made frequent trips by train to Galveston, where Mrs. Hunt visited her sister, Miss Clarissa Crawford, shopped, and attended social events.

But there was heartbreak in store for the Hunts. The clipping was headlined, "Local Woman's Funeral Planned for Friday." The story was short on details, but it reported that Mrs. Adam Hunt, of 306 Crockett Street, had died on October 14, 1888, when she mistook poison hemlock for wild carrot. Hemlock poisoning! The writer concluded the article with this caution for his readers: "This tragedy is a reminder that we need to be especially careful when we dine at Mother Nature's wild table. It is too easy to be seduced by a pretty (but poisonous) blossom or a tempting mushroom. Beware!"

How bizarre, I thought, and reread the clipping for the third time. Had Mrs. Hunt eaten the leaves as a salad? But fresh leaves usually appear only in the spring, and she died in October. Well, then, she might have cooked the root as a vegetable, mistaking it for wild carrot. Was she the only one in the family who ate it? Had Adam Hunt and little Caroline eaten it, too, and somehow managed to survive? But there were no answers to my questions in the terse newspaper report. It was a mystery.

And there was another puzzle, as well. A clipping from the *Austin Weekly Statesman,* dated October 25, 1888, reported the death of Mr. Howard Simpson, 34, of Galveston, Texas. According to witnesses, the man had calmly walked to the middle of the recently built iron bridge that crossed the Colorado River at the foot of Congress Avenue, and jumped. His body was recovered the next day at the Montopolis crossing downstream, where another bridge had recently been built. The clipping offered no indication of how this event might be related to either the Duncan story or the Hunt story. Another mystery.

But then the two separate stories became one, and the puzzling mystery of my ghost's last name was finally solved. "Local Couple Weds," a clipping informed me. On August 3, 1889, not quite a year after Delia Hunt died, Mrs. Annie Laurie Duncan and Mr. Adam Hunt—the widow and the widower—had married.

Ah, yes, I thought. I pulled out the wedding photograph of the twice-married man and the woman in the taffy-colored dress. So this was Annie. Annie Laurie, my ghost.

Assumes facts not in evidence, Your Honor, my lawyer self said, but weakly and without conviction. For there she was, very much in evidence, the woman with the remarkable eyes who (in my dream) had wanted desperately to tell me something. But what had she wanted to say? What was I supposed to learn from all of this?

I studied it for a moment, thinking of the first Mrs. Hunt's mysterious death and wondering if anyone had raised any uncomfortable questions about the circumstances. A wife is tragically poisoned; her husband (albeit after a respectable period) marries the next-door neighbor. It seemed like the kind of situation that might raise a few eyebrows.

But I still had no answers. I propped the photo against the saltshaker, noticing once again that the bride's eyes seemed to follow me as I moved. I went back to the clipping. The wedding took place in Annie's parlor, at 304 Crockett—in my shop! According to the article, the new Mrs. Hunt was attended by Mr. Hunt's eight-year-old daughter, Caroline. With that as a prompt, I pulled out the other wedding photo, the one in which the wedding couple was posed with the young girl in banana curls. Now I knew *her* name, too: it was Caroline. Her mother, Delia, was dead. Annie was her new stepmother.

And then Annie and Adam's story added another chapter. A clipping announced the arrival of their first child, Crystal, on June 14, 1890. Twin daughters Pearl and Amber were born in 1894. And then I found one more document, a gilt-edged page that looked like it had been taken out of a family Bible. At the top, in elaborate blue letters, were the words *Our Family.* In faded ink, in an old-fashioned Spencerian script, each of the four Hunt daughters was listed, with the marriages of three of them (Pearl, it appeared, had never married), plus the names and birth dates of their children and *their* marriages and the names and birthdates of *their* children. Annie and Adam had had ten grandchildren and sixteen great-grandchildren. He had died in 1927. She followed him in 1943. I did a quick mental calculation. She must have lived in the Crockett Street house—the building that was now mine—for over sixty years. Sixty years! No wonder the place was filled with her energies.

I was still studying the names when Lori knocked at the kitchen door, excited and bubbling over with some news. Winchester got to his feet to greet her. She was wearing sandals and he gave her a wet kiss on her toes.

She bent over to fondle his long ears, then straightened up again. "You are not going to believe this, China," she said, "but I have found my grandmother!"

"Wow!" I exclaimed. "Really? Lori, that's wonderful!"

"Yes, really!" Lori flung herself into the chair on the other side of the kitchen table. "I just got off the phone with Aunt Jo, who tracked her down through an acquaintance in Sherwood. She's in her eighties now, but she's apparently healthy and living not far from Dallas. I'm going to drive up and see her tomorrow. She's very excited about the prospect of getting together."

"Dallas!" I said. "I guess it's a small world, after all. You've been so lucky, Lori. Some people look for years before they find their families."

Her mouth trembled. "Not so lucky with my mother, I'm afraid. She died in a car crash three years after I was born. She didn't have any other children."

"I'm so sorry," I said. "But it's wonderful that you've found your grandmother. What did you say her name is? Her given name, I mean."

"It's Lorene," Lori said. "Why?"

"Lorene?" I pulled in my breath and the hair prickled on the back of my neck. "Take a look." I pushed the "Our Family" page across the table. "Under Crystal's name. What do you see?"

Lori looked down at the page. "Why, it's Lorene," she said, frowning. "What is this page, China?"

"It's a family genealogy," I said. "Crystal was this family's second daughter. Lorene was her first child." I got up and went around the table. Over Lori's shoulder, I pointed. "According to this, Lorene married a man named Gatley. Their daughter's name was—"

Lori gasped. "Laura Anne! *My* Laura Anne! This is *my* mother, China! My mother!"

I put my hand on Lori's shoulder. "I think your name belongs on that page, too." I pointed at the photograph propped against the saltshaker. "This is Crystal's mother. Her name is Annie. She used to live in the house where you have your studio. She is . . ." I calculated. "She is your great-great-grandmother."

There was a long silence as Lori took it all in. "But how in the world did you find all this out?" she asked at last. Her eyes were brimming with tears. "China, I don't understand!"

"I don't, either," I said, although I did, more or less.

Lori had been searching for her mother. Searching desperately, because she had lost everyone in the world she had loved. Because she needed to find out who she was.

Annie understood that need, because she had once been alone in the world, too.

And somehow, by some magic better known to shamans and sages than to us ordinary people, the two had found each other.

"Would you like some tea?" I asked, heading for the stove to turn on the kettle. "I'm ready for a cup."

"Oh, please," Lori said. "Tea would be wonderful."

I might have been imagining it, but I thought I heard a bell.

Author's Note

When I traveled through the countryside in Swabia and saw a savin [*Juniperus sabina*] bush in a farmer's garden, it confirmed what I had in many cases already suspected, that the garden belonged to the barber or the midwife of the village. And to what purpose had they so carefully planted the savin bush? If you look at these bushes and shrubs you'll see them deformed and without tops, because they have been raided so often, and even at times stolen.

> An 18th-century German traveler,
> quoted by Edward Shorter
> *A History of Women's Bodies*, p. 186

Rue in thyme is a maiden's posy.

> Scottish saying

Lad's love is maiden's ruin, but half of it is her own doing. [Lad's love and maiden's ruin are two folk names for the same abortifacient, *Artemisia abrotanum*, southernwood.]

> Devonshire saying

For several years, I've been wanting to include the history of women's use of herbal contraceptives and abortifacients in one of the China Bayles mysteries. But in our culture, today, these plants are almost never used for these purposes; in fact, the memory of these properties is buried and all but forgotten. So it wasn't easy to imagine a fictional context in which they would be appropriate. When I thought of creating a historical tale bracketed by a modern story (a ghost story of sorts), the narrative began to take shape.

But it hasn't been an easy story to tell, partly because accurate information about the plants women used in family planning has been difficult to come by. And partly because there are so many tragic stories—like the story of Delia Hunt, in this book, whose life was ended when she mistook one plant for another. (Or *was* it a mistake? There are many ambiguities, and to tell the truth, I'm not really sure how Delia died. All we know is that our fictional sheriff doesn't feel that he can press charges.) Over the centuries during which women have been seeking ways to avoid pregnancy or end it in the first couple of months, many such mistakes must have been made, and that's the real tragedy. Lacking a guide or adequate information, women took what they hoped would be an effective remedy. Sometimes it was. Sometimes it wasn't.

As for accurate information, the whole issue is clouded—and for some very understandable reasons. In most cultures, in both ancient and modern times, a woman's control of her fertility is a vexed question. A woman who wanted to avoid pregnancy could be faced with religious prohibitions, restrictive and punitive laws, and the disapproval of family and community. Whatever she did to control her reproductive process, she usually did in secret and in silence, with the support of only her closest female friends or a sympathetic sister or mother. She relied on folk knowledge that was shared among women, was rarely written down, and offered varying degrees of reliability.

What's more, the folk knowledge that women possessed in earlier centuries, *because* it was orally transmitted and rarely written down, has been virtually inaccessible to us. When knowledge about women's bodies was considered "black magic," it was important not to possess any written evidence of the practices, to avoid being burned at the stake. When few women could read or write, most got their information from family and friends, often in the form of folk sayings, like the Devonshire ditty about lad's love and maiden's ruin, or "Rue in thyme is a maiden's posy"—which often were not recorded until much later. In the early- and mid-twentieth century, modern medicine worked very hard (and quite successfully) to suppress information about all medical practices involving therapeutic plants. Documenting the uses of plants in the management of women's fertility has been difficult.

Thankfully, there is more interest in and respect for folk medicine today than there has been in the past century. A number of contemporary scholars have worked hard to discover and share with us the long, long history of women's uses of contraceptive and abortifacient plants. I have relied on the work of four for the herbal information in this novel. John M. Riddle's study, *Eve's Herbs*, is a history of contraception and abortion, primarily in the West. Ann Hibner Koblitz's *Sex and Herbs and Birth Control* is a cross-cultural study that includes examples not only from the ancients and from Western Europe, but from Algeria, China, India, Vietnam, and indigenous North American peoples. Her work gives us a glimpse into the methods that women of many cultures have used to regulate their fertility and control their reproduction. A third is the chapter on "anti-fertility technology" in Autumn Stanley's all-around excellent book, *Mothers and Daughters of Invention: Notes for a Revised History of Technology*. The fourth is Daniel Moerman's *Native American Ethnobotany*, a massive catalogue of North American plants and their uses by indigenous peoples. Moerman lists forty-one plant species that were used by Native American women as contraceptives and 102 as abortifacients. Women from different tribes frequently used the same plant. *Artemisia*, for instance, was used as an abortifacient by Blackfoot, Chippewa, Dakota, Kawaiisu, Menominee, Omaha, Pawnee, Ponca, and Sioux. Autumn Stanley made a comment that I find interesting: she noted that often during ethnobotanical studies, informants claimed that they didn't know or couldn't remember the names of plants that were used to control female reproduction. Stanley adds, "I suspect that the women knew very well what plants were used but would not tell a male anthropologist such secrets." Indeed!

Researchers who have tackled this thorny subject agree on a list of traditional herbal contraceptives that were used across cultures: parsley, rue, thyme, pennyroyal, juniper (savin), tansy, golden groundsel, artemisia, blue cohosh, acacia, assafoetida, Queen Anne's lace, slippery elm, calamus (sweet flag), and cotton root. Most of these were described as *emmenagogues*, plants used to provoke or induce menstruation by causing uterine contractions—good to know if your period was late. These herbal preparations were usually taken orally as a strong tea (plant material steeped in boiling water) or as a tincture (plant material steeped in alcohol). If you were more than a few weeks late, some of these plant remedies might have been administered vaginally. Koblitz, for instance, tells us that both slippery elm (in North America) and mallow root (in medieval Turkey) were used as an abortifacient: "fashioned into a probe and inserted into the womb" with one end attached to the thigh by a string. The probe remained in place "for as long as two weeks until bleeding occurred" (*Sex and Herbs and Birth Control*, p. 21).

To prevent conception, plant-based barrier devices were used, depending on what was locally available and culturally acceptable. In coastal regions, women employed vaginal seaweed sponges or kelp treated with honey (an antimotility agent) or lemon juice (a spermicide). In North America, native women made diaphragms of birch bark, while in Sumatra, women made tampons dipped in tannic acid (another effective spermicide). And there was the lemon-half cupped over the cervix, said to have been used by American female slaves (*Mothers and Daughters of Invention*, p. 261). Women's ingenuity was matched only by their desire to avoid pregnancy unless they could welcome the child into a supportive and caring family.

Both Koblitz and Riddle offer interesting comments on the use of the patent medicines that were popular from the 1870s to the 1940s. It is worth noting that Lydia Pinkham's wildly popular tonic contained several of the herbs that were known to prompt menstruation, and that Sir James Clark's abortifacient pills contained a potent mix of aloe, hellebore, juniper (savin), ergot, tansy, and rue, all of which could have acted as uterine stimulants, especially in the first eight weeks. Nobody knows how many women were tempted to swallow a whole bottle of the pills—and wash them down with a strong tea made of rue, thyme, tansy, and pennyroyal.

For the signature herb of this novel, I had many choices, but Queen Anne's lace, or wild carrot (*Daucus carota*), felt just right. It is well known to be one of the more potent antifertility plants and was locally available in many regions (including Central Texas). Brought to North America by colonial women, it spread quickly, probably because women settlers took it with them wherever they went. According to Riddle (*Eve's Herbs*, pp. 50–51), the earliest reference to wild carrot appears in a fourth century BCE work ascribed to Hippocrates, where it is mentioned as a powerfully effective abortifacient. In modern scientific experiments, extracts of the seeds tested on rats, mice, guinea pigs, and rabbits either inhibited implantation of a fertilized ovum or (if recently implanted) caused it to be released. Other, informal experiments by women have been reported online (for instance, at sisterzeus.com). Most online forums discussing the use of the seeds stress the need to correctly identify it, to be sure it does not come from its look-alike plant, poison hemlock (*Conium maculatum*)—the plant that so tragically ended the life of Delia Hunt.

If this is a subject that interests you (I hope it does!), you'll want to take a look at all four of the books mentioned above. They contain excellent documentation, full bibliographies, and handy indexes (useful if you want to look up a particular plant). If you're tempted to experiment with any plant for any therapeutic purpose, please, please, *please* do your homework. Plants don't wear labels, as the characters in this novel learn from tragic experience. And even labels don't always tell the full story. Be observant and careful, know what you're doing, and don't take risks.

Early on in the series, a *Booklist* reviewer wrote, "China Bayles is always trying to teach us stuff: it's not annoying at all but somehow soothing and fascinating." To that, I have to add that China Bayles is always trying to teach *me* stuff—and even when what she wants to teach me isn't soothing, it never, ever ceases to be fascinating.

I hope you feel the same way, and that China's herbal explorations will take you in directions you might not have thought of going by yourself.

Susan Wittig Albert
Bertram, Texas

Recipes

Carrots, wild carrots, and their Daucus relatives are worthy of a recipe collection all their own. Here are recipes for some of the foods mentioned in this book, to add to your own collection of favorite carrot recipes.

Cass' Couscous Carrot Salad

If you prefer (I do!), substitute 2 tablespoons candied ginger for the grated fresh ginger. For an entirely different taste, omit the basil and add ¼ cup chopped fresh mint. I've also made this dish with white and brown rice instead of couscous.

> ½ cup slivered almonds
> 1 cup water
> Grated rind of ½ lemon
> 1 teaspoon salt
> 1 tablespoon olive oil
> 1 cup couscous
> ¼ cup raisins
> 1 cup grated carrot
> 1½ tablespoons grated fresh ginger
> 1 teaspoon allspice
> ½ cup chopped fresh basil
> Juice of 1 lemon

Toast the nuts in a skillet over medium-high heat, stirring constantly, until they are golden (about 3 minutes). Set aside. Combine the water, lemon rind, salt, and oil in a saucepan, and heat until almost boiling. Add couscous and raisins, remove from heat, and cover. Let steam for 10 minutes, then fluff with a fork, breaking up any clumps. Add carrot, ginger, allspice, basil, lemon juice, and nuts. Serve warm or at room temperature to 4.

One-Dish Moroccan Chicken and Carrots

A slow-cooker recipe, easy enough for weekdays, exotic enough for a special meal. Traditionally served over warm rice, but it also goes well with pasta.

> 1 pound carrots, peeled and cut diagonally into 2-inch
>   lengths
> 6 skinless, boneless chicken thighs
> Juice of 1 lemon
> 3 cloves garlic, minced
> 2 teaspoons cinnamon
> 1 teaspoon cumin
> ½ teaspoon coriander seeds, crushed
> Cayenne pepper, pinch
> 1 teaspoon salt
> ½ teaspoon black pepper (or to taste)
> 1 lemon, sliced as thinly as possible
> ⅔ cup sliced onions
> ¼ cup golden raisins
> ¼ cup sliced almonds, toasted if desired
> Rice, for serving (optional)

Place the carrots in the slow cooker. Layer chicken thighs on top. Brush lemon juice evenly over the chicken. Mix together garlic, cinnamon, cumin, coriander seeds, cayenne pepper, salt, and black pepper. Sprinkle evenly across the chicken. Add lemon slices and sliced onions. Cover and cook on high for 4 hours or on low for 8 hours. Add raisins and almonds before serving over warm rice. Serves 4–5.

China's Peach-and-Carrot Cobbler

I use canned peaches for this easy cobbler. If you're using fresh fruit, you'll want 2–3 large peaches, sliced. If you like coconut, add ½ cup to the filling.

START WITH THE BATTER:
½ cup melted butter
1 cup flour
1 cup sugar
2 teaspoons baking powder
¼ teaspoon salt
⅔ cup milk
1 egg

Melt the butter in a 9x13–inch oven-proof dish or pan. In a separate bowl, mix together flour, sugar, baking powder, and salt. Stir in milk and egg, making sure there are no lumps. Pour evenly over melted butter.

TO MAKE THE FILLING, COMBINE:
1 (28-ounce) can sliced peaches, drained
1½ cups shredded carrots
1¼ cups sugar
1 teaspoon cinnamon
1 teaspoon ginger
½ teaspoon nutmeg
½ cup coconut (optional)

Mix all ingredients well and spread over batter—but don't stir it in! The batter will rise to the top during the baking. Bake 35–45 minutes at 350 degrees F. Serve warm with ice cream to 6–8.

Queen Anne's Lace Jelly

For refrigerator jelly, start by washing and sterilizing six 4-ounce jars and lids. If you want to store your jelly on the shelf, you will need to process the jars in a hot-water bath, following (carefully!) the instructions on the pectin box.

> 2 cups rinsed, prepared, and tightly packed Queen Anne's
>   lace flowers
> 3½ cups water, in a large saucepan
> ¼ cup lemon juice
> 1 package powdered pectin (Pomona's, Sure-Jell)
> 3½ cups sugar
> 1 drop red food coloring (optional—makes a pretty pink jelly)

Rinse out any nectar-loving insects from the flowers. Snip the blossoms from the bracts. Bring the water to a boil, add the flowers, and cover. Let steep for an hour. Strain, discarding the flowers. Measure 3 cups of the liquid into a saucepan. Add lemon juice and pectin. Bring to a rolling boil. Add sugar, stirring, and return to a boil. Boil for 1 minute, and remove from the heat. If you want to color the jelly pink, add 1 small drop of red food coloring. Pour carefully into prepared jars and apply lids. For refrigerator jelly, cool and refrigerate. For shelf storage, process in a hot-water bath, cool, and store.

Pesto Chicken and Carrot Wraps

A great use of that leftover rotisserie chicken. Or you can quickly cook and shred two boneless, skinless chicken breasts.

TO MAKE THE PESTO:

2 cups fresh basil leaves (no stems)

2 tablespoons pine nuts or walnuts

2 large cloves garlic

½ cup extra virgin olive oil

½ cup Parmesan cheese, freshly grated

Combine first three ingredients in a blender or food processor. Process until finely minced. With the machine running, add the olive oil in a slow stream, scraping down the sides (carefully). When smooth, add the cheese and refrigerate. You'll have enough for the wraps, plus more for salad.

TO MAKE THE FILLING, MIX TOGETHER:

4 cups cooked chicken, shredded

½ cup pesto

1 teaspoon cumin

FOR THE WRAPS:

4 wraps (tortillas, wraps, or thin pita bread)

4 slices Swiss cheese

2 cups shredded arugula or spinach leaves

2 cups thinly julienned or grated carrots

Olive oil for brushing

To assemble: Lay out 4 wraps. On each wrap, place 1 slice of cheese, followed by 1 cup chicken mixture, ½ cup shredded greens, and ½ cup carrots. Roll up tightly. Brush each wrap with olive oil and heat in a hot sandwich maker, a Panini press, or a nonstick pan on medium heat.

Tomato Basil Soup

The carrot lends body, flavor, and nutrition to this homemade soup. If you prefer a creamier soup, substitute cream, half-and-half, or evaporated milk for a portion of the chicken stock.

> 2 tablespoons olive oil
> 1 medium onion
> 3 cloves garlic, minced
> 2 stalks celery, diced
> 1 medium carrot, thinly sliced
> 1 (28-ounce) can tomatoes, crushed or diced
> 1½ cups chicken stock
> 6 tablespoons chopped fresh basil
> Sour cream

Heat the oil in a large saucepan. Sauté the onion, adding garlic, celery, and carrot when the onion is translucent. Cook together until the carrots are soft. Add tomatoes. Puree until smooth with your immersion stick or in a blender. (Careful: it's hot!) Return to heat. Add chicken stock and basil. Bring to a boil and simmer on low heat for 4–5 minutes. Season with salt and pepper to taste. Ladle into serving bowls, dollop sour cream on top. Makes four 2-cup servings, eight 1-cup servings.

Healthy Carrot-Maple Muffins

The whole family will love these tasty muffins—and they're nutritious, too. This recipe makes 12 regular-size muffins, 22–24 mini-muffins. To cut the prep time, double the recipe and freeze the extras.

1¾ cups flour

1½ teaspoons baking powder

½ teaspoon baking soda

1 teaspoon ground cinnamon

½ teaspoon ground ginger

¼ teaspoon ground nutmeg

½ teaspoon salt (may be omitted)

½ cup raisins or Craisins, tossed in 1 teaspoon flour

2 cups peeled and grated carrots

½ cup chopped nuts (walnuts, pecans, or almonds)

⅓ cup olive oil

½ cup maple syrup

2 large eggs, beaten

1 cup plain yogurt

½ teaspoon maple flavoring (optional)

1 teaspoon vanilla

Prepare your muffin tin (grease or insert paper muffin cups). In a large mixing bowl, mix together flour, baking powder, baking soda, cinnamon, ginger, nutmeg, and salt. Blend thoroughly. Toss the raisins or Craisins with 1 teaspoon flour (to keep them from sticking together). Add to flour mixture. Add grated carrots and nuts and mix well. In a medium bowl (I use a 4-cup glass pitcher for easy pouring), combine the oil and syrup and whisk together. Add the beaten eggs and mix well, then add the yogurt, maple flavoring, and vanilla. Stir all together. Pour the wet ingredients into the dry and mix with a big spoon, just until combined. As with all muffins, don't overmix: a few lumps won't hurt. Fill the muffin cups two-thirds full. Bake at 450 degrees F for 13–14 minutes, or until the muffins are golden on top and a wooden pick inserted into a muffin comes out clean. Turn out onto a rack immediately.

Spinach and Carrot Quiche

Great for brunch or Saturday night supper. Prebaking the crust of this custard pie keeps it from getting soggy. If you prefer, you can bake the filling in a greased (or sprayed) casserole dish, as a crustless quiche. For individual servings, you can bake the filling in a muffin tin (instructions below).

> Unbaked crust for one 9-inch pie, prebaked for 15 minutes
>   and cooled
> 1 tablespoon olive oil
> 1 onion, diced
> 2 cloves garlic, minced
> 1 (10-ounce) package frozen spinach, thawed (about 1½ cups)
> ¾ cup shredded carrots
> 2 cups shredded cheese (Monterey Jack, cheddar, or
>   mozzarella—or a mix)
> 6 eggs
> 1 cup half-and-half or evaporated milk
> ⅛ teaspoon ground nutmeg
> ½ teaspoon salt
> ½ teaspoon pepper

In a skillet, heat the oil. Sauté the onion and garlic. In a large bowl, mix the spinach and carrots. Stir in the sautéed onions and garlic. Evenly spread the cheese across the cooled pre-baked crust. Spread the spinach-carrot-onion mixture over the cheese. Beat eggs, then beat with half-and-half or evaporated milk, nutmeg, salt, and pepper. Pour egg mixture over filling. Bake at 350 degrees F for 40 minutes. (The quiche will set more firmly as it cools.) Serve warm or cold; slices may be reheated in the microwave.

For individual servings baked in a muffin tin: Spray the tin generously. Cut piecrust, tortillas, or thin bread slices in circles to fit the bottoms of the cups. Add cheese and spinach-carrot mixture. Fill cups two-thirds full with egg mixture. Bake until almost set and tops are puffed and brown, 20–25 minutes.

Cosmetic Carrot-Infused Oil

There are two kinds of oils commonly called "carrot oil." The first is cold-pressed from carrot seeds and mixed with a carrier oil; the second is a carrot-infused oil you can make at home from the flesh of the carrot. Both oils are rich in beta-carotene, vitamins A and E, and pro-vitamin A, and may help to heal dry, chapped, and cracked skin and condition hair. Here's a recipe for the carrot-infused oil.

> **2 pounds carrots**
> **Oil, enough to cover (Some excellent choices: olive, coconut, almond, avocado, grapeseed, jojoba—all good for your skin)**
> **Vitamin E oil**

Peel about 2 pounds of carrots and grate with a food processor or hand grater. Place the grated carrots in a slow cooker and add enough oil to cover. Set to warm (the lowest temperature) and infuse the oil for 66–72 hours. Strain through a fine-mesh or cheesecloth. Label and store in the refrigerator for up to 8 months.

To use: Carrot-infused oil may stain lighter skins. Make a sample by diluting the carrot-infused oil with a carrier oil, starting with a 1:10 ratio—that is, ½ teaspoon of infused oil to 5 teaspoons of carrier oil (one of the above). If that doesn't produce a stain, increase the ratio of carrot-infused oil to the carrier oil. Once you're satisfied with the ratio, add several drops of vitamin E oil. Apply to skin, lips, elbows, heels. You may also mix with your favorite cream, lotion, makeup remover, shower and bath gel, or shampoo.